The Makers of Magic

THE FOUR WINDS

A.M.Burn

Grosvenor House
Publishing Limited

This book is published by
Grosvenor House Publishing Ltd
Link House
140 The Broadway, Tolworth, Surrey, KT6 7HT.
www.grosvenorhousepublishing.co.uk

A CIP record for this book
is available from the British Library

ISBN 978-1-80381-654-8
eBook ISBN 978-1-80381-824-5

🏮 Problems

William had now been at Lakefield's school for nine months, his third school in as many years. He hated the constant changing and always being new, and knew without a doubt that it was because the teachers and headteachers saw him as difficult to teach and a disruption in the classroom and wanted him gone.

But he loved learning, he just struggled with all the reading, writing and maths, none of which ever made sense to him. He struggled to keep all the words, letters and numbers still on the page, they seemed to have a life of their own, sliding and spinning around on the ice rink white paper.

Sitting down, still, *every* lesson was also a problem. He wanted to move, run and build stuff with his hands that he had designed, reviewed, tested and built in his head. He had no choice though but to sit still on an uncomfortable plastic chair, knees tucked under the imprisoning table, while he battled the fizzing energy building inside him that would eventually explode like a bottle rocket launching off at the sound of the end of lesson school bell.

On one particular occasion, his Latin teacher, who was a dragon of a lady, had called him to the front. "William Taylor!"

He looked up from the rocket ship he was drawing in his notebook, "Yes Miss?" he replied with apprehension.

"Ah good, paying attention for once! Please come to the front and read the first section of chapter three, if you have remembered your textbook."

William's brain panicked, "Not me!" he thought, while his heart started to beat rapidly with dread. He hated reading and even more so in front of the class, during a pointless lesson. Who spoke Latin anymore? It was, as the teacher put it, "A dead language."

Now there *were* old ancient Latin type things William did find interesting such as catapults and castles but the teacher did not care or know anything about them. It was all numbers, letters and words, boring gibberish to him.

Despite his feelings of dread and panic, he had been asked to do it, so he did. Taking a deep breath, he pushed his chair back slowly, screeching the legs across the floor, as if the chair was protesting to being moved and sounding just how William felt. He hated having to do this, but he had a plan to get it over and done with. He would read with lots of long and slow "ums" and "ers" and joke around asking the class to fill in words he could not read. At the same time, he would laugh to make it all a joke.

William knew that if he could get the class to laugh at him, the teacher would have to step in to regain control, and would then ask William to stop and sit down. Yes, it was a bit of a humiliation to William, but it was worth it and it worked perfectly. It worked every time.

This was the normal story for William because...

School was not for William and
William was not for school.

In most lessons he would daydream and invent machines, gadgets and create stories in his head. Sometimes he would imagine machines that would stop the teacher from talking, tie them up in their chair and then catapult them out of the classroom window!

Other times, when he just could not cope any longer, he would end up in the sick bay with a headache, waiting for his parents to come and pick him up. He always hoped for his dad, as he was always more understanding than his mum, who just said he was not trying hard enough.

There was one lesson that William really loved though and that was Design and Technology. Here he was top of the class, a natural in that environment. For William, this class was like a duck taking to water, it all just meshed and made sense. He understood everything that was being taught. He could even do the maths involved to solve a problem, and for once *he* was the one being approached by others in the class asking for his help! The teacher would even ask him to go and help others with their work when he'd finished early, yet again.

William loved that he was not forced to sit at a tiny prison cell of a desk for an hour or two, to stare at a textbook with moving words he didn't understand. In the workshop everything was alive, making fantastic noises and smells that talked to him about what was going on, and he knew how everything worked. He loved the feel of the machines through his hands as they rumbled away, allowing the cold, dimpled texture of the metal surface to come alive under his hand.

He could tell just from listening to the rhythmical screech, screech, screech sound a lathe was making in the metal workshop next door, that the metal stock the machine was cutting was not quite round yet, and the object was only at the very beginning of revealing what it was going to be.

He loved the smell of all the glues and paints, even though they probably were not good for him. They were sweet smelling and thick in the air, making him feel happy. Lastly, there was the woodwork shop, a magical place of hard wood-handled tools that had not changed their design for hundreds of years and beautiful wood shavings all curled up on the floor.

This was William's type of lesson and he was good at it, in fact he was better than good – he was the best! He knew what to do and how to do it and he had a teacher who he thought was brilliant and not out to get him like all the other classroom-based teachers.

His teacher was called Mr G. Stephenson. William called him Mr Stephenson or Sir for short. He was a very relaxed and friendly teacher, although his build and posture spoke of military service. Rarely having to shout at his class to get their attention, he would tell interesting and exciting stories about how the item they were making had been used in history, always leaving the class transfixed, even if it was just about a clock. William had always felt that Mr Stephenson trusted him. It would be

William who he would put in charge of tools and machinery when he had to go and help another student or talk to another teacher. Mr Stephenson would also talk with and be interested in his work, as it would always seem to be that little bit more complex or bigger than the rest of the class.

During William's spare time he would often enter design and engineering competitions he found in his favourite magazines and websites, which often involved designing bridges, cars and problem solving. He had won a lot of the competitions and had the paper certificates on his bedroom walls to prove it, but that did not count at school. He even had to lie about his age to enter some of the competitions, as they were for adults only, and he still won.

But none of this made him feel less of a school failure and a boy with no future. However, little did he know that he was about to be talked about by some very interested and important people called Thomons, who lived in a world invisible to William and the rest of the people in his visible world. Thomons saw the abilities of William's unique brain as being very useful and important...

*

... "Order! Order!... for the sixth-hundredth-and-seventy-second meeting of the Igmon-Seeking, Selection and Integration Council," called an elderly gentleman in silver rimmed square glasses, who sat in a very high-backed, ornate looking chair. He clapped a metal looking object between his hands three times, creating a powerful

"BANG! BANG! BANG!" The sound echoed around the space and brought the hundred-or-so Thomon Councillors, Igmon Scouts and Integration Engineering Tacticians to silence under the broad-leaded glass-domed ceiling, which held back the slashing and pounding dark weather outside.

The space was lit with hundreds of tennis-ball-sized, perfectly spherical glass spheres, that lazily bobbed up and down in mid-air like stars above the attendants' heads, running in direct contrast to the violent fire storm raging inside them, that shot light in all directions.

The old gentleman, who was called a First Rate Councillor, sat on top of a raised up wooden plinth in the centre of the space, directly under the glass dome. Three other Second Rate Councillors sat around him on a lower platform and looked just as used to and as comfortable with their power as the First Rater.

They all wore similar uniforms, consisting of a dark purple bowler hat with a badge of two golden interlocking circles on their fronts, and a heavy black jacket covered in intertwined golden prime shapes in straight lines like chains.

"Which Scouts wish to put forward an Igmon subject to be considered for Thomon integration to the Council?" announced the elderly man over the quiet hall, in a voice that was much stronger than his face allowed for.

Several Igmon Scouts stepped forward to stand on a wooden ring that ran around the First and Second Raters platforms and bowed.

"Glad to see so many of you have a hopeful Igmon subject to present to the Council," the First Rater said, looking down around him with a practised smile at the hopeful Scouts. "But before you begin might I remind you that this Council has been very unimpressed with the subjects put forward for the last few years, many of whom had to be disposed of within the first year. It is your job, might I remind you, as Igmon Scouts to find the gifted children that Igmon's so ignorantly overlook. They are to be a benefit to us and should deserve a place in the Thomon world, to help drive us forward into the future. So, if you feel your subject is going to improve the direction of the last few years then please present your Igmon subject, but if not, then please sit back down and don't waste our time!" said the First Rater finishing his little impassioned speech with clear frustration.

A flash of sharp lightening outside the dome brightly lit the space for a few seconds, allowing the columns which lent heavily over, as if frozen mid-fall, that supported the glass dome, to cast long shadows that jumped and turned sudden angles along the uneven stone floor.

The First Rater signalled with the point of a soft hand to the female Scout to his left to begin.

"Thank you, Sir," she said, as she pulled a playing card-sized notebook from her pocket, covered in unreadably-small black lines, and a solid block of black ink. She then proceeded to pull a metal object from her belt called a Hadron-Tool, and pulled the top right corner of the small pad and stretched it until it was A4 size. The small black lines had turned into readable words and the block of black ink was now a clear portrait of her subject.

"Which Academy do you scout for?" the First Rater asked while the female scout was fiddling.

"Tradwall Sir," she replied, finally getting her papers in order.

"Aah, one of the Doggerland Academies very good, please continue."

"I present the case for subject zero six four seven. She attends Heathhall School for girls, has two older brothers and is part of a highly-thought of Igmon family. She is fourteen…" she started.

"FOURTEEN!!!" the First Rater exclaimed with impatient disbelief, the room falling instantly tense with everyone watching, realising what was about to happen. "… What did I just say? This subject is far too old, she will be too hard to integrate," the First Rater said with frustration.

"But Sir sh…" she tried to say over the top of the First Rater's voice but was not given time.

"You know she is too old! There have been numerous lectures and training sessions given to all Scouts about this and why it is, and so you should know better than to waste the Council's time!"

"Yes I do know that, and thank you for providing all the excellent training, but she is particularly gifted with numbers. I have not seen this level of ability in a long time! I understand that she is past the normal acceptance age for an Igmon child, but not by much and she…" she tried to rattle off the information as quickly as possible before being cut off again.

"But you know the requirements the Council is looking for," the First Rater said forcibly, interrupting her. "We have extensive years of experience with trying to integrate children above the age of eleven into the

Thomon world with very poor results. Might I remind you of case seven four two, when the Thomon world was almost revealed at an Igmon location they call Area 51." He paused to let the feeling in the room grow even heavier. "That is something I hope you would like to avoid happening again. And it is the view of the Second and First Raters of this Council to see the successful integration of any Igmon child and the safety of the Thomon world as a priority. Thank you Miss... Miss..." he said angrily as his face grew more and more fiery red every second, before pausing again as he could not recall the scout's name, and calming down.

"Roserod," the Scout said with disappointment, realising her case was over.

"Thank you, Miss Roserod, but this subject will not be taken any further," he said, taking one last moment to glare in annoyance at the Scout, before he moved on to an Igmon Scout to his right. "Do you have any subjects suitable for this Council's requirements?" he said pointing.

"Yes Sir, I have a boy of ten years old, who suits the Council's requirements, and I am scouting on behalf of Belbury Apprenticeship Academy," he said, happy to know his case would not be dismissed.

"Excellent, please carry on," the First Rater said, pleased, as he relaxed back into his chair and stacked his soft weak hands on his lap.

"Subject number seven three one eight, a William Taylor. He is currently at Lakefields School in Guildford and as far as I have been able to find out all his Igmon schools have struggled with him..." he began after going through the same routine as the previous Scout of enlarging his notes.

"All his Igmon schools!" the First Rater interrupted, repeating the phrase, "How many?"

"Five so far Sir."

"What struggles do they have with the boy?"

"They say he is a disruption to the rest of his class and seems incapable of learning and keeping up with the others," the Scout said confidently. "No fighting or violence though," he quickly added to ensure the First Rate Councillor did not misunderstand the problem.

"Ok, good, how did you first find out about this boy?"

"I teach his Design and Technology class Sir, and from very early on I noticed he was gifted far beyond his classmates. So, I started to place very specific engineering competitions in his favourite magazines and websites I knew he visited. Each competition was designed to show and test different areas of his gifting. He entered all of them and won pretty much every one, even ones that I would normally only give to adults!"

"Very good, and good thinking on your part, and what have you learnt?" the First Rater asked, clearly interested.

"He has some strong gifting towards engineering and invention, along with being an impressive visual acquirer of knowledge, with a strong visual perception and remarkable level of spatial awareness. He is a good physical athlete, very quick on his feet and as his Igmon school calls him heavily dyslexic. He is an only child of a financially struggling Igmon father and mother who try their best for him, but they are at their wit's end as to what to do with him," the Scout explained.

"Do you find him a problem, in the ways you mentioned earlier?"

"No Sir, quite the opposite, he is in fact my best student."

"What's your name Scout?"

"George Stephenson, Sir."

"Very well George, seven three one eight sounds most promising, good work. A no-hoper in the Igmon education system, dyslexic, an only child, the right age, physically capable and a potentially gifted engineer. Yes, he sounds like just what we are looking for," the First Rater said happily while leaning forward and looking down at the three Second Raters for their visual approval, who nodded their purple bowler hat-supporting heads in silent agreement. "Excellent, I don't need to hear much more on seven three one eight and I see that there are no objections from the Second Raters either," he paused to allow for any last-minute objections from the floor. "Good, send him an intervention and see where we get to."

"Thank you, Sir. Before I go… I've heard along with many other Scouts about rumours of a Krevak Ragwort starting to dissuade by the use of violence, Igmon subjects we select for intervention. Is this true and what is being done about it?" asked Mr Stephenson, bringing the room to a nervously interested quiet.

"Krevak Ragwort is not a problem for us in this Council despite the rumours, and that is all it is, rumours. The Protection and Security Council are dealing with him and those that are spreading these lies. I do not wish to hear his name mentioned again in this chamber. Is that understood," the First Rater snapped, sounding annoyed with the question.

"Yes, very good Sir, thank you," the Scout said while bowing his head before turning to leave, full of confidence that he would finally succeed with an Igmon subject, and be the one who found a truly special and gifted subject from the Igmon world.

*

William, being totally and utterly oblivious to this glittering review of his skills and talents, was angry, upset and mentally exhausted! Yet again he had been in trouble at school and sent home for causing problems in his Year Six class, which he felt was totally unfair and that the teacher disliked him instead.

So, he sat slumped over his desk in his bedroom surrounded by the certificates he had won and pictures he had drawn of machines and mechanisms that were stuck to his walls. Scattered over his desk were bits of construction sets and partly finished aeroplane models. Feeling frustrated, his eyes began to well-up with tears. He just did not understand all the other lessons and he was being punished for it yet again! William thumped his table with his fist in annoyance.

"I just don't get it! Why can't I learn like everyone else? I really want to be able to!"

With a deep sob, he rested his forehead on the table and closed his eyes, wishing to hide from the world that did not want him.

It was at this point that William heard a very confident knock downstairs at the front door. Without moving his head, he opened his damp eyes and heard his dad walk from the kitchen, which was under his bedroom, and along the tile-floor hallway to the door (which was looking in desperate need of a fresh coat of blue paint). His dad opened the door with a metallic click and said,

"Hello, how can I help you?"

William did not recognise the voice that spoke next straight away, but it very quickly introduced itself.

"Good evening Mr Taylor, I am William's Design and Technology Teacher, Mr Stephenson. I heard William was sent home from school today by the Headteacher for being what she called a disruptive influence to the class." He paused a few seconds to allow Mr Taylor to make the link. "I realise," he started again, "that this is not quite normal for a teacher to do a house call, but may I come in and have a chat?" Mr Stephenson had been waiting patiently for days just for a moment like this. A moment which his training had taught him would make the acceptance of the intervention far more likely.

William shot up to his feet, almost knocking over his chair, which he quickly caught and stilled, before delicately lunging over to the door to put his ear to the gap between the bedroom door and frame to listen. "What could he be doing at my house?" William thought. Things can't have gotten that bad at school, surely? He listened intently.

Downstairs, William's Dad, slightly taken aback, said, "Yeah sure, please come in," whilst taking a look at his watch to confirm that it was indeed late and school had finished a long time ago. Once again, the familiar hallway sounds punctuated upstairs as the pair walked through to the kitchen, followed by the squealing of pine farmhouse chairs being pulled out from under the round farmhouse kitchen table.

William could not possibly stay in his room for this – he had to hear what was being said about him. He slowly, quietly and purposefully pushed down the brass handle on his door. He could hear the bolt slide out of the lock in the jamb of the door and then he pulled it open. Popping his head around the corner, he looked down the stairs to check the coast was clear. Like a cat stalking its prey he crept ever so slowly and carefully to the steps, about half-way down the stairs, where the rungs of the banister ended and he could sit and listen to what was being said without being seen.

In the kitchen, Mr Stephenson was handed tea in a mug with a chipped rim and the words, KEEP CALM, DRINK TEA, written on the side in red.

"Thank you, much appreciated," said Mr Stephenson gratefully. "I was sorry to hear about your son being sent home today. I have no problems with him in my D&T class. In fact, he is by far the best student I have taught in my time at Lakefields, and he even teaches me a few things every now and then."

"So maybe you could enlighten me to what the problem is then? Why is he constantly being sent home or... or sent to sick bay with a headache," jumped in Mr Taylor, in bemused frustration that had built up over the years.

Mr Stephenson took a sip of tea before he responded.

"I think, Mr Taylor, William is very misunderstood… See, he is an immensely clever and intelligent boy and I've noticed he learns things very differently to the others in his class. Have you noticed how he thinks through things by physically doing something? He needs to move and do practical stuff to learn and understand, which for the most part in all the other classes, he is not able to do." He paused to take another sip of tea and then continued. "In the workshop I get to see him in a very different environment to all the other teachers – he is up and about, doing things with his hands. I often see him helping the other kids with their work when they get stuck. I have tried to explain my thoughts to the other teachers but as much as they would like to help they are not able to accommodate what he needs!" He paused a few seconds and then restated, "Lakefields just can't accommodate it. It's not that they don't want to do more for William, but they're concerned that if they give him the freedom to move around in the classroom then all the kids would want to as well. Before long the whole class would be running around, turning the classroom into break time! I can understand their concern."

"So, what do you suggest? To be honest we don't understand what is going on with him! He seems like any other kid in all other ways. Do we need to give him extra lessons with a tutor outside of school hours? But then who knows how we could afford that!"

The Taylor family was not well off. Mrs Taylor worked long hours as a secretary for a steel company and Mr Taylor was a self-employed gardener, but he currently had no work.

"Mr Taylor," Mr Stephenson said in a calm tone, seeing that William's dad was clearly at the end of his tether trying to figure what to do. "There is another option, which is why I am here. I am here not on behalf of the Lakefield School, but on behalf of another school organisation I work for. You will not have heard of it before as it is kept very quiet, almost secret from most people."

Mr Taylor laughed, "You're joking right? Let me get this right. You're here telling me…" he said, stabbing a finger into the table and leaning forward, "… that there is a secret school, which you are part of and that you're only pretending to be a teacher at Williams school?"

Mr Stephenson adjusted himself in his chair making it creak, as he controlled his feelings of annoyance at being thought of as only pretending to be a teacher. He gave everything to his teaching at Lakefield School, it was just part of his main job of being an Igmon Scout.

William could not believe what he had just heard! His favourite teacher was in his house, chatting with his dad about what sounded like a secret school! William leaned in even harder and listened even more intently to try and hear even more.

"It is a school for particularly talented and gifted children, like William," Mr Stephenson said calmly again, allowing time for Mr Taylor to understand that this was not a joke. "Sadly, I don't have much more time now," he said while pulling a vintage gold pocket watch on a chain out of his pocket, flicking open the lid with a well-practised thumb movement, to glance at the time, before standing up. "There is a lot to explain but I would like you to read these information packs before we next meet," he said as he produced some small postage stamp sized bits of paper from inside his jacket, which Mr Taylor looked at with confusion.

"Thank you for the tea," Mr Stephenson said, holding the cup up for Mr Taylor to take.

"No problem," Mr Tayler replied, turning and taking the cup to the sink to rinse it.

This gave Mr Stephenson just enough time to use his Hadron-Tool to touch the three tiny bits of paper and enlarge them.

"Here, please read these," insisted Mr Stephenson, holding out three A4 sized packets of information. Mr Taylor took them a little bit befuddled, as when he last saw the three bits of information they had been the size of postage stamps.

"Might I ask if you and William would be free this Friday evening say around seven pm? Could we meet at the Royal Arms Pub at the end of your road to discuss the information?"

Mr Taylor sat back down, slapped the information papers onto the table and lifted his hands above his head to stretch and let them settle behind his head, like a man who felt he had nothing to lose. "Sure..." he said, going along with the strange conversation, "... well... thank you for coming by!"

William quickly realised he had to move back to his room quickly before he was spotted out of bed, and like a silent flash he was off.

The two men walked to the front door, shook hands and parted company. Mr Taylor briefly stood in the open doorway and shook his head in disbelief, scratched his chin and turned to stare up the stairs at William's room. Suddenly Mr Stephenson's head reappeared around the door.

"Forgot to say that the ink on those information packs will disappear by Friday so read them while you can. Would not want the whole world to know about the best school in the world." He said in a very friendly tone before disappearing again.

"Right... ok," said a baffled Mr Taylor almost to himself, while shutting the door. He turned as slowly as the day had been long, and walked up the stairs with tired legs toward William's room.

William, who had jumped into bed pretending to be asleep, ignored the first knock on his bedroom door. When it came again, he answered, "Come in!" in his best sleepy voice. His dad stepped into his room, turned the light on and headed over to William's bed. Sitting next to William he exhaled a single long and hard breath and said.

"Well, that was an interesting conversation I just had with your DT teacher." He paused to unsuccessfully look around his brain for the teacher's name. "What's his name again?"

"Mr Stephenson?" William answered, sitting up in bed.

"Ah yes that was it. According to him you are a very special and gifted boy, who would benefit from what sounds like moving schools... *again*! Well..." he paused to rub William's hair, "we are going to meet him this Friday at seven pm to find out more. Anyway, get some sleep, as you still have two days left of school. In the meantime, I will chat with your mother about this and go over the information he gave us to look at."

The two days went slowly for William as he could not wait for Friday evening, he had so many questions! How was this new school going to be any different to all the others? What did Mr Stephenson mean that he was special? Never had he changed schools because of a positive reason, so this was very new to him.

A very normal English wet and grey Friday came around and William and his dad headed to the pub, without Mrs Taylor, who was working overtime.

The Royal Arms was a vintage pub. As they approached, warm light from the open fire inside glowed through the small, thick bottle green glass windows and laughter could be heard inside. William's dad pushed the heavy wooden door open with the familiarity of a regular, nodding to the barman and was greeted with recognition.

Quickly Mr Taylor scanned the room, and spotted Mr Stephenson sitting at a round table in a quiet corner with two wooden armchairs available. William was sticking very close to his dad as he knew this place fairly well, but not for good reasons, as The Royal Arms Pub was not known to be kid-friendly, especially when the football was on.

"Good evening William," Mr Stephenson said warmly as he stood up to shake Mr Taylor's hand. "Please sit," he said, pointing to the empty chairs. "I have got you drinks already, I hope that is ok?"

Mr Taylor looked stunned by the gesture, but managed to say, "Thank you."

Mr Stephenson took a sip from his pint and started to talk, "Well, thank you for coming. Now I want to talk with both of you, that means, William, you are also involved." He saw William nod in understanding and so carried on. "As I said before, I work for an organisation which is little known in mainstream education and we like to keep it that way. This is why the writing on the information packs will have disappeared by now." This was confirmed by Mr Taylor nodding his head and placing the blank A4 packs on the table. "Now you must understand…" Mr Stephenson said, emphasising the point with his hands, "… I cannot tell you everything you will want to know, but only what you need to know to make a decision. Belbury Apprenticeship Academy has been around for a very, very long time and often selects students from schools around the world to come and join who show particular gifting's or talents."

William downed half of his glass, hoping to hide the nervous excitement he was feeling, that was making his hands sweat, and placed it back on the coaster.

"Your son," Mr Stephenson continued, "caught my eye a while ago and we feel he would benefit from joining us."

Mr Taylor stopped Mr Stephenson, "Right ok, wait a minute. So, William and I would like to know what you see in him that is so special?"

"Well Mr Taylor, over the time we have been watching him, we have seen that he sees the world differently to those around him and interacts with the world differently than others. In the current school he finds himself in, he would be called heavily dyslexic, and it is seen as a problem because he does not fit into the standard classroom environment." He paused to give William and Mr Taylor a minute to process. "In very simple terms where your brain," he said pointing at Mr Taylor, "and my brain make connections between point A and point B, Williams go from point A to point E, and sometimes point A doesn't connect to anything at all. This makes him very good at things like visual acquisition and 3D perception. At Belbury Apprenticeship Academy, he is exactly the type of boy we want to work with and teach."

William was somewhat taken-aback at what his teacher had just said, but a smile grew on his face as he thought about being in a school where he was wanted. He reached for his glass to take another drink to find to his confusion it was full again. William was perplexed and looked around the pub for who had refilled his drink, but concluded that no one had brought a fresh drink from the bar. No one else had been near the table since they had sat down. He looked at the two other pints of beer on the table and both were as full, as if they had never been drunk. But William knew that both men had quickly drunk at least half a pint each.

Mr Stephenson saw William looking at the drinks glasses with wide open eyes and knew he had noticed the drinks were full again. He caught William's eye and gave him a wink, while never breaking conversation with Mr Taylor.

William focused back into the conversation feeling that there might be a connection, just as Mr Stephenson began saying, "There is however one catch if William is to become part of Belbury Academy."

"Right!" exclaimed Mr Taylor, "I knew there would be a catch. What is it then? Pay all my money into a random account, well I don't think so!"

Mr Stephenson quickly butted in, "No, no, no, it is not like that, the catch is very simple. We keep the academy very quiet, and so anyone who decides to accept an offer and become a pupil must board full time, and will only come home twice a year at Christmas and the summer holidays," Mr Stephenson said quickly, and visibly saw Mr Taylor calm down.

"Only twice a year," Mr Taylor replied with some concern. "That's a long time for him to be away, but then again it could be good for him," he carried on while turning to look at William, thinking about how much he would miss him.

"Yes, I totally understand that it is a long time that William will be away for, and it is a common sticking point for parents, but it helps with the new way of learning William will experience," Mr Stephson explained.

"A new way of learning," Mr Taylor repeated, remembering back to what he had read in the information packs. "Yes, those packs you gave me did make the school, sorry, the apprenticeship academy classrooms sound very different!"

"Different!" William thought, "Different how? Could a classroom really be any different?" he wondered, as he had not seen the information packs.

"Yes, that's right, and the difference is partly why Belbury is called an apprenticeship academy and not a school. In fact, there aren't actually any classrooms at all, which is one reason why it is often so good for kids like

William. Instead, all the lessons take place in the business and facilities around Belbury town, which Belbury Academy is part of. Apart from the academy houses and main hall you would not know there was an academy in Belbury town at all," Mr Stephenson explained.

"No classrooms, amazing! I hate classrooms!" William thought.

Mr Taylor sat back, making the wooden chair creak and thought for a minute, "Well William, you have not been able to fit into any other schools so far, so what do you think?"

William looked at the full drink in front of him, and knew that if he said yes then he would get to learn about and see more strange and more amazing things than a glass refilling itself. William looked up into his dad's face, his eyes bright with excitement, "No classrooms sounds really good, I would really, really like to try."

Mr Taylor could see William was excited at the prospect of fitting in at school, being special and going off on an adventure. He knew that all the switching of schools had taken its toll on William just as much as it had on him and William's mum. He turned to Mr Stephenson and tentatively said, "Well William is in and I think, by the sounds of what you have said it's his only hope. However, I will need to finally convince his mother, especially because it's boarding. I will see her when we get home."

"Fantastic!" Mr Stephenson exclaimed, clasping his hands together with happiness, making drinkers on the next table put their frothing pints down and turn in their chairs to look at this very un-pub like emotional outburst.

"When you've spoken to Mrs Taylor and hopefully she has decided to accept, all you need to do is be at the post box at the end of Downhole Road at eighteen thirty-four this coming Thursday."

William thought both the time and day were very strange but that made him all the more keen to be there on time, once his parents had agreed to let him go of course. They had to let him go, surely, he thought.

Mr Stephenson stood up to leave saying his goodbyes. Walking past Willam, he bent down to say, "If I were you I would keep your coaster, as it probably has a few drinks left in it." With that he left, calling behind him, "See you at school!"

Both Mr Taylor and William paused and sat in silence briefly before turning back to the table, where William snatched up the remaining coasters into his pockets.

The next few days passed as fast as a rock is eroded by the wind for William. Several times he could hear his parents heatedly talking about the decision in the kitchen below his room. For him the decision was easy. He had even planned to do a runner if his parents said no.

His bag lay open on his bedroom floor, ready to be packed. It was now eighteen o five on Thursday and William's parents had still not made a decision. Nervously he waited at his desk, sketching an idea for a time machine in one of his many books to stay calm.

Finally, his mother's voice called from the kitchen, "Come down here William!"

William threw down his pen and ran down the stairs so fast his feet barely touched any of the steps and then down the corridor into the kitchen.

His mum and dad were both sitting around the table and both looked tired as a result of all the back and forth talking.

"Well!" William's mum said. She was a very thin, short lady and had a sharp voice. "We have decided that under one condition you may go."

William could barely believe it, "Yes?" he said. "Anything!"

"I know it does not sound like much, but you must contact us after two weeks to let us know how you are getting on. Your dad and I understand that this is a chance that you may never get again and so we want you to try."

William lunged towards his mum and dad, hugged them, then rushed back off up the stairs to pack his bag, almost faster than he came down them. His mum also came upstairs and gathered clothes and a wash bag for him and placed them in the already open green canvas bag.

William's idea of packing was very different, in went his sketch pads and pencil case, his books about big mining machinery and ancient weapons, and of course some Lego. He forgot all about how to stay clean and what to wear, he was going on an adventure!

"If you are going to make it we need to leave now!" His dad called from downstairs.

Before William knew it, he was doing something between a walk and a run down the road, trying to keep up with his parents, and reached the red post box with three minutes to spare.

The Taylor family had a few quiet moments as they stood on the curb, waiting in the cold dark.

"How are you feeling boy?" William's mum said while placing a hand on his shoulder.

William looked up at his mother, recognising a gentleness in her that was normally missing.

"I'm really nervous mum, but very excited. My tummy is full of butterflies, feels like they are trying to take off!"

Down the road came a very standard white minibus, with the word coach on its side. It pulled up next to the post box at exactly eighteen thirty-four.

Mr Taylor chuckled quietly to himself saying, "I thought coaches were meant to be bigger."

The minibus's side door slid open to reveal Mr Stephenson standing on the first step, beaming at William. "Excellent, I knew you would accept!" came his happy greeting.

William turned to his mum and dad, "Well it begins... I guess! Bye then!" Giving them both a hug, he stepped into the minibus, and poked his head back out of the door for a last chance to wave goodbye.

Mr Stephenson shook both Mr and Mrs Taylor's hands and said that he would take good care of William. Then stepped up into the minibus and slid the door shut.

Excitedly, William turned to look down the minibus for a place to sit and froze.

From the outside this had been a very normal white minibus, despite wearing a rather optimistic name on its side. Inside however, it was anything but, it seemed to extend forever! Winding its way back and back and back with kids and adults scattered on the seats down some of its length, with an equal amount of luggage above their heads on racks. There was also an area that looked like a romantic French bar where people could get food and drinks. Further down William could see rows of stacked hammocks, some containing gently swinging sleeping people.

Mr Stephenson gave William a gentle push on his upper back, saying, "Let's go find you a seat."

William looked up and said, "But Sir the bus, look! What's happening?"

"Ha! Yes. Well. This is what happens when you experiment with infinite mechanics after a game of 4's," Mr Stephenson replied with a laugh. "I have yet to find the back, but it does come in handy when there is lots of kit to carry. Ah perfect, here we go. Take a seat here William and we will be on our way." Mr Stephenson walked back to the front, talked to the driver, and William felt the infinitely long minibus pull away, leaving his mum and dad waving innocently from the pavement, none the wiser about the Tardis-like inside of the minibus that was right in front of them.

William, braving a look backwards, saw the infinitely long minibus snaking and curving all the way down, like a train without an end as it drove.

▣ A New Beginning

The journey to Belbury Apprenticeship Academy was not only an adventure to William, but also a fresh start. No longer being thought of as stupid by other kids and teachers, or having to humiliate himself to get out of things he was not good at. That is, if all that Mr Stephenson had said was true, and William trusted him now more than ever.

The non-existent back of the bus scared him a little, and hurt his brain to think about and so he occupied himself by looking out the window at the fast-moving view. When a face with untidy hair that stuck out from underneath a grubby flat cap squeezed into existence between the two seats in front.

"Hi, I'm George, what's your name?" the head asked.

"William," he replied to the cheerful face.

"This your first time on the bus?"

"Yes, one as strange as this anyway!" William said, quickly glancing behind him.

George's eyes flicked up also to match where William was looking.

"My dad says that this is the only infinitely long minibus in the world and it was created by mistake!"

"By mistake?" William repeated, turning to look at George.

"Yeah, that's what he told me. My brother went down as far as he dared go once, came back terrified, which made me scared to ever venture down," George said before his head disappeared behind the seats and reappeared attached to his body next to William.

George was William's age and very normally dressed for a ten-year-old boy. He wore a woolly jumper which was averagely dirty, slightly muddy trousers with a hole in one knee, that hung over second hand looking brown boots.

"Ah perfect," said a tall lady with waist length brown hair and wearing a black jacket with sparkles on the shoulders, who had appeared from the front of the minibus. "William Taylor and George Meldul, yes?" She waited for a reply and received a nod of the two heads. "Good both together, that makes life easier. I have a round letter for each of you new First Years from Belbury Apprenticeship Academy. It tells you what house you will be in when we arrive. Please read it now and learn the name and colour of your house, you will need that when you get off." The lady ticked their names off her clipboard, before disappearing around a bend in the minibus looking for the next on her list.

William and George both opened their round letters, with William asking George to read his aloud, as he felt embarrassed about struggling to read.

Dear George Meldul,

Thank you for accepting your place at Belbury Apprenticeship Academy.

Your academy house is Starley, whose colour is blue.

You will be meeting your House Captain on arrival, please follow their instructions.

Yours

Sir Seamus Coalbrook – Headmaster

"What house do you have?" George asked his new friend, showing William his letter.

"I have Starley as well," William replied, stumbling a little over how to say the house name.

The two boys smiled at each other, happy that they knew someone already.

After having a quick rummage on the floor between his feet, George produced a brown paper bag, covered in writing and pictures in black pen. The writing on the bag raced around the outside of the creased paper bag, much like William had seen on advertising billboards in London. It said, "George Meldul's Lunch Only". George smiled at the damp brown bag which he held towards William.

"My mum made me a packed lunch, want some? The roudit and pea pie is really good!"

William peered into the increasingly gravy sodden bag. "Roudit and pea pie! What's a roudit?"

"Are, you're an Igmon then." William looked confused at this description, but George carried on talking. "A roudit is like a really long rabbit. My dad hunts them as they are a bit of a nuisance, eating everything, and their long bodies are a real trip hazard. Tastes great though. My dad said he once caught one that was three metres long! Here, my mum made two," George said while handing over a heavily gravy covered pie, wrapped in an equally gravy covered brown paper napkin.

"Thank you," William replied. Gently cradling the pie into his lap trying not to get too covered.

"I have never seen a roudit before."

"Oh you won't have. They are hidden from Igmons."

"Hidden, how? And what is an Igmon?" William asked, still confused.

"Ah yes, you wouldn't know," said George, while taking a bite from the pie, gravy dripping into his lap to join the other stains covering his well-worn jeans. "Well, there is a whole world hidden from the Igmons, that is people where you come from, by the Thomons, who are the people that I come from. The Thomon world has been hidden for thousands and thousands of years from the Igmons apparently. My mum used to tell me a story to try and explain it, it went something like:

At the beginning of time there were two families.

One family was the Whomos and the other, the Thomons.

These two families both worked the land day and night and would help each other where possible and got on very well.

But one day the head of the Thomon family met a traveller who promised him wisdom and knowledge beyond the gods if he would get him a drink of water from a well in their village.

The head of the Thomon family quickly jumped to the task and sent a bucket on a line down into the well, pulling it up full.

The traveller took a cup from his bag and filled it from the bucket and drank.

After quenching his thirst the traveller gave him an apple to eat.

A single bite of the apple made the Thomon man collapse asleep.

When the man awoke the traveller was long gone, so he walked home where he met his family who had been worried, for they had not seen him in days.

He explained what had happened and normal life started again.

As time moved on the Thomon family farm began to be very very productive with the head of the family inventing better tools and understanding what to do with the land and new ways to get more with less work.

This made the Whomos family very jealous as they worked even harder but with less results and were too proud to ask for advice and help.

The two families began to bicker and fight.

One night the head of the Whomos family crept into the Thomon's house and tried to kill the head of the family, but only managing to take his eye before running away.

The two families then moved away from each other, rather than go to war.

The Thomons, fearing their jealous neighbours, used their knowledge and wisdom to hide their farm and family.

And the two families grew and filled the earth but the Thomons never revealed themselves to the Whomos ever again.

My mum would then say, because of jealousy and pride we have the whole world and the Whomos only have some of it." George paused, thinking, checking that he had the story right. "Yes," he said, nodding his head, "that's all of it. Now I don't know if it's true or not but it's a mad story."

William just stared at him saying, "WOW, but you called me an Igmon not a Whomos!"

"Ah yes, well my dad says we now call the Whomos, people like you Igmons, because of how ignorant and stupid they can be. Not a nice name really."

Taking this in without complaint, William sat back into his chair, thinking that this view of the Whomos or Igmon people was probably quite fair and took a bite of George's homemade roudit and pea pipe. He was right, roudit's were very very tasty.

*

"Could all passengers for Belbury Apprenticeship Academy please take a moment to gather their belongings!" came an announcement over the speaker system in a poetic tone, "We will soon be arriving, thank you."

Mr Stephenson walked up from the front of the bus to see Willam before he got off. He tapped his hand on William's bag, that was now on the seat between him and the walkway and said.

"You got everything, because this next stop is yours?"

"Yes, I think so," William said while looking around to check.

"Great, stick with George here, as I am sure you know by now he is a Thomon and should know what he is roughly doing. There will be a teacher from Belbury Academy ready to meet you when we next stop, along with your new House Captain."

William asked if he was coming with them but the reply was no.

"I am heading back to Lakefields to carry on teaching, and finding more talented kids like you. You will do great here, you're a gifted kid so enjoy growing into what you will become."

With that the infinitely long minibus stopped, William picked up his stuff and shuffled off, lining up next to George and the other kids on the pavement. William took a quick look back just to confirm that the minibus was normal size and to remind himself of the infinite length of the inside. They had got out in what looked like a village or town, the name of which William did not know, and because it was dark he could not see well enough the sign posts that were only a few metres away from him.

In the dark he could just make out the surrounding landscape against the dark blue sky, showing dark black shapes that looked like mountains and hills all around.

Creating a picture in William's head that the village or town was nestled in a crater or bowl-shaped valley.

In front of William stood five people, lit by the light flowing from the minibus's open door. They all wore long coats which finished at the knee. Four had jackets coloured Green, Blue, Yellow and Red with matching caps. Each also had a polished brass gear-shaped badge on their left chest pocket with the letters HC in the centre. The fifth person was much older and taller than the rest, dressed in a white jacket that went down to the floor, with a very high collar, and decorated in what looked like golden dots and dashes of morse code. Her hat was white and flopped over her left ear. Emblazoned on the front was a large golden badge showing five horizontal lines stacked above one another.

All had the air of Victorian formality about them in clothing cut, style and materials.

"Good evening First Years, I am the Deputy Head of Belbury Apprenticeship Academy, Mrs Volta," announced the lady dressed in white and sounding just as Victorian as she looked. "With me are the House Captains and by now you should all know your house and colour. So please follow your correct captain to the Belbury Hall when I instruct you. There you are to be addressed by the Headmaster, Sir Seamus Coalbrook. Drop your bag off when instructed to, and they will find their way to your rooms."

"But Mrs…" a plump boy with slick hair put up his hand and butted in, "… how will my bag get to the right room? I don't even know what room I am in yet!"

"Archie Pivoting, a good question, one that you will learn the answer to during your time here. Do as you are instructed and your bags will be at your bedsides waiting for you. House Captains please lead on."

"You heard Mrs Volta! Follow your colours, stay close and keep up! James and Philippa please stay at the back. Jason, with me," the boy with the blue jacket said with an air of authority and self confidence in his voice.

Clearly, William thought, the boy in blue was not just a House Captain but probably the academy Captain also, or otherwise just very arrogant.

The gaggle of 10-year-old kids huddled together, all equally unsure of what to expect next, but excited by each new thing they saw. William and George stuck close together, dragging their bags along behind them, bumping them over the cobbled pavements and curbs. Even George, who had grown up in the Thomon world was a picture of nervousness and excitement mashed together, eager to not make a mistake and make a good first impression.

After many winding paths and staircases, past glittering windows and heavy looking monuments, they arrived at the start of a long but narrowing alley. This forced the herd of children into two lines to be able to fit and keep up with the boy in blue, who was walking at a frantic pace. He constantly called out behind, "Come on, come on, keep up" and "We are running late, hurry up everyone please!"

The fast-paced walk eventually stopped at a very strong looking oak and metal door, with a door handle on the left and the right. William could also see through the dim light flickering on either side of the door, that there were massive wrought iron looking hinges on the left and the right side. This puzzled William's mind as he tried to figure out how the door worked.

"Maybe it's a puzzle or not really a door at all, you know, like those trick boxes, where the front is not really the front at all and you open the box from the back," William said quietly to George.

The door opened towards the waiting group, its right-hand hinges squeaking a little as it swung outwards. Out backwards, oblivious to the group of children watching him, walked a slightly swaying, stocky man shouting in laughter, looking back at a group of people sitting in what looked like a pub, with tables heavy with jugs of foaming liquid. He turned around while placing his hat upon his head to be on his way, and looked briefly surprised to see tens of little eyes staring at him out of the gloom. A brief awkward moment followed until the man composed himself, said good evening, and then hurried off past the students, down the alleyway with a single loud hiccup echoing off the walls, leaving the door open behind him.

The boy who wore all green approached the same door, shut it, then used the right-hand door knob to swing the door inwards on the left hand hinges. It was now no longer a pub that could be seen, but an empty and welcoming entrance hall.

"Right in you all go!" The boy in green instructed, "Put your bags into the hole below the fire and then stand against the right-hand wall on the striped rug."

In the First Years went, just as they were told. Inside there was a roaring fire, not in a fireplace, but hovering above the floor in what looked like a clear sphere of glass, and below it was a hole about the size of a dustbin lid.

The children approached it nervously to place their bags down what looked like a bottomless pit, not quite believing what they had been asked to do.

William thought the fire raging around inside the sphere was beautiful and he could feel its heat as soon as he stepped through the door. The closest student to the hole looked down the circular abyss and then back at his bag with worry all over his face.

It took some quick commands of encouragement from the House Captain wearing the blue jacket to get the bags dealt with, "Hurry up please this room won't exist forever, your bags will get to where they need to go, no need to worry."

In went the first bag and then the rest, tossed into oblivion with each student wondering if they would ever see their bags again, and if so if all the contents would be broken, like at an airport.

The blue jacketed boy piped up again, "Come on come on, by the right-hand wall. Yes, that one over there, all stand on the rug," he said, while pointing at a thickly-made stone wall which towered over the top of a rather worn rainbow striped rug. "Right this is very important everyone, no one is to move, *got that*!" He said forcefully.

William nodded his head furiously and said yes along with everyone else. After seeing what had to happen to his bag, William was wondering what was going to happen to them.

The next thing he knew there was a rush of air and he descended along with everyone else down through the rainbow rug. He looked over and could see that the green jacketed boy was holding a metal object in his hand and turning something on it, almost like he was reeling in a fishing line after catching something but without all of the physical effort.

William looked down again, the rainbow rug had risen up past his knees, he could see a warm glow filling the space around his feet. As the rug approached his head he closed his eyes and held his breath. For some reason William thought and felt that he was going to drown.

Moments passed before William heard cries of, "WOW!" and sharp intakes of breath coming from those around him, forcing his eyes open. He was physically ok but his brain was not, he could not believe what had just happened to him. "It is impossible," he thought, "I just passed through a solid floor."

These thoughts were quickly taken over by more amazement as he looked out. It was a vast hall of a cavern, glowing warm, bright and busy with activity and noise. There were many other similar platforms, gliding up and down all the walls, packed with strangely dressed people, monstrous-looking caged creatures and other boxes and equipment carried on trollies that hovered just above the ground.

"Welcome First Years to Belbury Square, the centre of the greatest academy in either of the two worlds. When we stop please follow me and stay close so we do not lose you. Philippa and James would you shepherd the students from the back again please."

"Wow this place is amazing," William said to himself.

William had a few moments left before the fast-paced walk began again. He studied the space with darting eyes, it was the biggest space he had ever seen. He thought you could fit both new Elizabeth class Royal Navy aircraft carriers in here and still have room to spare.

The construction was a mix of raw rock, massive timber, stone work and high-tech structural work. William thought that he could probably see every type of construction age past, present and future in just this one place.

"Come on, come on keep up," called the blue jacketed boy again as he strode along weaving in and out of the busyness they had just arrived in.

In the centre of the ceiling was a preposterously huge glass bowl, about the size of the millennium dome in London, made of lots of huge glass panels and upside down like a cereal bowl. Inside the giant glass bowl William could see strange and unfamiliar creatures swimming around.

"Oi First Year!" shouted the yellow jacketed girl, clearly used to telling people what to do. "Get moving!"

William thought that for a girl with such a gentle name as Philippa, she had a very commanding voice.

"Hurry up!" she said again, pointing after the rest of the group.

"Sorry." William ran to catch up.

This was a busy place, people and things moving everywhere. William passed an amazing looking mechanical instrument playing beautiful background music. He tried to stop to look at the machine but was hurried on by the yellow jacketed girl, "You can look at that later, keep up with the group!"

From the quick glimpse he got, he could see many large gears, lifting and dropping balls onto keys. All controlled by a single man turning handles and pulling levers.

Around the square people were sitting and drinking, some playing games and others were clearly hurrying around on business. A very social space William thought.

One thing was clear that linked all the people, they all dressed slightly Victorian, but modern with splashes of the future.

After navigating the huge numbers of people and creatures that were also trying to dodge each other, the group reached a set of wide stone steps. They did not go very high but angled steeply in at the sides, funnelling people through an equally massive doorway at its centre.

Once through the doorway, William looked back and saw that the door was made of tendril-like things growing out of the wall and floor, knitting and weaving together so tight that no light could be seen from the other side.

This very special door guarded a very long hall with a ceiling that curled up and away, leading to a point above a high platform at the far end. William now stood in an enormous hall, which he could see was made with an intertwined root system, similar to the door. The structure was also covered in things that looked like mushrooms, and all connected with threads of white mycelium that weaved in and out of the root structure.

"Belbury Hall, I've heard about this place," George said to William in a stunned, awestruck voice. "They started to grow it roughly a hundred years ago and it's the only living root system building in the whole world."

"First Years please go with your House Captains to find seats with your new houses. Right, where are my Starlies?" the blue jacketed boy announced over the sound of hundreds of voices chatting in the hall.

Hands shot up across the group.

"Good come with me," the boy in blue said before walking off, continuing to talk as he led his new First Years to where they would be sitting.

"I am Marcus Mardic, I am Starley House Captain along with Captain of the academy." William and George were jogging to keep up as Marcus continued to talk. "Starley is the best house in the academy and current 4's champions. If you're an Igmon, you will soon learn about the greatest game in either of the two worlds and we are always looking for new players. The Headmaster, Sir Coalbrook will speak to us before we can eat, so sit down and say hi to your new families. We don't bite and we look after our own like we are flesh and blood. I will find you all at the end of the meal and show you to your house." He finally stopped and placed a hand on an empty chair. "Here we are, two seats for you two…" he said looking at William and George, "… and with other new First Years. Perfect." Then off Marcus went to seat other new First Years, before seating himself with a group of older-looking students toward the front of the hall.

🔔 An Introduction

William was thankfully settling into a seat and beginning to turn to the girl next to him to say "hi", when there was a shout from the front and everyone suddenly stood again. William and George, a little slowly and uncertain, copied everyone else, while looking around to find a reason.

William saw the main door slithering silently open, allowing a procession of people, who could only be teachers, to parade in, and who were being led by Mrs Volta who stood out, as she was the only one all in white.

The rest were wearing a selection of top hats, bowlers and flat caps, along with an array of colourful knee-lengthed jackets. William saw boots of every type, some tall, some short and some highly polished, others in need of repair. All the teachers were decorated in different bronze, gold, and silver brooches, badges and graphics, showing gears, symbols and prime shapes of all styles, types and sizes.

Belbury Hall was silent, apart from the loud and rhythmical hammering of hard-soled footwear on the stone floor. Once at the front they took their places on the raised wooden platform in highly decorated chairs, some futuristic and some old-looking. William noticed that each chair lowered itself as it took the weight of the teacher sitting in it, before gently recoiling up to a suitable height. This made his mind go wild, creating different mechanisms and ways that could be done.

Once they were all seated, Mrs Volta stood and announced with authority, "Stay standing for the Headmaster."

William looked back at the main door, but it did not slither open again.

"Good evening everyone! I trust you have all had a good summer holiday. And welcome to our new First Years! Please do sit down."

William turned around while following the instruction and saw someone that could only be the Headmaster had somehow appeared at the front, where there were no doors.

Turning to George, William whispered, "Where did he come from?"

"Through the back wall, in the middle," George replied with a smile and suppressed laughter.

William was gutted he had missed it. Yet another thing that he thought was impossible, in a day of impossible things happening and he missed it! This place was getting more and more amazingly crazy every moment.

"Thank you, let's hope that level of listening continues through the year," said the Headmaster, to the laughter of the hall. "To those who don't know me yet I am Sir Seamus Coalbrook, the Headmaster of Belbury Apprenticeship Academy, the best and greatest academy in either of the two worlds!" he said, beaming with passion and excitement, as the cheers from the academy rose.

Sir Seamus Coalbrook was a man of average height, with bushy brown eyebrows that matched his bushy brown moustache. His jacket was long and coloured like the sky and covered in small golden gears, symbols and shapes like stars in space. He wore a tall black smoke-stack top hat, with a golden badge on its front showing two gears meshed together, one big, one small. Underneath the jacket he wore a red waistcoat with two golden chains hanging from the centre button, each leading to a pocket on opposite sides. On his feet were brown workman's boots, which definitely looked like they were used for the purpose.

Sir Coalbrook continued, "It is now time to welcome our First Years to the academy. As I call your name, please come to the front and collect your Hadron-Tool. Through your time here you will learn how to use it and create your own additional functions and controls to add to it. So now without further waiting..."

The First Years were called up one by one, each one was applauded by the entire hall as the cold metallic-looking object was bestowed to them, and then cheered by their house as they walked back.

"James Jackson of Rutherford house... Goran Henbane of Fermi house... Millania Plinkton of Blanchard house..." The list of names continued to grow, while William grew ever more nervous, waiting to hear his own.

Finally, "William Taylor of Starley house," was called.

He stood up nervously, seeing hundreds of pairs of eyes watching him take the lonely walk to the front, to stand next to Sir Coalbrook.

"Welcome William," Sir Coalbrook said, while looking him confidently straight in the eyes and holding out his hand to be shaken. The handshake was very strong, making William wince with the pressure.

"I have heard you're quite something! I look forward to seeing what you can do and what you turn into," he said with an excitable sparkle in his bright blue eyes.

Out of the same bottomless pit of a pocket that had produced all the other Hadron-Tools, Sir Coalbrook produced another metal object, about the size of a hand-held torch and handed it to William, leaned in and said in a more private and quiet tone, "Learn to use this properly and you can change the world."

"Thank you Sir," William replied and could feel himself beaming with excitement inside. Turning the cold, unfamiliar object around in his hands, he walked back to his chair to the cheers of his new house.

Belbury Hall was now thick with the sounds of cheering and clapping as the last of the First Year students sat down at their house of Blanchard.

Moments later, two loud cracks sounded around the hall, as Sir Coalbrook clapped a similar-looking metallic object to those he had just handed out twice between his hands. The sound was all enveloping, like it was coming from every plate, cup, light, from everywhere and everything all at the same time. Belbury Hall crumpled into silence once more and every face turned to look at the front.

Sir Coalbrook now began to speak again with more formality and direct speech, to the hushed room of young faces. The excited playfulness of the first part of his speech had gone.

"For all of you, this year is a fresh start. One where problems and failures of the past can be forgotten, and one to use to build upon the progress and success of the year you have just had. If you feel lost, look to those who your houses are named after and uphold the memories," he said with a clear belief and passion that every student could indeed better themselves and create a better world.

Turning and pointing to a large planetary gear clock-looking object on the wall behind him he continued, "House points have been rolled back to zero." The clock-looking object began slowly moving and changing shape with the silent sound of well-greased gears. The item was beautifully made out of something like polished brass or bronze, making it twinkle and sparkle like a jewel, reflecting light onto the hall's walls and ceiling like stars. There was a single large central gear called the Pin Gear, which had four more smaller gears sitting around it called the House Gears. Each House Gear contained the first letter of the house name in ornate script. All four gears were now slowly all becoming the same size. As the year progressed, they would increase and decrease their size depending on how many points the house had.

The House Gears also rolled around the Pin Gear to show which house was winning. The leading house would be at the top position with the largest gear. The house in last place would sit at the lowest position, with the smallest gear. As they rolled and moved, the house Gears would overlap and overtake each other as house points and positions changed. This slightly mad and overly-complicated way of keeping score was contained by an outer ring called the belt, which stopped the whole thing falling apart.

"So, there is always a chance that your house could win Best House this year, or maybe the coveted 4's trophy, currently held by Starley for the last two years," he continued.

A cheer came up from the Starley tables as House Captain, Marcus Mardic stood up and encouraged more cheering from his house.

"You can do better than that," he shouted to his house, who responded with even more volume and stamping of feet and banging of fists, to the boos and heckling shouts of all the other houses. William joined in with the cheers and beat his fist upon the table.

The cheering and noise quietened down as Sir Coalbrook raised an arm to restore order and Marcus sat back down.

"Will any of you be holding the 4's trophy at the end of the year? Well, that is up to you!" Sir Coalbrook paused for a moment. "It is now time to eat our first meal together, so be bold, make friends, learn and strive to better yourself first before trying to fix those that are around you... You may begin."

From somewhere music started to play and happy excited conversation filled the hall. William looked around confused about where the food was, since the tables were empty. As if by magic, the woodgrain in the centre of each table split, allowing scissor mechanism, metallic arms to quickly spring out. Moving in sweeping arcs over the length of the table to place food and drink, before shooting back down like a rubber band. The arms returned again moments later with more food and drink, making springy, stretching noises as they moved.

William and George found it hard to have a conversation with the other First Years around them, as they all were transfixed by the arms appearing and disappearing, carrying food and drink and making a noise like an Anglepoise light as they did so.

Breaking free of this transfixing spell the spring arms cast over those at the table, William turned to a girl on his left with straight blonde hair that flowed freely to her lower back. She had a soft pale face with round gold rim glasses on her nose and was called Isabel Howl. Then to George's right was a short, slim girl with thick brown hair platted in a single ponytail with a long fringe that partly covered her right eye called Jasmin Bloom. They had all taken fried chicken, bashed potatoes, peas and gravy while excitedly starting to chat with each other.

"Where are you from William?" asked Isabel, while eating very properly with her cutlery.

"Depends on the year," William said, leading with his normal joke and enjoying the confused reaction from Isabel, "I have moved around a lot due to schools. I live in Guildford, Surrey, at the moment, just south-west of London. You?"

"I have lived in Thadworth all my life, that's a Thomon town, and I'm guessing you're an Igmon, as I have never heard of Guildford?" William nodded his head in confirmation. "Well, I have never met anyone from the Igmon world so nice to meet you."

"Likewise," interrupted George, while dripping gravy over the table. "William is the first I have met."

They were all playing with their Hadron-Tools while talking and eating, trying to get used to the unfamiliar device.

"I have been so excited about getting mine, I can't wait to start building it," said Jasmin, whilst spinning her Hadron-Tool on the table.

"Building it?" William asked. "Firstly, what is a Hadron-Tool and what do you mean by build it?" he said looking at the rather basic looking metal object in his hand.

"Ah yes, you're an Igmon! All students in the Thomon world are given this basic tool, called a Hadron-Tool when they start their development academies," Jasmin said.

"We use it to create and change the world around us," Isabel butted in, eager to show what she knew. "This is the basic version that everyone is given at the start. I have read that as you get good with it and find out what you want to do, you can add tools and abilities to it. Eventually everyone ends up having a very personal device that others find very hard to use," she went on, smiling to herself, impressed with her own knowledge.

"That's right," George said, waving his fork in Isabel's direction. "My dad has had his since he was my age and it looks way different to this one. I have seen him do loads of cool stuff with it. He is a Mechanical Fitter for the Bodger and Builder Society, and can build pretty much anything and everything," said George proudly.

As the meal continued, the table's wood grain split open again and the mesmerising dance of mechanical arms started to clear away the main course and replace it with pudding. William found this a little scary as his brain gave him a 'frozen' error warning as he tried to work out how this worked.

He then turned to his new friends and asked them to explain what 4's was, having never heard of the game, but recognised that it sounded pretty important.

Jasmin jumped in, "My eldest brother plays 4's professionally for the Iron Water Team. It's amazing to watch and I hope to get into a team. The game is simple really, you have a square pitch with a team in each corner. Teams win points by getting the ball into their opponent's goal. The team whose goal was just scored in, then loses a point."

William, with his elbows on the table, listened with interest and said, "So it's kinda like rugby but with four teams not two?"

George looked confused, "What's rugby? Anyway, teams can also negotiate with each other, teaming up against other teams during the match. Simple really," he said before taking a bite from a plate-sized chocolate donut.

"That sounds very complicated," William said, trying to keep up with the game.

"Don't worry," George said, this time spitting some pudding crumbs over the table. "The house will teach you how to play. I love watching it. There is no better game."

The conversation went on for the rest of the meal, talking about stuff from both the Igmon and Thomon worlds.

"Look, there are more interesting things than wrestling and tackling each other!" Isabel said as she became bored with the non-stop talking about violent sport.

"Like what?" The two boys said in unison, and both with food in their mouths.

Before she got a chance to say what was more interesting, two more cracks sounded within the hall and the tables fell silent as all eyes looked to the front again to see Sir Coalbrook standing.

"Well, I hope you have enjoyed our first meal together, but it is now time to leave for your beds. You will be able to find your lesson timetables and maps in your house common rooms. Lessons start when the first hammer drops so don't be late. House Captains please show your First Years to their dorms."

And with that the hall began to empty through the large door at the back of the hall, which had pre-emptively slithered fully open, as if the living door also had watching eyes.

"Keep up Starley First Years please," Marcus shouted above the noise of hundreds of moving students.

The walk to the Starley dorm took some time, as they had to walk down endless corridors and passageways. Some were round, some were square, some made the First Years crouch, to avoid banging their heads. One passageway had doors tightly lining the floor, walls and ceiling, with gravity having little effect on those walking out of any of the doors. There were staircases, slopecases, flatcases and more moving platforms. William felt totally lost and wondered how he was ever going to find his way back out.

They also walked through many small squares, each with many other passages leading off them. Each square had its own feel, but each had a high ceiling with a white cast-iron signpost with black writing at its centre. The signs in one particular square pointed to areas such as Engineers Toy Box, Stone Fabrics and Lightning Control Centre. The group ran scared past one door that roared terrifyingly at them and peered down stairwells full of water. Many Humans, Elves, Dwarfs and other strange looking creatures and beings passed the other way, wearing all sorts of different jacket colours, decorations and items on their persons. They all looked busy and William could feel that there was a great energy to the place.

Eventually they came to a halt inside a very tall red brick shaft that rose up and out of sight.

"Right, your first lesson, so listen carefully," Marcus said, turning to the group. "Take your Hadron-Tool and push the round end of it into one of the holes at the bottom of a groove going up the wall and don't let go! Your Hadron-Tool is like a key that will allow you access into your common room and yours only. You will see these holes and grooves everywhere," Marcus said as he pointed to a small round hole in one of the red bricks. "The groove tells you the direction of travel," he added, while running a finger along a straight groove cut into the brick. "Most of them you can use, but you must look at your map first to see where it finishes or you may end up very, very far away from where you actually want to be." With that, Marcus pushed his Hadron-Tool into a small hole located at the bottom of a long groove that ran up the shaft and instantly vanished out of sight.

Jasmin Bloom was the first to give it a nervous try, followed by the rest of the group who found that there were hundreds of holes and grooves, covering the inside of the shaft.

This made William very worried indeed. He could see that mixed in with all the grooves going up, were many grooves going down through the floor and some holes had no groove at all.

"If it were dark you could very easily end up somewhere you did not want to be," he thought aloud.

"Yes, I was thinking the same thing," replied George with trepidation, and thinking William was talking to him. "Oh well, up we go"

Together they pressed their Hadron-Tools into separate holes in the shaft's curved brick wall, and William once again held his breath. Wwwwoooosssssshhhhh. No sooner had they pressed their Hadron-Tools into the holes, they were standing in a new space similar to the one they had just come from.

Marcus counted them in, "Everyone here? One, two, three, four, five, six... great, no one let go. Brilliant!"

"Um, Captain!" called a blond-haired boy.

"Yes," Marcus replied, searching the group, to find the body belonging to the voice.

"What happens if we do let go?" the boy said, saying what all the other First Years were thinking.

"Good question and one which no one actually knows the answer to. The few who have let go, have never been found again, so have not been able to tell anyone what happens. Just best to not risk it and hold on tight!" replied Marcus with a smile.

They had walked into a space where modern and old design clashed comfortably with each other, much like the rest of Belbury Academy that William had seen so far. Threadbare sofas sat alongside brand new high-tech ones, and a similar situation with the rest of the furniture. The room was a mix of high- and low-tech materials and objects, showing the best of old and new. Roughly down the centre of the room and evenly spaced were two large floating spheres of fire that heated the jumbled space, with many smaller tennis ball-sized spheres of light floating just below the ceiling rafters, shedding light around the comfy space. Large notice boards stuck with formal academy papers and posters showing people playing 4's and clubs to join, were dotted in the space between the windows. The house crest painted gold and blue hung above the entrance that they had just walked through, like an ever-watching gate keeper.

"It is the exact same thing to go out and down from here, just push your Hadron-Tool into a hole at the top of a groove going down. Let me be the first to welcome you to the Starley common room. The boards on the right have your timetables and maps on them. Please take one of each and study them tonight as you will need to get to each class on time, and as you should have learnt from all the walking this evening, nothing is exactly close together," he said while picking a map up and waving it around. "The corridor to my left leads to the girls' dorm and to my right is the boys' dorm. You don't enter each other's dorms!" Marcus paused to firmly stare around the group to check they all had been told. "The one behind me leads to the House Prefects and Captains area. You do not enter down there unless you are invited. Right, it is getting late..." he said while glancing at the side of his Hadron-Tool "... so off to your rooms now and we will see you at breakfast. Remember..." Marcus said, raising his hand to mark the importance of the next point, "... lessons start at the drop of the first hammer so don't be late! Off you go."

The number three dorm William and George entered was a very pleasant wedge-shaped room, with the door being at the point of the wedge. The opposite wall was a single huge window, with four comfy chairs looking out at the infinite dark night sky. Even so, William felt like he could see for miles and that he was very high up. There were four captain's beds, two each side, with personal space, consisting of storage and desk space located underneath.

As promised, their luggage was placed neatly next to their desks. Happy to see his bag again, William quickly unzipped it to see if everything was still inside. To his surprise everything was better packed than how he had left it, clothes were ironed and neatly folded and his Lego was all sorted neatly into colours and types and all his pencils were perfectly sharpened.

The two boys, exhausted from a day of long journeys and longer walks, and their brains suitably frazzled from seeing many impossible things become possible, this was true even for George. Wearily they dressed for bed, dragged themselves up their short wooden ladders and under the covers, falling asleep before their heads hit their pillows.

🔲 Control and Manipulation

A sound like a big bell rang around six thirty in the morning, waking the boys abruptly from the depths of luxurious sleep.

William, excited for the day ahead dressed quickly in his new uniform, which both he and George found hanging neatly on their desk chairs when they arrived with a note pinned on top saying:

Academy Uniform

William Taylor, First Year, Starley House
Items included: 1 x Blazer, 2 x Trousers, 2 x Shirt,
2 x jumpers,
1 x Tie, 1 x Cap, 4 x pairs of socks, 1x pair of boots.
Wear from this morning.

William's blazer was made of heavy maroon-coloured material and ended at his knees, and covered a white shirt that had a very solid, starched, cut-away collar. The blue house tie and maroon flat cap made him feel very smart, and both showed his house emblem of a seven-spoked wheel. His trousers were black and floated about a hand's-width above his smart black leather lace-up boots. William admired himself in the full height mirror, feeling great pride in the uniform and what it meant for him. A new look for a new start, he thought to himself.

"Yesterday wasn't a dream," William said to his reflection in disbelief.

"No mate, definitely not, and I think we've not seen anything yet," George replied, full of excitement for the day ahead.

As they chatted and walked around their room getting used to their new clothes, they tried to figure out what the first drop of the hammer was and where the first class was from the bizarre map they had been given, unhelpfully with no instruction on how to use it.

William walked over to the heavy curtains, testing his shoes as he went, stiff, he thought. He flung the curtains back, revealing an awesome view. He then looked down at his feet and saw the immense height he was at, making him grab the curtains tightly to stop himself from feeling like he was going to fall. William had been right the previous night; he could see for miles and he was definitely high.

Looking out, William could see a small town spread out below him. He could see three other towers like the one he was in; these must be the other academy houses, William thought. Each tower must have been about half a mile high, with birds circling below their roof lines.

All the towers had bases like great redwood trees, and grew upward through stone, steel and finally into glass at their tops. The towers dominated the small town below, but both were set in an even larger and deeper valley that contained fields, woods, lakes and rivers, with roads leading out of the valley in four directions.

"Well, this view definitely makes the map make a bit more sense, and boy do we have a lot of walking to do!" George said while staring out of the window.

"You any good with a map, George?" William asked.

"No, you?" George replied.

"Not really no, but we better get good quick or we're going hungry!" William said, already feeling his tummy start to rumble.

The map was on what looked like high quality handmade paper, that flexed like leather. The boys now regretted not spending the previous evening studying it as instructed, as they were finding it very tricky to read.

When William first held it, he could see a plan view of the town below in all its detail, he also found he could even zoom in and out. Red dots were scattered over the map, which when touched expanded to show location names, timetables and advice on how to get there. When he flipped the paper end over, a new lower floor level was shown, with more streets, corridors, rooms and spaces than could comfortably be conceived in William's mind. Each time the paper was flipped a new floor level would appear. George found that he could flip the map up to six times before it showed the ground level again.

"Right, well first things first I guess. Let's silence my tummy," William said. "Breakfast! George, lead the way."

Without too much trouble the boys found the correct floor where the main Belbury Hall was located, and navigated there quite successfully. They took only one wrong turn on their way, that left them face to face with a wild looking scientist. Explosions of bright white hair made him look like he had taken a few too many electrical shocks that day. The crazy looking scientist wore a thick monocle and a long white rubbery coat. He was busily wiring up a pulsing, humming contraption to his co-worker, who looked more than a little bit reluctant to be attached to the device. The wild man chased the boys away before they could see the effect of the device.

Breakfast was again, all-you-could-eat, and delicious. The meal was dominated however, with William and George, who had managed to find Isabel and Jasmin sitting at the same table as the previous night, figuring out what their lessons were that day, where they had to be and at what time. As far as William could see there were no normal subjects like maths, science, English, history and thankfully no Latin. There was however a class called "Looking After Yourself", which took place at a mixture of places – from the hospital, a couple of restaurants and a sports centre. "Your Culture, Your History" took place in the library, museum and one or two of the town's pubs. "Building the Future" took place in the industrial district, and "Work, Earn and Live" took place in the town's bank along with a number of other general shops and businesses.

The list went on and on, but the first lesson was called, "Control and Manipulation". This lesson was located across the other side of town in what looked like a mix between a shooting range and a housing estate.

Not knowing what time the hammer dropped, but seeing the hall quickly emptying, the new friends set off at a run, crossing the main square with William leading the way, map in hand to find the first groove that would take them in roughly the right direction. William successfully found the groove as shown by the map and to his relief was also heading in the right direction.

"You better be right about this one," said George, "I don't want to end up in some random location."

"Well you will just have to trust me!" William said, confident that he had the right groove. "Right, I will go first. See you at the other end!" he said while placing his Hadron-Tool on the edge of the hole, before muttering, "please be right," and drove it home into the hole. Wwwwoooossssshhhh.

Before William had even thought he had pushed the Hadron-Tool in all the way, he had arrived at the base of a very tall spiral staircase, leading up to sunlight and a blue sky. The rest of the group had now arrived, and together they shot up the cast iron staircase. They burst through the disk of blue sky and sunshine to emerge into what looked more like a battlefield than a classroom, just as a crisp and clear, CLANG, sounded twice in the distance.

Piles of material and partly collapsed buildings were everywhere, with smoke oozing from piles of rubble, caused by whatever action had taken place. Crater holes littered the ground, some the size of dinner plates, others the size of houses, and debris covered everything.

William could now see more groups of First Years walking and running out of various locations and objects around the hellscape. Some ran out of an old phone box, others a hollow in a tree. One unlucky group fell out of one of the remaining first floor windows of what used to be a house.

Intrigued, William looked back to see what he had come out of. He could no longer see a hole leading to a staircase, but a small pond complete with fish and fountain, which Jasmin was now standing up to her ankles in and complaining about having wet feet.

"Sorry I am late, all of you walk to me!" shouted a very loud voice, off to William's left. It was a man in a forest green and brown knee-length jacket that had pockets at thigh level. It was held in place with a stout brown leather belt, which held many pouches tight around his hips. A pair of brown boots rose up his calf, supporting a single scratched pad covering his right knee. A helmet sat over his head and was decorated with scraps of loose material. He gave the impression of looking smart but yet ready to run off into the woods at a moment's notice.

He strode into the angry mess, touching his Hadron-Tool to remnants of piles of broken buildings as he went. Before Williams' eyes buildings began to rebuild themselves, like a video in reverse.

Seeing that the gathering children were staring and pointing in firework excitement at what was happening, the man began to explain in a loud voice as he worked.

"All the buildings in this training area are built with a global proton magnetism. This means that each block, tile, particle of dust, everything has been given a set location on the planet where it should and wants to be." The man carried on touching piles of rubble as he continued to talk in a raised voice. "When it is removed from this preset location, say from a practice battle, it longs to be back where it was created to be.

However, it must wait until it is allowed to do so, which is what I am doing now. No matter where all the parts have been thrown to, once they are allowed, they move back to their original global proton magnetic position without delay. This takes all the pain and effort out of clearing up and rebuilding after each session, as if by magic!"

"That's impossible!" William said under his breath. "How on earth does the global proto thing work? There must be some sort of electronic micro sensor built into everything," William thought. His mind racing from question to question, as it swirled with excitement about what he was seeing.

They all met in the middle just as the man finished talking and everything was reassembled, with not a brick out of place.

"Well good morning First Years, I am your Control and Manipulations teacher and I will answer to Sir or Mr Warthard. I am here to teach your most important lessons: how to control and manipulate the world around you. Master this class and you will be able to use your Hadron-Tools to their maximum. And maybe, just maybe, you might become one of the greats."

William felt a little shy in the presence of such a confident-sounding and together looking man. He found himself rolling his Hadron-Tool around in his pocket out of nervousness.

"Right, you all have your Hadron-Tools, yes?"

"Yes!" a few voices nervously said.

"Well, let's see them. Get them out and hold them high so I can have a look."

There was a rustling as the First Years produced their Hadron-Tools from all different locations, as no one was quite sure where it should be best kept.

"Great, let's have a closer look now then," Mr Warthard said, walking around the children and looking at the type and condition of the Hadron-Tool they had been given.

"Well, you all have a decent basic model, that is good to see. Now with this tool, yes even your basic version, you can manipulate the world around you. As you get better you can add additional items to your tool to suit your needs. But, as you are First Years, there are to be no additions made to your tools, is that understood?"

"Yes Sir!" a few more voices answered a little more bravely, while the group felt a little disappointed.

"As you gain experience with your Hadron-Tool, you will be able to change the shape and size of objects around you." He demonstrated by touching the ground with his Hadron-Tool and dragging the ground up into what could best be described as a wall or barrier, but which looked exactly like the ground that it had been pulled from.

"You will be able to project objects through the air." With a flick of his wrist the ground dropped back down, flowing back to where it had come from. Picking up a stone in one hand he touched it with his Hadron-Tool, it shot off, smashing into the nearest building, creating an explosion of dust as it was obliterated against the brickwork.

"You may even get good enough that you can create lightning bolts, or create something out of nothing!" he added, looking at the children with excitement in his eyes. The children responded with wide-eyes of excitement and amazement; he knew they were now eager to start learning.

"But another rule first. You are now standing in the live practice zone. Here you will learn to defend yourself and if required – attack. So never come here without a teacher as you might not come back. The mock fights, battles and wars that are practised here by the senior students are no joke! Is that understood?"

There was no reply from the group, but Mr Warthard could see the message had been taken in.

"Good. Now the tool can be held in either hand, but you must hold it round end out, like this," he said, holding his tool up in the air for everyone to see. "These tools don't work by force or magical words," he said with a slight laugh. "They work by connection, imagination and confidence. You need to create a clear image in your mind of what you want to happen, have no doubt that it is going to happen, and a strong connection with the object for it to change. If you have those three things, then your Hadron-Tool will do what you want to that object. Does everyone understand?" Mr Warthard finished his checklist, tilted his helmet back and looked around checking everyone was keeping up, and had their Hadron-Tools the right way around. With two large, quick steps he was standing in front of Jasmin Bloom pointing at her Hadron-Tool.

"What's wrong here?" he said, firmly but kindly.

Jasmin looked at her tool and quickly flipped the tool the right way around. She gave him a sheepish smile and saw a light green glow around him.

This was nothing unusual for Jasmin as she was gifted with soul synesthesia, meaning that she saw people with a different coloured haze around them dependent on the character she felt they had. People who were trustworthy and safe had a green haze, and those who were untrustworthy, she saw in red. This gift of seeing in colours was not only related to peoples' characters, but also to numbers and letters. When she did not want people to know what she was writing, she would swap letters for colours, or paint a picture to remember information from a class.

Jasmin had often been told by her parents that in the Igmon world her gift was viewed as a problem and was something to be medicated or taught away. But in the Thomon world it was celebrated and sought after, which often made Jasmin feel sorry for those in the Igmon world who were not encouraged to enjoy their gift.

"Ok class, watch me for a demonstration of what we will be learning today. I will say what I am wanting to happen aloud so you know what to expect to see. Let's have a play with... this car." Next to Mr Warthard was a very standard blue Ford saloon car. It had been quietly procured from the Igmon world for research purposes and not at all for fun, during a joint operation between the Thomon Research Engineers and the Protection and Security Council.

Mr Warthard squared up to the car and positioning his feet firmly in the dirt with a twist, over-emphasising the movements, he drew his Hadron-Tool and pressed it on to the body of the car, saying:

"Raise!"

The car without vibration, effort or noise, slowly rose calmly straight up from the ground, following Mr Warthard's arm movement as if he was as strong as Big Carl, the largest mobile crane in the Igmon world.

"Halt!"

The car stopped rising and floated mid-air, at shoulder level, as if frozen in time and space, with its wheels dangling ridiculously below.

"Lower!"

Back to the ground the car floated like a feather, landing daintily on all four wheels and gently compressing the suspension.

"Ok, a very basic-looking skill but great fun, and useful. Now, how about one more thing? Making it smaller! Remember you must have good contact between your Hadron-Tool and the object you want to manipulate. Best practice is to push into the object as it shrinks, as if you are trying to compress it, this helps maintain that all important contact."

He looked back at the car, touched it and said.

"Shrink!"

The car began to shrivel, like a balloon losing its air.

William could just about make out a blur of movement at the end of his teacher's Hadron-Tool that he did not notice before. Like hundreds of tiny legs, wiggling around, like a spider pulling in its thread.

The students could see Mr Warthard pushing into the car, leaning over it to never lose contact with it as it moved away from him as it shrank. He stopped shrinking the car when it was the size of a match box and he was on his knees. Unfolding himself from his kneeling position, he stood and addressed the line of students, who applauded.

"Thank you. Remember it is not about words. Saying 'abracadabra' will do nothing. It's about how strongly you can imagine it and feel what you are wanting to happen and how well you can start and keep the connection. Being able to shrink objects is immensely useful, as it means you can carry a lot more stuff in your pockets, but only if you also learn how to make it grow back to its original size again. A volunteer to pick up the car for me?" Hands shot up. "Jasmin, on the double if you please."

Jasmin ran over and slid to a halt next to the small toy car. She picked it up carefully so as not to break it, and took a long close look to check it was still the same car and not some sort of magic trick, before placing it into Mr Warthard's open hand.

"Thank you. This car can now fit in my pocket, and I can still open the doors. If I wanted to I could shrink one of you and have you get in, start it and drive around. Right, thank you, Jasmin. Please place it back on the floor."

Happily, Jasmin grabbed the car and placed it on the floor where it had come from.

"Grow!" Came the command, once Jasmin was back in line. The car slowly grew, like bread dough proving. Mr Warthard stopped the enlarging of the car once it was back to its original size.

"Everybody understand what I am expecting to see and any questions? No? Good! Who would like to try then?"

Hands shot up along the line.

"Great, first you need to find a small item like a leaf, stone or twig from around here and hold it out flat in your hand like you are feeding a horse."

Everyone shot off, running around what now looked like a posh commuter tower to William, looking for something they could use. A minute or so later all of the First Years were back in line holding their chosen objects out in front of them, hands flat as instructed.

William had chosen a small brown pebble, George an oak leaf, Jasmin a slightly mouldy twig and Isabel had somehow been able to find a tiny flower.

"Perfect, everyone, well done, and lots of different items. Right, now time to manipulate the objects you have into your practice cubes. So, who wants to go first?"

William stepped forward so fast, he surprised himself, he did not think he had volunteered. He held out the small, round, brown pebble he had collected from near one of the surrounding buildings that looked like an outdoor bike lockup.

"Good, thank you William. Hold it steady now. Don't want to change the shape of you by accident now do we?" Mr Warthard said while moving his Hadron-Tool in a smooth and controlled yet stylish way towards the pebble, like an artist moving a paint brush toward the canvas.

Slowly and without saying a word he touched his Hadron-Tool to the pebble and like magic the pebble began to swell, twist and bulge into a perfect cube, a little bigger than the original pebble. William guessed that all the sides were about twenty millimetres long.

William could now clearly see hundreds of tiny legs working away at a blurred pace. Small electrical flashes along with a blue glow could also be seen, as the Hadron-Tool changed the pebble.

He now walked down the row of children changing the objects they had into perfect cubes, all the same size, and carrying the same colour and texture as the object from which they had been created.

Mr Warthard walked back to the centre front. "I want you to practise lifting your new cubes and changing their size as I have shown you. Keep these cubes on you for all classes as you will use them throughout your first year," he instructed.

The rest of the lesson was spent trying and failing, or trying and sort of succeeding at the task. While Mr Warthard walked around the class giving tips, pointers and odd motivational speeches.

"What you are now doing is learning what the Igmons ignorantly call magic, but this is nothing of the sort as magic does not exist. The magic they make stories and myths about is made by a combination of our advanced technology, science and engineering. Right now you are trying to compress, stretch and move the very fabric of the physical world, the very stuff your practice cube and the world around you is made of. All thanks to a well-engineered Hadron-Tool." He tailed off from his little speech as he approached another member of the class to offer help.

George was struggling to lift the cube. His first attempt ended in sending his cube careering into Isabel who was next to him, causing her to drop her tool and clutch her leg with both hands in pain. Shouting at George, close to tears she cried out,

"How could you be so incapable? Go practice away from me!"

His second attempt sent the object burrowing deep into the ground at his feet, which Mr Warthard had to retrieve for him.

William was having far greater success with floating and changing the size of the cube. It was coming very naturally to him and he felt at one with what was happening.

"Alright for some," a frustrated George said, flashing a jealous sideways look at William.

Lessons went on like this all day, with William, George, Jasmin and Isabel rushing all over the map by foot and by groove.

They arrived late at "Your Culture, Your History", due to taking the wrong wall groove. They had ended up somewhere very cold, like a beautiful winter wonderland, until they encountered a savage looking eight-legged bear, which had sword-like teeth, on full snarling show, with slobber slopping out of its mouth, running down its fur as it charged them. The group only just found a groove away from inevitable death with moments to spare.

William found the, "Your Culture, Your History", class interesting after having been dreading the class, as it reminded him of history lessons at Lakefields. He was correct about the amount of books and texts involved, which he had to read very slowly. But the teacher was like Mr Stephenson and told stories and tales of the past, about why things are like they are now and William was fascinated.

One story in particular got the group talking for the rest of the day. The story was about the Dynacube, which was the source of endless energy. If you looked closely at the Dynacube on a full moon when the planets were in alignment, you could see lightning bolts striking around a mini sun.

In the story, the Dynacube became lost during one of the many battles of the Great War, between two powerful Thomon families. One family had been tasked as its protectors and had used it to bring life to the earth and the people who lived there, helping to develop and advance human life on earth. They lived a life of selflessness, since none of them owned anything but gave what they had to those in need.

The other family wanted it for themselves. They hated all others who lived in the world, seeing all others, Thomon and Igmon as being no better than slaves or cattle to be worked. They wanted to use its endless power to enslave all those who stood against them, who they saw as inferior and to take what they had not earned for themselves and to rule all others.

*

Sitting on a comfy, battered sofa, near a floating sphere of fire that bobbed up and down gently in the Starley common room. The friends talked excitedly about where they would look for the Dynacube and what they would do with it if they found it, when William became distracted by the floating glass sphere in front of him. He realised that he had not taken the time to look and see how these spheres worked, which were everywhere. So, ignoring his friends, who continued to talk, he knelt down on the old carpet beside it as it silently bobbed up and down. He could feel the intense heat on his skin, but when he touched the glass-like surface it was cool to the touch. He looked under it, around it, stared hard into the violent furnace inside hoping to see what made it float, but saw nothing. Confused, he closed his eyes so that he could fully focus on feeling through his fingers, then gently slid both his hands over the smooth, cool surface. Then he felt it, a gentle almost unnoticeable vibration, that rippled from top to bottom. The surprise of this discovery sprung open his eyes to try and see it but the feeling was instantly gone as if it was afraid to be seen. William's brain began churning over ideas of how it worked before it was interrupted by Marcus Mardic jumping onto a table in the centre of the room. He clapped his Hadron-Tool, creating a loud BANG sound throughout the room. All eyes snapped to look at Marcus, who was holding a single piece of clean white paper.

"It is time… to sign up for the Starley 4's team trials," he called excitedly before touching his Hadron-Tool to the paper in his hand. Instantly all four corners folded into spikes. He then released the paper as if to drop it and it took off across the room, shot forward by his Hadron-Tool. It flew low, skimming heads and knocking one particularly tall student's academy cap off as it shot across the common room, before burying its four corners in the notice board like nails, holding it firmly in place.

"The trial is next Wednesday evening after lessons at the top pitch. Everyone is allowed to sign up and try, but only a few will be selected to compete," said Marcus as he stepped down from the table.

No one moved for a few seconds. Then noise suddenly erupted as the sheet was surrounded by students signing up. It was mainly the older years signing up at first, but the scrum calmed down after a few minutes giving the younger years their turn.

George looked at his new friends, and then jumped to his feet.

"I am in! Come on. What's the worst that can happen?"

William wrote his name, his pen shaking a little with nervousness on the sheet, followed by Jasmin.

"Not going to try out Isabel? Too much muscle needed?" George said while flexing his thin ten-year-old arms.

"Why would I want to take part in a game that could put me in hospital! No, I enjoy watching it, but playing it no thank you. I am perfectly happy, thank you," she said. While outwardly this was said with confidence, inside she was desperate to sign up, but could not bring herself to do it as her parents had always pushed books and discouraged sport, thinking it was a waste of time.

8 Try Out

A wet and grey Wednesday evening met the line of hopefuls on the 4's top pitch. All waiting for a chance to show Marcus, the House Captain, what they could do and be picked for one of the 4's house teams. Damp evening mist had descended, making the grass slippy under-foot. Ghostly outlines of people, barrels and distant trees, helped to add to the nervousness for what they were about to go through.

William was standing with George at the centre of the line of hopefuls, with neither boy daring to talk to each other and break the nervous silence. William apprehensively looked out through his breath at the first 4's pitch he had ever seen. He could make out that the pitch was big, much bigger than a rugby or football pitch, and he started to realise that this game would involve a lot of running. In anticipation of what he guessed would be coming he started to wiggle his fingers and toes to combat the stiffening cold and be ready to run.

All the hopefuls had swapped their normal academy uniform for basic sports gear, of mid-thigh length heavy-duty, cotton shorts, a long-sleeved top, long socks in the house colour and studded boots.

Half the house had turned up for the try outs and were facing the current first team players, standing in their blue glory, with boiled leather helmets under their arms, looking like an army ready for battle and being led from the front by Marcus, who was also holding something that looked like a giant brown egg.

Marcus stood without moving or saying a word for just a few seconds, he just looked slowly up and down the line. William could tell that Marcus had a thing for theatrical performance speaking as he would always make it into a bit of a show. Marcus then walked past in front of the hopefuls while starting to talk about the game and what was required. The hopefuls were now all starting to feel the cold and started to jog on the spot to stay warm.

"4's is not a game for the faint-hearted. Those who play put *everything* on the line every game! They do it for the pride of the house and to retain the cup, but also for personal glory. It is great to see so many of you here but most of you will not be picked. You will need to be fit, fearless and clever to become a champion at 4's." Marcus paused to look down the line. "So, fitness – let's see. Run and touch each goal on the pitch four times – three – two – one – *GO!*"

Like startled rabbits, the line of soggy and frozen hopefuls shot off in all directions to touch each goal four times, all trying not to be the last to finish.

The evening went on and on like this, with one test rolling into the next one. Tackling, running, catching, running, wrestling and running. No break was given, leaving William's lungs feeling like they were going to explode. William willed his aching body to keep going, "You're my legs and you will keep going," he forcefully commanded himself. The quantity of hopefuls still going was slowly diminishing with every new test. All finding they did not have what it took, and dragging their sore wet feet back indoors to warm up and console their failure.

While more and more trials and tests were given to the remaining hopefuls, they were also being shouted at by the members of the house team.

"Keep going!"

"Get up, don't quit now!"

"You call that running!"

"I said tackle not cuddle!"

The loud voice of Marcus carried clearly over all of the exhausting activity and the shouts of what was apparently encouragement, as he himself shouted the instructions and rules for the game of 4's.

"The pitch is a hundred and ten metres square. Each team has an oak barrel goal, which they need to protect and it sits five metres in from the corner. Each goal is surrounded by a one metre no go zone, shown by a white line around it. No one! I say *NO* one is allowed inside that area – of your goal or the opponent's. Who is allowed in the no go zone?" He asked the huffing and puffing hopefuls.

"No one," came a gasping reply.

"Come on, you need to do better than that!" he called, while cupping his ear with one hand.

"NO ONE," the hopefuls managed to shout back.

"Good, you're all still listening! There is a four-metre gap between the outside of the no go zone and the edge of the pitch so you can play behind the goal as well as in front. Your team gains points by throwing this ball," which he held up aloft above his head, "into your opponents' barrels. When you score, you gain three points, and the team whose goal you scored in, loses three points. Everyone following me so far?"

"Yes," came an effortful shout from the remaining exhausted hopefuls.

"Good, you are all learning," he shouted before carrying on.

After more running, testing and shouting, it was over. William, tired, battered, soaked and broken, had made it to the end, and collapsed onto his knees in a muddy puddle to get his breath back.

"Well done, well done all of you, great work this evening. Keep an eye out on the notice board, if you have done well enough you will see your names selected," Marcus said to the bedraggled group.

With a sigh of relief, William, George and Jasmin hobbled back together to the warmth of the common room, a hot shower and then a deep exhausted sleep.

"That was much harder than I thought it would be," said George to his two exhausted friends who just grunted in reply.

William woke early the next morning, while George was still sound asleep. Quietly he climbed down his short ladder, his body still sore and stiff from the previous day's 4's trials. He spun the small light on the desk under his bed to turn it on before sitting to write a letter back to his mum and dad as two weeks had passed at Belbury Apprenticeship Academy. William did not know where to start, it had been two weeks of excitement, seeing impossible things made possible and learning so much that he had almost forgotten that the Igmon world existed.

It was in that moment of quiet contemplation, while he was sitting alone in his room that he realised something very important, something that would change his life forever. Not once over the past two weeks had he struggled in class. Yes, he had been his normal slow-reading self, but it had not felt like a problem. Not once had he come back to his room in tears. Not once had he felt like the teachers were against him. Not once had anything except enjoyment and fascination passed through his mind. William, inspired, put pen to paper and began to write.

To Mum and Dad,

I am loving mi time heer. This skool is so amayzing and so unlike all the other skools I have deen to. I am not sure I wood really call it a skool as it is very a small town and we have lesons in the bifferent shop and workshops around the town.

I have som good friends heer as well as deing in a great skole hous called Starly, which is at the top of a realy tall tower, you would lov the views.

I have never deen so happy in skool.

I am also trying out for the hous 4's team, which is kinda like four way rugby.

Thank you so much for leting me come heer.

I hop you are wel.

Lov Will.

Folding the letter up, he dropped it into one of the infinitely dark holes in his dorm. The pupils had started to call these dark circles 'anything holes', as you could pretty much put anything in them, that needed something happening to it, and that something would happen, and no one knew how it worked.

🔲 Time to explore

The day was Saturday, William and George were planning to explore the map to fill the day. Since starting at Belbury Apprenticeship Academy, they had never been lower than level two. They knew from the map that there were lots more levels to explore, and hopefully more amazing things to see if they went lower. The two boys also noticed that as the map levels went lower and lower, the amount of information dots that could be touched reduced dramatically and eventually totally disappeared on level six.

Before setting off George studied his map, to find a way to reach level five. The map showed that once they passed level three, there were hardly any grooves to get any lower. This lack of access and lack of information dots made the boys curious, and they began to think that maybe, they were not meant to go down so far. So of course this made them even more confident that level five was the right one to get to and explore first before trying to head even lower another day.

They set off "down the groove", as was said in the academy, to get out of the house common room.

They reappeared on level two, George ready with his map out to navigate William and himself to the closest down groove to take them to level four, bypassing level three. There was no direct route from level two to level five and level three did not interest them enough to want to explore.

The boys emerged onto level four, which had a polished clean red brick floor, the walls and ceiling were tiled in computer beige rectangles, again polished clean. Tennis ball sized spheres of light floated along the top centre of the arched ceiling, lighting the space.

The throng and hubbub of people wearing all sorts of hats and knee length jackets was even more electric and energetic than on the levels above. The boys could see that much work was being carried out and daily business clearly still happened on the weekends.

William stepped out of the alcove into which they had arrived, promptly got shouted at for getting in the way by a very small lady who looked like a cross between a dwarf and a goblin, whose coat tails were dragging behind her on the floor.

"Where to next then?" asked William, looking left and right, up and down the packed corridor.

"Ur... Ur... let's go... Um... Right, we should find a square where we can work out where to go next," George said hurriedly, but confidently as he was not enjoying being knocked about by all the people passing this way and that.

"Sounds like a good plan," William said, while squeezing off in the direction given, making sure to keep close to the wall and stay out of everyone's way.

They emerged into a very grand square as the map had predicted. The red brick floor filled the whole square like a great desert and polished to such a gleaming finish that it looked as slippery as ice.

The computer beige wall tiles carried on along the sides of the square, but gave way to a tall glass dome above. Through the glass dome the boys could see the raw rock that made up the ground above, on show, bright, cleaned and lit up for all to see as if on display in an art gallery. The natural forms of the rock created an artistic sculpture all around the square.

What amazed the boys most was a window in the centre of the dome, because it did not show rock but blue sky, idyllic clouds and a perfect sun. Birds also flew in and out of sight. The window was framed with a large gold ring, imprisoning the beautiful view. The whole architectural spectacle gave the feeling of looking up and out of a great shaft cut through the solid rock above, all the way to the surface.

"Wow!" William said, staring up.

Both boys stood still, looking around the room, as the energy of daily Thomon life hummed on around them.

"That must be a graphic or screen of some sort," said George, pondering the possibility, "we are hundreds of feet below the surface."

William thought how real it looked, and how nothing in his Igmon world came close to this in terms of realism, if it indeed was a screen at all. It felt so real that he thought he could smell the air, feel the breeze and hear the birds.

"Maybe our engineering teacher will be able to tell us how it works? We have our first lesson with him next week right?" William said to George while still looking around. "I would love to learn how to make amazing things like that," William said privately to himself.

"Right where to next?" George said, trying to break the spell of the room.

"Well, what does the map say?" asked William.

There were three options George could see, and he headed to the closest one. This took them past a thrift market, some sort of modern blacksmiths and a gym where everyone was floating around the room. There was a sign on the window, which the boys paused to read:

"Giving you the latest in zero gravity exercise, build that body and save those joints."

This to William seemed like a contradiction, as even to his young mind he knew that it was gravity that made things heavy, and so how could people work out when they were weightless? William made a mental note to ask a teacher about weightless weight next week.

"A new fad probably," George said, staring in through the window. "My mum got really into a fad once, which had her always walking backwards. I suppose in the Igmon world you have things like that as well?"

"More than I would like to admit," William answered with a chuckle.

The two boys found the groove they were looking for, which headed straight down into the floor.

Trust was very important when using these grooves, as they often sent the user through a solid object, such as a wall or floor. One could imagine that if the groove was fake or not made correctly, then the user was not coming out of the other end in the same shape they went in.

This made for much amusement and joking with his class when a new groove had to be used for the first time. Thankfully all the class were still alive and the jokes were just that, jokes.

William pulled his Hadron-Tool out of his pocket and pushed the end of it into the snug fitting circular hole, wwwwooooosssshhhh.

*

Joyless was the first thing that William noticed when his senses came back, moments after reappearing, just before George appeared next to him. Immediately George started to flip the map over and over quickly, until he was on the correct level and so could give directions.

Level five had lost the energetic energy of level four, and felt more like a graveyard than a place of work.

The floors were still clean and highly polished, but this time it was a single smooth white surface. "Painted maybe," William thought.

The corridor was much narrower than the floors above and had a low and sharply angled ceiling, covered in glassy black tiles, as were the walls. Together the floor and the ceiling gave a clinical, wipe-clean feel, and again it was lit by the very common floating tennis ball sized spheres of light. Here they were unevenly spread along the top of the angular ceiling and some looked so dim, and in need of stoking.

"Ok I have us," George said thankfully and stabbed a finger at their location on the map, "it looks like if we head left we will get to another square, where we should be able to find a sign post," he said while folding up the map and putting it in his pocket.

William looked at him, nodded in agreement and set off down the corridor, leaving echoing footstep sounds behind them.

Level five had no hustle and bustle of people moving around, indeed very few people were walking around at all, leading William to walk with caution as he did not feel like this level was nearly as friendly as the levels above. Those that were working and moving around on level five all wore slightly more serious clothes, which matched the wipe clean look and feel of the level.

The two slightly nervous boys emerged out of the long doorless corridor to a square, which as the map had shown contained a sign post that pointed in seven different directions.

In the short time William had been at Belbury Academy the map had never been wrong, not even slightly wrong. William had therefore assumed it must constantly update itself somehow, as work was always being carried out to build new passages, grooves and buildings around the town and on all the levels.

Looking on to the small square was a small food and coffee shop, which was clearly getting ready for the lunch time rush and sold drinks like, "Coffee explosion, start your day off with a bang", "espresso to help you sleep, drink ten minutes before the effect is needed".

The signpost at the square's centre was like all the others, old fashioned cast iron and painted white, with black letters, making it feel reliable, dependable and correct.

Its many signs pointed to:

The Past,
Dead End,
Dangerous Testing,
Power Core,
Future History Research,
Night Time,

The last one was blank, but still pointed down a corridor.

"Well Will, which shall we choose?" George asked.

"Dead End sounds interesting! Do you actually think it is a dead end? Odd to sign-post something like that, don't you think?" William said more thinking allowed, but George still answered.

"Yes odd that, on the map it does show a corridor which goes nowhere, no rooms lead off it either. Just one straight corridor. It's not that long so we could go look at it first and then come back."

"Done," William said.

After a few minutes of quick walking, the boys arrived at the slightly disappointing, but totally expected dead end.

"Well, that was definitely worth it!" George said sarcastically, while he touched the wall to see if there were any grooves or holes; none could be seen or felt.

"Look there, footprints on the floor facing the dead end so it must go somewhere," said William, pointing to some very clear boot marks on the highly polished floor. Looking like someone had been standing there, waiting for something to open.

"Doubt we can get this dead end to do anything other than be dead. Let's go back. The Power Core sounded like something worth seeing and it is probably not dead," William said in expected disappointment.

The two boys headed back to the sign post, checked the direction to head in and then saw three people in white coats, hats and boots walk out of the Dead End corridor where they had just been.

"Well clearly we missed something down there, but let's look at the Power Core, surely we can't miss that," William said while looking at the sun dial on the wall, which showed ten fifty-seven. He wanted to make sure that they would not miss lunch.

As they headed off down the new corridor, William noticed a man sitting in the coffee shop. He was not having a drink or any food, but was just unblinkingly staring down the Dead End passageway. William thought he looked a little out of place, as his clothing was all wrong and clashed with the clinical surroundings. The man was clothed in a heavily woven dark jacket that flowed to his ankles, covering some very muddy dark black leather boots. He had bright, wild, red hair and between his fingers he fiddled with his gold pocket watch. William shrugged off his interest in the strange man as he had other things on his mind, and wanted to see the Power Core.

They headed west down another corridor that at the start was the same white floor and black tile walls and ceiling as the rest of level five. William was happy to find a groove in the wall, which they used to save some time walking, as this corridor looked unendingly long.

They reappeared in a very different environment. The corridor had changed and was now a skeletal, intertwined root system-looking tunnel with a stone floor. The end of the tunnel was near and opened out in a bell shape to the top of an ornate staircase that slithered down the side of a rough white chalk cliff face that reminded William of the White Cliffs of Dover.

They walked out of the tunnel and could see for what felt like miles. The sky was bright blue and unfocusable, with a great forest rolling out in front of them, like some great sea ebbing and flowing with the breeze. As they walked down the staircase, they caught glimpses of flashing lines and glowing lights below the dense forest canopy.

At the base of the stairs they paused to take in the sight. Huge and ancient-looking oaks, ash and beech trees towered above them, gently swaying under the gentle sky, dancing to some unheard music.

This moment of peace was abruptly interrupted by an elderly lady in a green and brown tweed three-piece suit, matching flat cap and olive green zip up wellingtons.

"And what are you doing here?" the lady demanded. "I have told the Headmaster that visitors must be booked in if they want to look around the Power Core!"

"I am sorry, we didn't know, we just wanted to explore our map," William said a little worried.

"And who might you be?" the lady demanded again, with hands on her hips.

"I am William Taylor, Miss and this is George, er, er, George Meldul," he replied quickly while George nodded his head quickly and pointed to himself.

"William Taylor… are you really! I have heard much about you boy, I hear you are particularly gifted," the lady said, her voice passing from anger to interest, when William said his full name.

"Dyslexic yes, not sure about gifted though," William said, flushing red with embarrassment at being thought of so highly by a stranger, and in front of George.

"Confidence boy, confidence! I hear great things about your gift, and it is a pleasure to meet you. All the great engineers and world changers have gifts like yours. In fact, the man who created the Power Core was dyslexic and like you came from the Igmon world. Would you like to see what he created?"

"Oh yes please," William said, suddenly becoming excited.

"Well then we will need to make an exception to the booking-in rule this time, follow me," she replied.

"Gifted," George said jokingly at William, before elbowing him in the ribs causing him to wince.

They followed the lady who had still not said her name ever deeper into the darkening forest, constantly stepping over a growing spider's web of glowing and pulsing hoses that snaked over the floor. The hoses cast their multi-coloured light onto the tree trunks and branch of the canopy roof above their heads as the lady began to speak.

"Many lifetimes ago, Jaxson Perbrighton invented the Power Core System that powers the whole of the Thomon world. It is such a simple system that most people never thought of it. But he saw the world differently and that is part of his and your gift. These trees…" she said while continuing to walk along pointing to different trees, touching some and allowing her fingers to be bounced around by the rough and craggy texture of the different tree barks, "... are constantly drawing water from the soil up into their trunks, think of them as a big water pumps. What Jaxson found was that he was able to collect the tiny amounts of electrical energy this process created as a by-product. Jaxson created these," she said, pointing to what looked like a semi-translucent glowing blanket, wrapped around the tree next to her. "They are called 'SUCK' jackets, which stands for 'Simultaneous Uplift Collection Kit', the energy byproduct could then be collected and transported to be used for everything we need."

"So how many trees wear a 'SUCK jacket'?" George asked while prodding one of the slightly squidgy and glowing jackets.

"About two in every three trees are used. We constantly move the jackets around to allow the tree a break to grow, as the jackets have to be wrapped quite tight for the system to work."

"Miss... errr...?" William paused as he realised he did not know her name yet.

"Ash," she filled in.

"Miss Ash, what is in the pipes and why do they glow?" William said, wandering over and touching one of the white, silicone-like hoses that pulsated and vibrated under his fingers.

"They are filled with a liquid called 'Denolight', which again was invented by Jaxon for this purpose. The Denolight liquid glows in proportion to the amount of power it contains from the trees. The more energy it has in it the brighter green that section of Denolight glows. It is beautiful isn't it?"

"Yes, amazing!" the two boys replied as they twisted around to look at a few hoses that were all in different stages of colour and brightness.

William came with another question. "Since we are underground, how is there a blue sky? It can't be a screen as it spreads out over the whole forest, which is how big?"

"Great questions William. Let's see, how big is the forest," Miss Ash thought for a moment after repeating his questions. "As far as the mountains in the distance is the best answer I can give for how big the forest is. Now the sky question is definitely an interesting one. You are correct that it is not a screen. That would be too big even for our best engineers to get working. I would have thought one of you would be able to answer that question by now," she said, pausing for a moment to smile and look at the boy's expressions. "You are no longer underground! Yes, you entered the Great Forest from one of the entrances underground on level five, but you are now well and truly on the surface. Remember grooves don't just stay on the level where you started it."

This answer made William feel a little bit stupid as it was obvious really. He could feel a breeze passing through the trees and thought he saw a large deer-like creature in the distance being chased by something William could not quite describe, of course this was on the surface. No amount of tech could support this level of life underground.

"Now William and George, it has been a pleasure to show you around but don't you think it is time you should be leaving for lunch?" said Miss Ash while looking at the side of her Hadron-Tool. "Better get a move on so as not to miss it! And next time please book in with me first if you want to come see the Power Core again. It is never good just to turn up to the Great Forest. Not everyone and everything in these woods is as friendly or safe as me," she paused, *"understood?"* she said with force to ensure she was taken seriously.

"Yes Miss, thank you. Come on George," William said while turning to leave.

The boys set off at a run back through the forest, leaping hoses and dodging tree trunks until they reached the base of the staircase. William started up the stairs taking them two at a time reaching the top in a puddle of sweat and out of breath, only to find George waiting at the top, leaning against the cliff face.

"I found a groove in the end of the hand rail, clearly some people here are really lazy," George said, almost laughing.

"Like you then," William retorted while placing his own Hadron-Tool into the next groove to go back down the corridor.

Running back past the sign post the boys saw that the Dead End corridor was now closed off. Monstrous-looking official guards were stopping people going down it with their tree trunk arms and troll-like faces. The people being stopped did not look best pleased about it, with lots of shouting and waving of irate arms, that was clearly not getting them anywhere.

William could just about see the soles of some boots, toes down to the ground, indicating someone was lying face down in the corridor. Sir Coalbrook was standing in front of the guards having a very stern conversation with a spikey looking man who looked like he was dressed for a funeral instead of the weekend. The weasel man had his Hadron-Tool strapped to his belt above his right hip in a brown leather case, and a brass whistle was attached to the lapel of his coat by red and green twisted twine.

Upon seeing the two boys, the lady who ran the coffee shop rushed over to Sir Coalbrook, wiping the dirt on her hand from cleaning up spilled food from the floor on her apron as she went. She tapped Sir Coalbrook on the shoulder, interrupting the conversation of the two men and pointing at the boys while saying something to him. Sir Coalbrook looked with fixed eyes at them without emotion, and thanked the coffee shop lady.

"Wonder what's going on there," William asked George while continuing to run across the square. There was no time to stop and see more, as he thought they must be running close to lunch ending in the main hall. He was right because they made it back just in time to be allowed in by the slithering door for lunch, and to get the last of the food before the mechanical arms, shot out and cleaned the tables.

The boys found Isabel sitting in her usual place surrounded by playing card-sized books.

"On your own? Where's Jasmin?" William asked, looking around the hall trying to spot her.

"Jasmin said she was going to the Belbury art gallery to spend some time painting her, your history, your culture notes with Mrs Tint the art teacher there," Isabel replied.

"Everyone to their own I guess," George replied with little interest, as painting was very low down his list of fun things to do.

"So what have you two been up to? You both look quite damp!" Isabel asked, looking curiously at the two sweaty boys.

"We've been exploring level five on the map! Did you know there is a whole forest down there, but on the surface that powers this whole place!" said William, looking a little bit confused by his own description of the forest's location.

"Well of course! That is the Power Core invented by Jaxon Perbrighton, I read about it in preparation for coming here," Isabel said in a tone that thought you were strange if you had not.

"It's amazing, it all glows and hums like it is happy," said George, partly interrupting Isabel.

"We also found a Dead End passage, which turned out not to be a dead end, if that makes any sense!" William said once again confused by his own inability to give non-confusing verbal descriptions.

"No not really," Isabel replied equally confused.

"Well, we followed the sign post for 'Dead End' as it sounded interesting," William said before being interrupted by Isabel.

"Only boys would find something that stupidly basic interesting!"

"But who would sign a dead end if it were not something more," George said in counter argument.

"Well, when we went to the end of the dead end it was what the sign post said, a dead end. But here is the cool thing, we later saw people walking out of the Dead End corridor," William continued.

"Three people all in white clothing came out of nowhere!" George added while holding up three fingers.

"They must be using their Hadron-Tools to disperse the wall then," Isabel said, making it sound totally obvious to anyone with half a brain cell.

"What's dispersing the wall?" George asked.

"Have you boys really not done any reading around what you can do with your Hadron-Tools once you get good enough and have the correct extra items?" She paused to look at the boys with motherly disappointment on her face. "By placing an authorised user's Hadron-Tool against a wall set up for dispersion, the molecules that make up the object disperse, allowing the person's molecules just enough room to pass through the solid object. It works, because as everyone knows, you are made up of more space than stuff! That sort of security is only used when it is of the utmost importance, like a vault. If you are not allowed through you just end up walking into a solid wall and looking very stupid."

"Ah right ok, like Sir Coalbrook did at the start of term, when he walked in through the back wall of the hall," George said.

"Yes that's right, but we don't learn how to do that until final year," Isabel added.

"So the Dead End is not really a dead end but a locked door? I wonder what is behind it that they need to protect it like that?" William said, before briefly pausing to let an old memory appear. "And remember, when we came back to the square something had happened down the Dead End corridor. There were loads of dangerous-looking black clothed security guards, and the Headmaster was talking very firmly with someone very important-looking. Remember George?" William asked, but did not wait for an answer. "And there was someone lying on the floor, but I couldn't really see any more than their boots." William finished with a great thinking look on his face.

"Yeah that's right, it didn't look good. Something was stolen maybe, or an accident had happened! That could explain the person on the floor," George replied.

"Well, it is nothing for you two to go sticking your noses into, you'll get in trouble. The Headmaster will sort it out," Isabel said.

At that moment Sir Coalbrook appeared behind William and George. Isabel suddenly found a section in her book about the history of Thomon paperweights very interesting.

"Had a nice afternoon boys?" came his low and strong voice.

William and George did not need to look around to know who it was. They looked at each other fearing that it was too late and they were already in trouble, even before any sticking of noses had been done.

"I require both of you to follow me to my office now! Up you get!" he said, in a manner that gave no wiggle room to not do as they were told.

The two boys nervously stood up and followed on behind. As they left, George looked over his shoulder at

Isabel, who had now looked up from her gripping book, shrugging his shoulders and mouthed to her silently, "What's going to happen?"

Isabel replied in kind, shrugging her shoulders and mouthed in reply, "I don't know."

The boys followed Sir Coalbrook as he walked up and down staircases, along endless corridors and through two stout-looking walls, with Sir Coalbook keeping the wall dispersed for the two boys to pass through. One of the long, grand corridors was hung with rows of oil paintings, showing past Headmasters and Headmistresses, sitting enthroned in their offices of power and control.

They finally came to the end of a long broad walkway, which had one side open to a view of the mountains beyond over a classic stone balustrade. The worn stone called to William to touch it, and run his fingers along its top. Williams' hands and fingers responded as if they had a mind of their own, moving to rest upon its cold top. William thought about how many other students had walked along this very same path to the Headmaster's office, worrying about what was going to happen to them. William imagined he could feel their emotions and hear their footsteps walking on the smooth stone floor as he felt the weathered and roughly-pitted surface of the stone that was connecting him to the past.

The hallway led not to an office door, but a beautiful hanging tapestry that showed a large castle surrounded by the house emblems.

Sir Coalbrook stepped up to the life-sized door in the centre of the castle, placed his Hadron-Tool against the wavy fabric door lock and twisted it like a key. Click!

"In you go boys," he said as he pushed the door open on the gently swaying fabric, to reveal his office beyond.

It was a circular room with a quarter of the wall straight ahead filled with a large floor-to-ceiling leaded window. It was made with small cylinder glass panes, which increased the shimmer of the view due to the imperfections of reeds and bubbles in the glass.

In front of the window was a wide wooden desk, supported on a single leg at the right front corner, and looked like it should be falling over. The centre of the desk was covered with a green leather pad that had the wear marks of many years of constant use.

In the centre of the room was a large fire sphere that floated above a pond, which glistened with the reflection of the fire above. The fish in the pond swam through the reflected flames without getting burnt, and around an uphill flowing water feature, making a relaxing bubbling sound. Wooden chairs with great backs surrounded this feature, each grandly embroidered with what looked like a story, almost like a stained-glass window in a Igmon country church.

The remaining wall space was taken up with shelves that matched the wood of the desk and sat upon a box section metal frame. This was home to books, photos, tool boxes, dirty overalls and old boots, along with many other objects, which were of unknown use and type to William.

At the left end of the shelving, close to the window was a black cast iron ladder with an interesting scroll decoration on its sides that could be run all the way around the shelving on brass wheels and track, to allow access to the many shelves. It also led up and above the shelving to a walking platform around the base of the fish scale glass dome that made up the ceiling.

William felt the presence of the established power that this room was meant to convey. Interestingly he also noted that this room had no edge of the future about it or any organic structure, like he had so often seen around the town. This made him think that Sir Coalbrook was more a man of history and tradition, than of pushing forwards at all costs.

Sir Coalbrook moved to his well-practised and established place in his chair, behind his impossibly balancing desk and invited the two boys to stand on the other side of it facing him.

"Did we have a nice adventure earlier today?" the Headmaster asked.

But the boys did not answer. They just stood there in silence, not daring to look him in the face.

"It is not against academy rules to explore, so you can say yes!" he said while smiling, trying to relax the two boys.

"Yes Sir, it was very interesting, the Power Core especially," George said.

The boys looked up a little more, noticing the non-angry tone the Headmaster had taken, and realising that they might not be in trouble after all.

"You saw me after an incident down on level five, with the head of the Protection and Security Council or PSC, one Arthur Rebibox. There was an incident with a member of our level five team, which I am sure you saw. The member of the team in question is now in the medical centre receiving emergency care, and will have all their limbs back in place in a few days. You may be wondering why I am telling you this and have asked you here." The boys nodded their heads. "Firstly, you will hear about the event anyway and secondly I need to know if you saw anything on your explorations that could help Arthur here catch the person involved."

Arthur had apparently appeared in the room and was now standing behind the two boys, as the Headmaster pointed behind them in indication.

William thought for a minute. Closing his eyes he tried to put himself back in the level five square and relive the event, trying to rewind his memory like a movie. His head began to move and sway around as his mind navigated the images in his head.

"Well, there was a man sitting in the coffee shop who didn't look quite right. I saw him as we left the Dead End corridor to go to the Power Core."

"Good, please go on," the Headmaster encouraged.

"He had bright red, messy hair and a really thick, heavy-looking black coat. He was also fiddling with something gold between his fingers, probably a pocket watch, like yours Sir. I thought he did not quite fit with the look and feel of level five. He was also staring really hard down the Dead End corridor." William paused for a moment and looked at George and asked. "Did you see anything else or was that about it?"

"Nope! Most of what you just said was new to me," said George, while shaking his head.

"I think that is all I can remember," William said while pausing to think hard again. "Oh, it was around ten fifty in the morning when I saw him, according to the sun dial on the wall."

The Headmaster raised an eyebrow at this rather accurate time.

"I didn't want to miss lunch and so kept looking at the clocks as we explored," William quickly added, after seeing the disbelieving look.

Sir Coalbrook, happy enough with the answer, stood and turned to look out the window. Without looking back, he said, "Thank you boys for your time. Please go back to exploring and enjoying your day. Leave the same way you came in, the doorway will still open for you."

After waiting for them to leave he addressed Arthur.

"It's him again isn't it?"

"Yes, it is! It's the hair that really gives him away, but he never hides and he seems to be growing ever bolder and ever more confident," Arthur said in a husky concerned voice.

"Are you close to catching him, he is getting closer and closer to it? This is the third attempt!" said Sir Coalbrook in a worried voice. "We should never have agreed to keep it here, and now the students may be at risk! It should have been destroyed with all the others. It's causing us nothing but problems."

"We will continue to do our best and will strengthen the protections around it," said Arthur definitely before pausing and taking some steps forward. "Seamus... he will try again, we have no doubt about that, we got lucky this time and only one person was injured. We all know what he and his followers are capable of when they get close to what they want. Look, I know this is getting harder and harder to justify keeping it here, but we really must. If Krevak ever does manage to resurrect the Hemlock family name and regain their strength, then we must be ready. It is my utmost priority to protect it, you have my word on that."

"Thank you Arthur, we must stay vigilant. Please carry out your plans immediately," Sir Coalbrook said with fresh determination in his voice.

With that Arthur Rebibox turned on his heels and left the Headmaster's office the way he had come in, which was through the pond. Leaving Seamus alone to think, ponder and plan.

After a quick journey using the map to navigate the network of grooves back to their house, William and George reached the common room and were instantly bombarded with questions from Isabel and Jasmin.

"Well, what did the head want?" Isabel asked with concern.

"Are you getting a detention or even expelled?" Jasmin asked.

"No, no, no, we are fine," George said, trying to calm the two girls down and trying to act all unworried himself. "He just wanted to ask us about what we had seen on level five."

"Well, what did you see?" Jasmin asked.

"Not much really, we told him no more than what we told you earlier. Sir did say that whoever was on the floor was missing some limbs! I reckon they were attacked. You don't get that sort of injury from just tripping over your own shoe laces!"

"They were missing limbs! How many?" Jasmin exclaimed.

"Don't know, Sir didn't say, only that they would get them back in a few days, which is kinda amazing. He did seem very interested in that guy you saw Will, the one with the red hair."

"You're right, he did seem very interested in hearing about him, didn't he. The guy just looked all out of place and so stood out to me. Thinking about it now, Isabel you said that the Dead End is probably not really a dead end but a high security door. Right?" Isabel nodded in conformation. "Well, the guy was really staring down the Dead End corridor, almost like he was waiting or planning something. You don't... you don't think it could have been that red haired man who de-limbed the person on the floor do you?" William answered.

"Well, it would make sense. But who was he? Must be someone really bad for the head of the Protection and Security Council to be involved," George replied.

"But what could that door be protecting? It's got to be something very important or expensive to be worth risking being caught and causing that much damage to someone?" William thought quietly for a second, before the group began to talk all at once again, trying to guess and understand what might have happened down the Dead End passageway.

🔔 Train Like We Play

William finally started to feel like he had got into his stride with the unique academy. He and his new friends had even worked out what "the drop of the first hammers" was and where it came from.

In the reign of Belbury's second Headmaster, Sir Fletchly Carrington Plugsworth, the town's clock was destroyed by a protesting, rogue troll, who had had enough of moving heavy things around for a living and wanted to paint tiny porcelain figurines instead. The troll was not allowed to though by the Council for Humans, Creatures and Monster Work Relations, as he only ever broke the tiny figures with his massive spade-like hands and club-like fingers. In anger the troll had thrown a cart and its two horses, crashing into the town's clock. The clock had been smashed and so there was no ringing across the town for when the day's work should start.

This caused a lot of problems for Belbury town, because every business and activity relied on every other business or activity. If no one started work then no one else could start work either.

The blacksmiths, who were the loudest business in the town, had decided among themselves, due to being the self-reliant types, that they would be the signal to start the working day. This was going to be controlled by a single blacksmith who became known as having the key to the day. He would land the first blow on his anvil at whatever time he chose. This could be early or late, depending on the amount of time and money spent in the pub the night before. All the other blacksmiths would hear the clang and start their clattering work.

The noise was loud enough that the whole town worked to it even once the clock was working again. William thought that this was amazing, that it was the start of physical work, the smashing of hot metal, that would start the day off for all.

Walking through the common room on a bright and clear Wednesday morning, there was a great commotion around the house notice board. Looks of disappointment, pride, and happiness were showing across the range of faces surrounding the pinned-up notice. William, George and Jasmin all realised what this meant.

"The 4's teams are up, come on!" George said excitedly as he urged William and Jasmin to help him get close enough so he could see. After wriggling, squeezing and pushing their way through the crowd to get close enough, George stretched his thin neck to see and read the names that were due to attend practice that very evening. He was quickly scanning up the list looking for his name, muttering under his breath.

"Where am I, where am I?" Finally, he saw his name, he had made it into the thirds team and was over the moon. "Will, look, I am in a team. That's flippin awesome! Hey Jasmin, you're in the thirds team too, put it there team mate," George said, turning to Jasmin for a high five.

Now it was William's turn to view the board and could scarcely believe where he saw his name.

"I am in the first team," William said, stunned.

"Wow, you got in the first team, now that is impressive for a First Year who does not know how to play the game! Marcus must really like you," George said with broken proudness toward his friend.

"I really need to learn how to play the game and quickly, George, will you help me?" William asked, turning to his friend with panic.

George paused looking back, jealous of his Igmon friend, but saw this was a question that could only have one answer.

"We may be on different teams and somehow you may be better at a sport you have never played before than me but, yeah I will help you as long as you help me also to get better, I want in on the first team also!"

"Deal," William replied, shaking George's hand, both boys smiling at each other.

*

4's practice started that week after class. The air was bitterly cold, stinging William's nose and rasping in his throat. He stood on the pitch in a large circle with many much larger boys and girls, all who looked like they could crush him if he crossed them the wrong way. Marcus was in the centre of the circle and holding the heavy looking brown leather egg.

"Well a new season is here, and new battles are about to begin. Make no mistake, especially to those that have never played 4's before," he said looking at William who was the only new First Year, "every game is a battle. Many of us here will end up in the medical bay after a game, broken from committing our bodies to winning. That is what it will take to remain 4's champions three years on the trot. You can bet that the other houses are plotting and training to see our downfall. To that end we will always train like we plan to play. Everyone is to give two hundred percent at all times, no questions, no complaining and no quitting. If that does not sound like something you can do then please leave now."

No one left but everyone closed in, pushing a hesitant William in also. He was not so sure about the prospect of ending up in the medical bay, but did not want to let his house down. He also felt something powerful growing in him as he stood with others from his house, like warriors training for battle.

"Good... let's get to it... RUN, TOUCH EACH GOAL FOUR TIMES."

The order was obeyed like hunting dogs being released by their master.

The training session was exhausting. William was no longer cold, but soaked, covered in mud from head to toe and his chest felt like it was going to explode, but he was beaming with happiness when Marcus called William over.

"How you finding it Will?"

"Great so far," was able to be heard in-between his heavy breaths.

"Good, Will I picked you because you're a fighter and you are proper fast, I need that in this team. When all hell is breaking loose, I need someone who can see the holes, and will be brave enough to punch through those holes. Can you do that for the team?"

"I can do that," William said proudly.

"Good, your position is called 'narrow back'. You're to hang back and stay out of the main bulk of the melée. You need to always be looking for when the game is opening up for you and then not hesitate to dive in. I am the 'captain' and I control the team, the plays and when we use them. Jessy there," he said pointing to a girl with long blonde hair stuck to her back by mud and looking like a Viking shield maiden, "is our 'negotiator'. She will endeavour to get the other teams on side when I tell her to. The two monsters over there," he said pointing to two oversized brown haired twin boys who were rolling around in the mud with each other, trying to rip a brown leather practice ball out of the other's grip, "they are the 'defensive backs'..." William was very glad they were on his team and would not be tackling him, "... their main task is to protect the goal, they don't take prisoners when playing but they play fair enough to be legal. Everyone else is an 'attack defence' and will try to score where possible. They will also defend and block for you when you have the ball, and will clear the way for you when you ask. Understood?"

William nodded beaming with the thought of what he would be doing.

"Learning to play the game is one thing, but for your position it is vital that you get on with the others on the team, as they will end up in medical trying to protect you and make space for you to score. They won't do that so willingly if they don't like you. Right, enough talking, go join the group over there," Marcus said pointing to the far-right goal, where a group was practising tackling and ball capture drills.

🎇 Dirt and Grime
But Oh So Much Fun

A new week started, bringing along with it a new lesson called, 'Building the Future". To William this sounded like it could be his new favourite class as it sounded a lot like Design and Technology or Engineering.

William, George, Jasmin and Isabel had made their way across the town with a mixture of tunnels, stairs and grooves, finally emerging through a manhole cover in the centre of a wide cobbled street. They were now in what would be considered the industrial district of Belbury town. William's nose could smell it and his ears could hear it, making his brain tingle with excitement.

With every new sound and every new smell William became more and more eager to get inside to see what was going on.

Here the buildings were a mixture. Most of them were old iron, wood and stone structures that gave a feeling of tradition and reliability. The rest were more flowing modern buildings that looked like they had been grown out of the ground, with spiralling bars and curving walls, full of glass, space and optimism for the future.

The students walked into a building with a sign above the door saying, Diesel and Sons Engineering.

The building itself was part old and part new. Either the company was doing very well and investing in a brand-new building, or it was failing and being absorbed by the more successful company next door. But to William's mind that did not matter, what mattered was what was happening on the inside.

The whole class was now standing in the dirty entrance lobby, where the dust from the workshop could be clearly seen settling thick on all the flat surfaces, including on top of a low wall to the left-hand side of the rectangular lobby. This low wall separated the children from where a blonde-haired secretary sat at her desk answering circular letters, and what looked like some type of phone, all the while keeping on top of the businesses calendars that were bound in heavy leather covers.

A man burst in, walking backwards through some double doors in front of the waiting group, carrying a stack of rolled up drawing papers under one arm and having a loud conversation with someone on the other side of the door.

"That's what I said to do last week, we agreed that was the solution!" the backwards walking man called to someone. "I know that's what you think but we have agreed to do it my way, now get on with it!" he said firmly.

Along with his stack of rolled up drawings, he wore a blue knee length jacket with his Hadron-Tool and a small yellow and black book in his breast pocket. His black leather boots had the toes worn through so the metal toe cap could be seen beneath. Clear wraparound safety glasses sat on his dirty nose, which had got that way by being rubbed with a dirty hand. On his head was a black bowler hat, again dirty and worn.

"Ah... is it that time already? – Gosh the day has gotten away from me," the man said when he saw the lobby full of young students. "Well, give me one second to put these papers down and I will come and start your lesson."

He turned abruptly and walked off down a corridor to the left, appearing again a few seconds later, arms free of paper and started his introduction again.

"I am Mr Diesel and welcome to my company, you are all here, yes? Anyone missing?" There was no answer from the group. "Excellent, well then we will begin, please follow me."

The children followed Mr Diesel through the double doors and stopped in front of a single pair of shoes sitting upon a metal shelf. Next to the shoes was a shelf supporting a single pair of safety glasses and a shelf holding a single folded up blue jacket.

"Right, would all students please take a pair of shoes, glasses and a jacket, and using your Hadron-Tools, along with the skills you have learnt so far, please shrink and enlarge them to make them fit. There are benches to sit on just the other side of me."

"There's more than one of us!" William said to George while looking at the lonely looking single pair of safety shoes, to which George just shrugged his shoulders.

The students did as they were told and started to line up to take one of every item. In the end there were plenty of items for everyone, as every time a pair of shoes, glasses or jacket was taken from one of the little metal shelves another would appear in its place.

Once the students had gathered their kit, they found a place to sit and set about trying to resize the items to fit with differing degrees of success. After a bit of fiddling William had two shoes that were close to being the correct size for his feet and roughly the same size as each other. The jacket's sleeves were now somewhere above his hands, and the glasses stayed on his face, just. He had counted that as success and could be improved upon later.

"Come on come on, we don't have all day," came the call from Mr Diesel with a hint of impatience. "You can fiddle and fettle them to your heart's content later. Everyone look at me and listen now please!" Mr Diesel said, trying to make an effort to look at every child to make sure they were paying attention.

"This is stupid! I feel like a clown, no way I can walk around in these!" George said while looking down at his feet, where one shoe was half the size of the other, "I look ridiculous!"

"I will help you out when I get a chance," William said, trying not to laugh.

"When we go on to the workshop floor please do not touch anything until I have cleared you to do so. Everything on the workshop floor can create and give great joy and pleasure, but can also do great harm if not treated correctly and respected. If you are unsure on what to do or would like to use something please ask. We have not had any deaths with a student for a while, only mildly serious injuries on my workshop floors and I would like to keep it that way." He paused for a moment to check that all the eyes and ears had taken the warning in. "Good, please follow me."

Once again the train of children followed Mr Diesel through another set of swinging double doors, and William was now in heaven. The commotion of machines doing work, the smell of lubricating oil and the sounds of workmen talking and joking loudly with each other was energising.

The workshop floor was vast and there was not just one floor but many above and below where they were now standing. Many staircases and floating platforms led off in all directions to different levels and workshop areas, making William feel like he could easily get lost.

"Welcome to level seven, our main workshop floor, here we make everything metal. Anything from universal beams to decorative features, jewellery and the fabrication of mechanisms for doing pretty much anything and everything. This has been a family business for generations," he said proudly, "and we have educated countless academy years of students in all things engineering. In your class you will be expected to get your hands dirty. This is not a library class, although we will have some lab time alongside all of the practical work you will be doing."

They followed Mr Diesel around level seven, with him talking about what happens and what all the tools were and how they worked.

William could see rows of what he could only describe as lathes and mills. The machines held and spun material to be cut in the correct manner to what William was used to but that is where the similarities ended. The cutting tools were the engineers' Hadron-Tools, which they pressed into the material, cutting it with ease, and without creating swarf, sound and no smell either.

William's feet could feel the subtle vibrations of the machines carrying out their masters' tasks through the metal grated floor, making everything feel alive and giving the workshop a heartbeat. He also saw the workshop staff using their Hadron-Tools in many different ways and using so many different types of attachments that shot in and out of their tools. Some attachments were like pincers, measuring objects for accuracy. Others were moving heavy objects around or using a hammer-type feature to tap an object into place, another tightened nuts with a spanner-like feature. After each use the attachment would vanish back into the Hadron-Tool with a flick of the engineer's wrist and be placed back into their jacket pocket.

The First Years moved along the floor with Mr Diesel talking about some of the more unusual machines, what they did and who was operating them when they came to a basic cutting station.

William thought back to the Igmon world, where metal cutting stations are hot, loud, spark-bouncing places. But here a man was holding his Hadron-Tool like a pencil and cutting an intricate shape out of a metal sheet without any problem – smooth, quiet and clean, effortless.

William's hand shot up to ask a question, "Sir why are there no sparks or heat, and where is the noise from that man cutting over there?" he said pointing to the man he was watching.

Mr Diesel answered with understanding in his voice, "Good question, and you must be from the Igmon world, where that would be the case. The Igmons have to use abrasive wheels, saws or massive heat to cut metal because they are ignorant of better ways to do the same thing. In our world, with our Hadron-Tools, we are able to cut material by separating the molecular structure of the material from itself, meaning the cut is perfect, a form of ultrasonic cutting. There is also no heat or sound because the energy that is released from the metal when it is split is absorbed by the Hadron-Tool, which in turn helps power the Hadron-Tool. Does that answer your question?"

"Yes, thank you Sir," William said, amazed by what the small device in his pocket could potentially do.

"Any more questions? No? Follow on then."

They came to the edge of level seven and could now look over the edge and see the vast expanse of the workshop and the depth to which the floors penetrated the crust of the earth.

Looking up William could partly see inside the modern town that was slowly absorbing the older building they had just walked through.

"There are many ways to make objects, each has its pluses and minuses..." Mr Diesel said, lifting his hands and pretending they were scales, "... and to be a good engineer you must balance the good and bad aspects to get what you want out the other end."

He then pointed down over the edge and carried on. "Down on the bottom floor we have the casting facilities close to the earth's molten centre. If you want to go somewhere that is otherworldly and go back in time then go down there, it is such an escape from the present." William could hear from how he said this, that he loved the older ways of doing things. "Above us in the ivory tower where we have material manipulation. Up there materials are pulled and pushed into any shape you like using the Hadron-Tool, we will be heading up there another day." This sounded utterly amazing to William. "Ok everyone please step on to the platform and hold on to the edge." Once everyone was on, Mr Diesel took out his Hadron-Tool and started to wind it like a fishing rod reel and the platform started to rise. "Right, lab time and I hope everyone has their practice cubes with them? As we will be starting to learn how to cut and rejoin them today."

*

Back in the Starley common room William, George, Jasmin and Isabel had all collapsed into their favourite sofa, and were practising on their cubes. Isabel and George were both struggling a little, while Jasmin was having a little more success. William tried to help with some advice, as again this skill had come fairly naturally to him.

"You have to imagine it happening and see exactly what you want to happen on the block in front of you."

"Imagine, just imagine," Isabel said sarcastically, "give me books any day, I guess I am finding out where my skills really are!"

"You will get it," William encouraged, "you're already getting better."

George sweated as he strained his imagination to cut the simple small block in front of him. "I am done,"

George breathed out once the block was cut, "but don't give me books, give me a game of 4's, that seems much easier."

"George, you still have to rejoin the block," William chuckled while slapping his mate on the back, "I'll give you a hand."

🗼 Failure Returns

During William's time at Belbury Apprenticeship Academy he was having so much fun and he was happy, happier than he had ever been before. The lessons did not really feel like the lessons he had been having at all his previous schools, as they normally took place inside the businesses around the town. So as the day-to-day life of the business went on, of customers purchasing meals or products, management meetings and the daily grind was happening, William and his friends would be in these businesses learning and seeing their learning applied.

The students could see what they were learning applied directly to the real world, taught by people who were applying it to the real world themselves, helping everything they were learning – even the hardest subject – to make sense.

William had not had any major issues with his work yet either, which he thought was a first. He was still a very, very slow reader and often had to ask what certain words were, and his writing still looked like a chicken had done it with a pen in its beak. Some of the other students in his class thought he was writing in code, as they could not read and understand a single word he had written.

But he was keeping up and his brain was happily filling with learning. He had also not been sent back to his dorm room as yet, but that was all about to change when the lesson, "Look Confident, Feel Confident", came around.

This class happened in the Belbury Theatre, with a teacher called Mrs Plushoe. She wore half-moon glasses on a colourful chain, with a white shirt that had a frilly collar. Her skirt went down to the floor and was held high at her waist with a stout belt. She had tied her hair up in a tight bun at the top of her head and adorned it with a colourful Glopersip bird feather. She had a rather parrot-like face, which went hand-in-hand with her clear, sharp and crisp voice.

The whole class was sitting in rows of old red velvet seats, which sat upon an equally old and slightly sticky carpet. They all faced a stage about a metre tall off the floor with large, heavy-looking red curtains hanging at both sides.

Mrs Plushoe walked up and onto the front of the stage and banged her foot on the floor to get the class's attention. "Right, now that I have all your attention!" She paused, ensuring this was true. "This class has its roots in Thomon antiquity and the surroundings reflect that history. The agedness of this theatre shows its importance due to its longevity, and that it has not been knocked down and replaced with some ice cube modern monstrosity!" She paused for effect, clearly showing a dislike of the new architecture sprouting up around the town. "In these classes you will learn how to conduct yourself, here you will learn how to project," she said with a long rolled r, "confidence and so be self-confident. We will do this through the real magic of the theatre and with the art of acting." This was said with a dramatic lifting of the arms, her head tilted up to heaven and then an equally dramatic collapse into a perfect curtsy.

"But first," she stood and began again, "I must know where to begin with each one of you, so each of you will read aloud to the class and to me from the stage. There is no embracement to be had from this little exercise as everyone will have to complete and everyone will fall short of my standard, is that understood?"

The look of "oh no" that was on every face looking back at her was a good enough answer for her to continue.

"I have a script here for you to read from so please, in your rows, starting from the front left come up on to the stage and read the section given to you."

A girl called Henady Tipleton from Fermi house was first up. A girl who William thought, with her nut brown hair, slender shape and classic English looks was very beautiful, but he was too nervous to talk to her. She walked up the side steps of the stage and took the sheet from Mrs Plushoe's steady hand.

At this point Mrs Plushoe reminded everyone to flip the single page over to get a new section of script to read, and that everyone one was to treat everyone else like they would like to be treated when it was their turn, and then left the stage.

Once she had sat down, she signalled for Henady to begin.

Henady froze, looking out briefly at the sea of little eyes looking back, the paper trembled in her unsteady hand from nerves. She crossed her feet over and began to read what turned out to be the beginning of a story.

The class carried on like this with everyone reading in turn the next section of the story, which William thought sounded a lot like Hansel and Gretel. A story that his mum had regularly read to him when he was little.

About half the class had completed the task with mixed results, but all had completed the task when it was William's turn.

Like all the others he found his way to the centre of the stage using the stairs to the right-hand side of the stage, took the paper from Tyrop Clunk, who looked very excited to be getting rid of the hot potato he was holding, almost throwing the paper at William.

Like all the others William looked out, and the sheet of paper began to tremble. He swallowed hard and looked down at the words on the sheet, but could not keep the words in place and so could not read. They leaped about and danced on the page teasing and tormenting him. They would run in and out of focus as they swirled and twirled about the white paper dance floor.

William began to panic, his lips quivered and he wished hard that the stage would allow him to sink through it, like the rainbow carpet had done on his first day.

This was a nightmare come true.

His mind was churning over arguments for why he should not have come to Belbury Academy and anger that Mr Stephenson had lied to him. He said I was gifted and I would fit in and I would do great. I can't do this!

"You're a failure William." The phrase began to run around and around his head again and again like a rhythmic drum. "You're a failure, you're a failure," became louder and louder with each saying.

"What is the problem William?" came a call from Mrs Plushoe, helping to break the depression like trance William was now in.

"I... I... I can't read the words Mrs Plushoe." William stammered trying to hold it together. The crushing weight of the failure, after what had been the most amazing time, was almost unbearable. Bad memories from his past started to rear their ugly heads from the depths of William's mind and began to shout out their crushing words, reinforcing and building William's feeling of being a total failure.

"Ah I see, have you forgotten your glasses?" she asked.

"No, I don't wear glasses."

"Right then, what is the problem? What is your surname?"

"Taylor Mrs."

"William Taylor is it?"

"Yes."

"Ah right, the gifted one!"

A small laugh misted up from a group of boys in the back row from Rutherford House, who disliked William and anyone else not from Rutherford house and had a special dislike for Igmons.

"SILENCE!" shouted Mrs Plushoe, sounding like the crack of a whip and standing up to look around the seated class.

"To gain a gift, one has to sacrifice something else. Each of you will have your own personal problems to solve, and let's hope that all of yours are so easily revealed and so easily solved. You three boys…" she said pointing at the red-faced offenders, "… will stay late after class with me to sweep and clean this theatre." She then turned to William and in a much gentler tone said, "You may sit down."

Giving no reply William hung his head in embarrassment, shame and failure that he felt summed up his life. He slowly walked off the stage back to his chair and slumped down ready to endure the rest of the lesson, which rolled on as if nothing had happened. At the end of the lesson William left quickly not talking with anyone.

Isabel looked at George and said in a concerned voice, "Someone should go after him!"

"Leave the boy alone, he just needs some time," replied George and Jasmin nodding along.

"Some friend you are! Fine I'll go." Isabel jumped up from her chair and shot across the floor in pursuit of William. But once she was outside there was no sign of him. William had run around the corner and found the nearest groove and used it without checking his map first to see where it went.

William re-emerged and sank to the floor, bringing his knees to his chest, hugging them tight and resting his forehead on his knees, sobbing.

"Would you like a cup of tea?" Came a question carrying gently through the air to rest upon William's unhappy ears.

William looked up towards the voice, his red, wet eyes struggling to focus on where the voice came from. After a moment with a quick rub on his sleeve his eyes dried allowing the world around him to come into focus.

He saw that he was sitting at the base of a large white cast iron pillar, much like the sign posts found in each courtyard, but this one had no signs on it. It was however covered in holes in a random pattern, but no grooves.

The ground William sat on was scrunchy with leaves and twigs and he sat in the shade of an ancient and gnarled oak tree. Two night-black ravens sat on its lowest branches, tilting their heads to one side looking at him.

The upper branches of the oak were covered in tiny people like creatures with wings that sparkled yellow and white as they danced and flew around.

Finally, his eyes settled on a small man sitting at the base of the oak tree, who wore a striped waistcoat covering a shirt with no collar and grey, dirty trousers. His hair was long and braided down to his waist, where it was tucked into his pocket.

"Would you like a cup of tea, William?" came the question again.

"Where am I?" William asked.

"Where are you now... is it not obvious? You're sitting on the ground in front of a white post in the Great Forest. Now would you like a cup of tea and you can pull yourself together?"

William stood up and cautiously wandered over to the strange looking man, and sat on a log opposite him with a small fire in between them. The man picked up his Hadron-Tool and drew hot tea up from a battered pan that hung on a chain above the fire in a swooping arch and sent it into the cup next to William. The tea tasted sweet and helped William to quickly pull himself together, he however did not let himself fully relax around this strange, unknown little man.

"How do you know my name; I have never met you?"

"My ravens, Hugin and Muninn told me who you were," he said, pointing absentmindedly above his head. "They fly around the town seeing and hearing all that is going on. They thought you would be of particular interest to me."

"They talk to you? Who are you?"

"Talk is a bit of a stretch, but yes, we communicate in some curious way. I am Carrion and I am the keeper of thought and memory. I also have been known to prod the odd Thomon in the right direction and help the odd student to succeed where required. Only a small prod you must understand, the right piece of inspiration at the right time to ensure the Thomon's stay on the right track and so on."

William's mind was churning along with this new information that the little traveller looking man was saying. His mind raced, trying to make this new information fit, and eventually made what he thought was a link to something similar he had heard before.

"Are you the traveller from the stories I have heard? The traveller who gave knowledge to the Thomons?" William asked.

"Me – no, no not me."

William looked disappointed.

"But like him, yes. Why were you crying?"

"I thought you would have known that already!"

"Ha, ha, ha," the little man chuckled, "my ravens are smart and see a lot but they cannot see through walls, like into the Belbury Theatre auditorium. So why were you crying?"

Before answering William assessed the little man for a moment, although a little strange, he did not seem scary and someone to be wary of. He actually came across as warm and caring, with a sprinkling of clever mischievousness.

"I couldn't read a bit of a book to everyone in my class."

"Why?" came a surprisingly sharp snappy reply, briefly stunning William and putting a little crack in his character assessment.

"It is not cos I can't read or can't do stuff in front of people, but the words were dancing all over the page and wouldn't stay in place for me to read them, they were all jumbled up as often happens."

"Ah I see, yes that would be a problem. Not everyone is the same," the little man said calmly once again.

"Please don't say I am special, because I really don't feel like I am," William jumped in pleadingly.

"Special... Ha! Don't kid yourself boy, no one is more special than anyone else, but some are rarer and I hear you are one of those. My ravens tell me you have greater skill in one area than most. Now, most people are generally average at everything," he said while stocking the fire with his Hadron-Tool, "and not amazingly good at one particular thing. However, most people wish to be amazing at something, to be the best at one thing, but are not willing to do or lose what it takes to gain it."

It was at this point the little man brushed some of his loose hair aside that had been covering his left eye to show an empty dark socket, where his eye used to be. As if to say this is what I was willing to lose to gain my knowledge. William reeled back from the site of the dark grotesque hole which made him feel sick.

"People like you, who are very good in one particular area or have a particular talent often fall short of the average standard in other areas. This keeps everything in balance. But what you must understand is that you can cheat the balancing."

At this point Carrion reached into his pocket and produced a small metal cylinder.

"Pass me your Hadron-Tool," he said, holding out his small and dirty hand.

William complied and handed over his device. The man then busily set to work in his lap, the flames of the fire hiding most of what his hands were doing. Once the activity was done, he handed it back to William.

"What have you just done?" William asked, looking over his Hadron-Tool for any sign of the work that had just taken place, and none could be seen.

"You have been told that your Hadron-Tool can be adapted to suit your needs, yes?" Carrion asked and William replied with a silent nod. "Well then, the little addition I have made will fix the words in place and allow you to see them wherever they are."

"But I don't know how to use it, and I am not allowed to make any additions to my tool yet!"

"Details William, details," Carrion said, waving a hand in the air dismissively. "If you imagine strong enough and have contact enough, then your command will be obeyed."

Getting up he wandered over to his ravens and stroked them on their night black heads before they flew off out of sight up above the trees.

"My time here is done," Carrion said, "do not try and find me as that will only happen when you really and truly need my help. Any of the holes in the post will take you to where you need to go, just see it in your head and you will arrive there. Go now as your friends are worried about you." And with that he touched his Hadron-Tool to the great oak tree and disappeared.

William was now all alone, the fire dwindling to nothing, and feeling for the first time shivers of fear. He struck out at a quick scared pace to the post now that he was alone in the Great Forest.

The post was covered on all sides and head to toe with holes. He readied himself, pictured his house common room with its warm balls of floating fire and pressed his Hadron-Tool into a hole.

"William, where have you been?" said a very angry and worried Isabel as she ran over to hug him.

William had appeared at the top of the grooves that gave access to his common room.

"You had us all worried," said Jasmin following behind.

"I am sorry, I just had to leave, but I am feeling better about it all now, and think that it won't ever happen again," said William, with a strange feeling of new found confidence, with not only what was now in his pocket but also that somewhere out there were two ravens watching, looking and reporting back to a strange little man.

🏰 The Very First Game

The day of the first 4's game dawned bright, clear and cold. William was sitting having breakfast, dressed ready for the game in his blue knee length socks with red lines around the top, blue thigh-length shorts and a heavy long-sleeved blue top. He would change into his boots and helmet once in the team preparation room at the pitch.

Around him, his friends were offering him all sorts of hints and tips for the game, but none of them were helpful or useful. William was so nervous he could hardly eat, and the small amount of food he had been able to swallow kept wanting to come back up, so chatting over 4's tactics was the last thing on his mind.

When he had gone to sleep the previous night, he had been imagining the whole team walking out onto the pitch in slow motion with some epic music playing in the background, looking powerful and indestructible, like he had seen in movies back in the Igmon world.

But now none of that was happening, his mind could not have been further away from feeling like what those films showed. He started to think he was being a coward, as real warriors don't feel like this before battle, he told himself. He was now deeply aware of what he was going to be doing and how much the team would rely on him.

The pressure his mind was creating for himself was almost too much.

This trance was broken when Marcus came over to William and put a heavy hand on his shoulder.

"Time to go now Will," he said as an order.

"Right... wish me luck!" William said to his friends, while trying to put on a brave face.

"You will do great Will," George said.

"Remember what I told you," Isabel added.

Jasmin just looked at William and gave him a smile, a quiet yet very powerful expression of knowing William would do ok.

William followed Marcus out of the hall, the rest of the team in their blue kit starting to join the column of the Starley 4's first team as they passed each table on their way out.

The main 4's pitch was located in the north east part of Belbury town. It was immaculate and tended to like a person on life support, by the academy's estate manager Trevour Pilchard, a scarecrow-like man, who would chase off any students who dared stand on, jump over or look disapprovingly at his pitch. The only people who ever made it onto the pitch safely were the players and game officials. Everyone else needed a very good reason on a circular note, signed off by a teacher.

The grass had been recently cut by a sound blade, leaving every blade of grass perfect, and the fresh white line paint was crisp, straight and bright.

The tiered stands were filling up quickly with supporters from every house all mixed in together, surrounding the pitch with colour and noise. Flags for each house decorated the stands, fluttering in the southern breeze that swirled around the stadium. An academy band was playing a mixture of coiling green pipes of differing lengths with flexible paddles, below a massive riveted copper gramophone shaped horn, amplifying their music all over the stadium.

As the team carried out last minute planning and personal pre-match rituals ready for the game in the Starley preparation room, William listened to the shouts and songs being sung above, and he could hear how important the match he was about to play was to the house members above.

The noise was getting louder and louder as the stadium reached full capacity, indicating that the whole academy was in attendance for the first match of the season. There was just time for a last pep talk from Marcus.

"We have practised hard; you all know your roles. Give everything you can for the team. Discomfort and pain will disappear, but a loss will always be with you. So let's start off this year well with a win. Hands in." The team all closed in, placing their hands on each other's in the middle. "Win on three, one, two, three."

"*WIN*," the team shouted together, joining them all like an oath.

The four teams now made their way onto the pitch and took up their positions with the captains walking to the centre to meet the referee, who was from the national 4's association, who ran and organised all the 4's matches across the Thomon world.

He was a tall elf, about twice the height of any of the players, and had sacrificed width for the height, making him bean-pole thin. The referee wore black knee length socks, a thick long sleeved cotton top, again black, and some inappropriately short shorts, again black. On his head was a boiled leather helmet similar to the ones that the players wore, as it was quite common for the referees to get in the way and be tackled like any other player or hit by a runaway, heavy leather egg.

He spoke firmly to the captains, "This is my pitch, what I say goes and if you want my respect you must give me it first. I will not tolerate anyone other than the captains talking to me and fair play is a must. Go back to your teams and make your final preparations." Once finished he sent the captains away while he tested the egg-shaped ball by throwing it a few times into the frosty air. A few moments later he raised his Hadron-Tool with a flick of his wrist, allowing two small pads to flick out and touched them to his throat. The two pads collected the vibrations from his throat as he spoke and the Hadron-Tool body then projected his voice out to the whole stadium.

"Welcome, welcome to all of you, to the first match of the Belbury Apprenticeship Academy 4's tournament." Cheers erupted from the stands. "The game will last seventy-three and a half minutes, and I request that all the crowd stay off the pitch during play, I will not have a repeat of last year. Teams, are you ready?" He looked around making sure to make eye contact with all the captains and as many of the players as possible.

He flicked his wrist to hide the two vibration collection pads and then blew his Hadron-Tool, which created a loud whistle sound around the entire stadium, before he threw the ball unnaturally high in the air for someone so thin.

After shooting up higher than the top of the stadium, the ball plummeted back to earth, where it was caught by a large boy from Fermi house, who lasted all of two seconds before being tackled along the length of his body from all directions by a player from each of the three opposing teams. Resulting in the first game stoppage for a trip to the medical bay.

*

William was still feeling bruised, battered and exhausted the next morning when he was woken up by a newspaper hitting him on the head, thrown by Marcus Mardic with a shout of, "Well done superstar, you got your name mentioned."

William struggled to unstick his eyelids before managing a, "Morning," in reply.

It was the weekend and the students did not have to get dressed in their academy uniform to be able to head down to breakfast, which for William's battered and sore body was a grateful relief. He chucked his dirty 4's clothes from the match the day before into the anything hole in the wall to be washed, folded and returned to him. He pulled on a T-shirt, joggers and slid on some slippers, before wandering down to the Belbury Hall with the paper yet unread under his arm.

Jasmin, Isabel and George were already at the breakfast table munching into a full Thomon of scrambled Didi eggs, the cousin of Dodo wiped out by the Igmons.

The sausages and bacon were from the Winged Fumper, a boar-like creature that was well known for fighting viciously with the three poisoned horns that stuck out of its nose and whose wings were far too small to be used for anything other than cooling itself.

"Well, well, well, the hero finally awakens... Hungry Will?" George said in a cheery voice that spoke of being in a good mood.

"Morning, and yes very hungry," William replied, while filling his plate with the food on offer and taking a deep swig of tea from his mug, which was sitting on a cup-filling coaster.

William sat down and produced the paper called The Wisdom Weekly to read about the match. Its sports reporter Douglas Dasher had written a single page spread on the game. William flipped the page over eleven times, keen to get to the sports sections and see his name. The sports section included many everyday sports from across the Thomon world such as, the Hide and Seek Championship for invisible creatures and the two mile lake swimming competition with the rock people from the Andes coming in dead last once again.

William breathed a breath of comfort and readiness and began to slowly read the story of what had happened the day before. He did not want to test out the modification Carrion had made to his Hadron-Tool as there were too many eyes watching, so he resolved to read at his normal slow pace and unrushed, helping to ensure that most of the words where unmoving, only a few quivered to test William's calmness.

The match I am covering today is the first in this years Belbury Apprenticeship Academy 4's tournament, which has been running at this academy since it began during the Great War.

The house teams are Rutherford, Fermi, Starley and Blanchard. With Starley, captained under Marcus Mardic, aiming to keep the cup for a third straight year! A relatively unheard of statistic in 4's history. Holding on to the trophy for three years on the trot has only been completed by Fermi House more than a century ago. So this year, history could be equalled and I will have all of the information you need as the year progresses.

"I didn't know winning the trophy three years running was so unheard of," William said with a mouth full of egg.

"It's properly difficult to do," George replied, with a mouth full of sausage, "as all the other houses team up to stop that happening."

William looked back at the paper.

All four teams looked in very good shape for this first match and were all able to field full first team sides. The importance of a first match win and the momentum that would bring could be seen in the eyes of all the players.

The egg was thrown into the air at eleven thirty am, in front of a packed stadium of cheering colour and sound.

Play was paused almost immediately for the first medical removal of the match for Fermi house. Shirt number five, Dungouse Treepot, has yet to recover from his broken hip, fractured foot and dislocated shoulder.

Within moments the game was back underway and in full flow, with all teams making great inroads with goals across the board. After fifteen minutes Rutherford house was leading with fifteen points, followed by Starley on twelve and Blanchard on nine. Fermi house after a poor start and being a player down were struggling to get into the game, lagging behind on minus six.

No teams attempted to work together until twenty-four minutes into the game, with Starley and Fermi joining up against the winning Rutherford team. We don't know what was agreed between the two teams as they never say, but both seemed to be happy with the deal. This resulted in five goals being scored, with James Silver, Trever Trivet, Jessica Plankton all scoring one and Alex Long scoring two. Resulting in Rutherford falling into last place on zero, Starley on eighteen, Blanchard on twelve and Femi moving up to three.

The rapid fall from first place to last left the defensive backs of the Rutherford team struggling to get back to grips with the game. This shows the relatively short time they have had to prepare and develop a good team cohesion.

The third quarter of the game there were five medical removals from the pitch leaving both Starley and Rutherford houses short on players, allowing Blanchard the chance to take the lead with eighteen, with a goal against both Starley on fifteen and Fermi on zero.

The last quarter saw feverish play with the Starley team finally starting to click with each other and having some good passages of play with the ball. There was all to play for with the narrow backs on all teams struggling to find their place in this first game.

"Here, look, he is talking about me here. I can see my name in the paper!" William said excitedly.

"Well let's hope it is good, these media people can spin anything in any way," Isabel said.

William Taylor, the youngest player at age 10 on the pitch, would have to wait for the last few minutes of the game before proving himself. He ran two splendid actions that saw amazing footwork and communication between himself and the attack defence players, who on both occasions, when William had been passed the ball from the goal defence twins, were able to carve, at great expense, the smallest of gaps for William to accelerate through in the nick of time, scoring twice before the final whistle, giving the win to Starley House.

The final score at the end of this thrilling first match is Starley on twenty-one, followed by Blanchard on fifteen, Fermi on zero and Rutherford on minus three, who will be very much disappointed as the team showed great promise going into the last quarter. William Taylor will definitely be a player to keep an eye on for the future.

"Wow… that is a good write up," Jasmin remarked.

"If you keep performing like that you will be a famous player before you leave this academy! So can I have your autograph now!" Isabel said, pretending to be star struck.

William folded the paper up and thwacked it on the table next to his freshly filled mug of tea, that was slowly filling itself again, a broad grin across his face and a feeling of pride growing inside him after his debut performance success. He had always been good at sport, but to have done so well that he was written about in a newspaper, now that was a dream come true. William felt he was riding high once again and that nothing could go wrong for him today.

Isabel reached across the table for the paper to read a little while the boys talked about the 4's game and potential ways to beat the other houses and which players looked good and which looked awful.

"Hey look at this, it is talking about the incident on level five. That's what the Headmaster wanted to talk with you about, after your day exploring that level right?"

George and William stopped talking and asked Isabel to read it and listened intently.

"The well-known but secretive Krevak Ragwort, a distant relative of the disbanded Hemlock family attempted to break into a secure location on level five at Belbury Apprenticeship Academy last week. We don't have information on what he was trying to steal or what the academy is holding, but it must be of some value for him to take such a risk, when he is high up the Protection and Security Council's priority capture list. One man is thought to have been killed by Krevak in his escape, this has yet to be confirmed.

The head of the Protection and Security Council, Arthur Rebibox, in a statement said, 'They are renewing their attempts to look for Krevak Ragwort, and will review all the safety and security protocols around the entire Belbury town in the coming days.'

All previous attempts to catch him so far have failed, and Mr Rebibox declined to give any more direct information on the break in or their manhunt for Krevak Ragwort."

"I was right! There is something important behind the Dead End corridor," William said with excitement.

"Wonder what it could be? Isabel, any ideas who the Hemlocks are?" George asked.

"Why would I know?" she replied.

"You're the one always reading books and in the library, you must have come across him!"

"Well, I have not come across either of those names in my time spent reading my books or in the library. You know how vast a place it is! You can't be that blind to not know that!"

"Is it now!?" said George, pretending he had never noticed.

"Well look, if you really wanted to know who the Hemlocks are, and maybe what could be hidden down there, then we could stay late after lessons to have a look," Isabel said, floating the idea to William, George and Jasmin, who did not like spending more time than absolutely necessary in the library.

Despite the group's general dislike for the library they agreed to the idea as it sounded like a good plan and would do it this coming Monday.

As the group sat finishing their breakfast and now talking about the attempted break in and how to trap this Krevak character, William was knocked from behind, on purpose, by Goran Henbane, making him knock his teeth against his mug and spill his tea over his lap.

Goran was the leader of a small gang of boys from Rutherford house who disliked William and all the other Igmon pupils in the academy, because they were true Thomons.

"That was a bit of an easy win, but I guess it being your first match and all that the other teams went easy on you, probably felt sorry for you since you're a weak little Igmon. Don't start thinking you're a hero too soon. We will put you into medical before the year is out," Goran said in an aggressive tone, almost spitting through brilliant white teeth into Williams' face.

William rose to the challenge, pushing his chair back suddenly, sending the rear chair legs smashing into the shin of one of Goran's gang, who yelped in pain, clutching his shins. After all, that was a reason why he was on the Starley first team, because he was a fighter.

Just as he was about to throw his mug of hot tea straight in Goran's face in anger, Mrs Plushoe stepped in.

"And what is going on here? I hope nothing?" she said with the question not being for any other purpose than to diffuse the tension and did not expect an answer.

"Good, well on your way then Goran, your table is over there," she said, directing him as if he did not know.

"We'll get you next time," Goran said over his shoulder, sneering at William as he walked away.

"I see you have never heard of the term 'meek' William."

"No! And I am not a weak boy, Goran will get what he deserves if he does that again," fumed William, his heart still racing and eyes wide, ready to fight.

"Ah yes, the fight in a young man, now that is fine. No one should make a bully's life easy by giving them what they want, but meek is not weak, a common mistake to make. It is to have the ability to destroy, but choosing not to. It is the mark of a true warrior and a man," she said with an air of longing and dreaminess. "You best learn that quickly, since you will probably be in the newspaper a little more than everyone else if you keep performing like that on the 4's pitch," she said while pointing to the paper, which was laid on the table showing the 4's game report again. "Do I make myself understood?"

"Yes Mrs Plushoe," William replied, suitably confused and told off, suddenly coming over all tired as his body slowed down and the adrenaline returned to normal.

Mrs Plushoe left spinning on the balls of her feet so her coat flared out around her waist, like she was ballroom dancing with an invisible partner. The group laughed at this and returned to their breakfast.

⬚⬚ Being Nosey

William, George and Jasmin had just endured with some significant effort the "Work, Earn and Live" lesson in the town's bank called Gold Stones, with a dwarf called Turpit Cointis. He was of normal adult size for his kind, which was the height of a seven-year-old human child. He had a round head with long hair combed neatly back, mimicking his long neat beard, which was decorated with rings and jewellery. He wore a double-breasted pinstripe suit like many of the other bankers, along with a matching shirt and tie. He looked every part the description of a crisp, hardworking and cut-throat banker William knew from the Igmon world.

However, it was clear that even though these dwarfs were now in banking, they had not forgotten their love of the mine, and so like all the other dwarfs in the bank, Turpit still wore his mining steel toed wellies, although they were cleaned and polished to a shine. His double-breasted suit jacket, which had no buttons because chubby dwarf fingers find them tricky, was held in place with his old tool belt, where he still hung a head torch and set of gloves.

Dwarfs in Igmon myths are more known for mining deep into the earth for gold, silver and precious stones while singing and whistling catchy songs while they work, and being looked after by a beautiful maiden. But real dwarfs who lived in the Thomon world had become so much more. Being very crafty, they had moved into banking, which had quickly grown to be very profitable for them. They had found that by controlling the creation of gold and silver and then also the borrowing and lending of the gold and silver at the same time they could haul in quite the profit.

When the dwarfs wanted the value of gold for example to go up, they just mined a little less and made it a little more scarce and so more valuable. This gave them a big advantage over any other bank in the area who did not also have the mining capability.

Isabel was the only one who enjoyed these lessons and tried to answer every question to be top of the class. Her arm was constantly shooting up at every request for an answer. Turpit Cointis eventually had to purposefully ignore her to give others a chance. But everyone else was so uninterested in the lesson, Mr Cointis would end up having to choose Isabel anyway, given the lack of other high waving hands.

Her friends often caught her reading ahead in the lesson's textbook, so that she could be well ahead of all the other students during the lesson, which gained her no friends.

The morning's lesson had been about compound interest and writing balance books, which although important to understand, was so boring. William nearly fell asleep at the standing desk that stood to the side of the main hall of the bank, where customers would walk in and out, meeting with clerks to discuss business just over his shoulder.

He was kept awake by the architecture and grandeur of the bank. Gold was heavy everywhere, from gilded leaves that hung on black steel railings, to great solid looking statues that sat strong and proud in most of the corners in the building. William thought they showed past heads of the bank or great dwarf leaders.

The roof was a single slab of solid white marble, with a map of the world painted in thin black lines upon it. It showed more land than William had seen on maps in the Igmon world.

William was fixated by it, as the marble was not solid and still but solid and fluid, shifting from tomato soup smooth to great spikes suddenly in different locations all over the map. This, William had been told, was where the greatest trading values in any given commodity was at that exact moment in time, anywhere in the world. This resulted in a map that was constantly changing its texture as the values in the Thomon world ebbed and flowed.

There was also a gigantic polished grey, circular vault door at the far end of the bank, with three great turning wheels on its front, each the size of a human male. There were three holes in the vault door to receive the Hadron-Tools of the allowed operators of the door to insert as keys, and release whatever the overly complex locking system concealed inside. The students were not allowed beyond the vault door to see what was safely hidden away, and were quickly shooed away if they tried to touch it.

William did think it strange that if the bank's vault was as secure as it looked, then *why* was the object that was hidden on level five and recently nearly stolen, not hidden and kept safe in the bank? He continued to wonder and imagine what could possibly be hidden down in the depths below Belbury town? Who was Krevak Ragwort and who were the Hemlocks? William's mind spent the rest of the lesson tossing these thoughts around, but found no information in his mind that could answer them.

The lesson thankfully came to an end and the group walked around the corner to the library, which was Isabel's favourite place, where their next lesson was to take place. No one was allowed into the library without the say-so of the librarian, who sat at her solid mistletoe desk that smelt heavily of bee's wax polish, just inside the front door. She greeted Isabel with a friendly familiarity, as Isabel had almost lived in the library during her spare time. But her tone was stern to the boys, who were rarely there, informing them that noise must be kept low and running around was not allowed.

Through a window in the next brown wood-panelled door, William could see hundreds of towering racks filled with stacks of multi-coloured, tiny flat squares. Next to the racks were large dark wooden benches running in lines across the room and balconies above.

Hanging from the ceiling were lengths of winding and swooping brass track guiding two-wheel carriages that carried piles of tiny books slung underneath them. They flew along from one location to another at great speed, stopping and starting in total spooky silence. The track dropped down in great sweeping arcs to bench level, allowing the carriages to pick up items and transport them elsewhere or drop loads off.

In other areas long scissor-like extending arms reached down from the rafters, grabbing and flying up to disappear into the library's roof. This constant sorting and organising was all done in ghostly silence, while people and other human-like creatures sat loosely scattered around the wooden benches reading and writing.

It turned out that the library had so many books, papers and documents that to keep them all in the same space they had all been shrunk to the size of match boxes. The library user would then use their Hadron-Tool to enlarge the book they wanted to read and shrink it again after use.

Other rooms led off the main hall and contained all the dangerous and high learning books, which only the most highly trained Thomon were allowed to read. Access to these books was guarded by the very terrifying and scary looking obstacles of tiny, mousehole sized doors. This required that the person who wanted to read those books be skilled enough to shrink themselves down to gain access. Only the most highly trained Thomon could do this without causing themselves any long-lasting problems after they had re-enlarged themselves.

*

The "Your History and Culture" lesson always took place in the library for First Years and was taught by Sir Rudyard Welton, a traditional but lazy looking man who deemed looking presentably smart of secondary importance. His clothes were worn right through in all the normal locations for a man of the paper and ink. He wore a checked knee-length sports jacket that had a different coloured patch on each elbow. His worn green corduroy trousers sagged sloppily over brown leather unpolished slip-on shoes that had a ridge running around the toe. A white shirt with a worn unstarched collar was partially tucked in and a green and gold cravat was tied around his neck. The look was complete with a laughable combover of thinning brown hair on his head.

Once the lesson was over, the group of four stuck around in the library to begin looking for the name Krevak Ragwort and the Hemlocks, but where on earth to start? The group decided to split up, William and George took the modern history section, with Isabel and Jasmin taking historical newspapers.

The two groups parted ways and began to slowly run their Hadron-Tools over the spines and labels for each item in their section, allowing enough time for it to grow to a readable size before moving onto the next item if the title did not seem like a good place to start or looked really boring.

William and George quickly found a fun game to make the looking for the right book title a bit more fun. It involved running their Hadron-Tools along the line of books at a slow, quiet and secretive run. This created a wave in the books as each grew larger and then rapidly shrunk back down.

If they did it in the right section and suddenly enough a tiny creature like a pixie would be thrown out from behind the books where it was hiding, high into the air, emitting a high-pitched scream as it flew. Ending in the little creature having a thumping landing on the wooden desk.

The pixie-like creature was always very unhappy about this rather rude and traumatic experience, and before storming off back to its home behind the books it would shout angrily at the two boys in a language they could not understand. But expressive pointing of fingers and waving of arms like someone on holiday who could not speak the local language, told the boys all they needed to know.

Jasmin and Isabel rounded a corner while scanning stacks of old papers and caught the two boys playing out their little game. This provoked great annoyance in Isabel, but great laughter from Jasmin upon seeing a tiny little creature screaming as it flew up into the air and then went crashing down. Isabel whacked Jasmin on the upper arm to stop her laughing before turning on William and George.

"William and George! We are here to look for information, not to play games, leave the flicks alone," she said, hissing through pursed lips, while trying to control her anger.

William and George suitably dressed down after being caught in the act got back to what they should have been doing and actually started to look once again at the titles on the spines of the books they were enlarging.

William eventually took one new-looking book out entitled "The Last Of The Great Thomons" and started to turn through the pages looking for the key words.

Again, William had the problem of words not staying put, making seeing what he was looking for very difficult.

He then remembered what Carrion had done to his Hadron-Tool. What was it he had said? "It will fix the words in place and allow you to see them wherever they are." He quickly picked up his Hadron-Tool off the table top and tossed it over a few times in his hand, trying to think of how to get it to work. There were no teachers around to ask what to do, or what to think of or imagine to get his Hadron-Tool to keep all the words inplace, and even if there were, they would probably tell William off for modifying his Hadron-Tool.

"Contact and imagination, contact and imaginations is what the teachers keep saying. Well then, let's give that a go," William thought to himself.

He touched the tip of his tool to the page and let his unique brain do what it did best and imagine what he wanted to happen. William was able to imagine so well that it was as real to him as anything else, and at that moment the words on the page were in his mind really moving into straight lines. Purple ink started to flow out of the Hadron-Tool like a spilled ink pot, slowly flooding the page.

Amazed by this, William snatched his Hadron-Tool off the page to look at the tools tip, but could not see any purple droplets dripping from the end. Areas of the page that had just become purple had also instantly turned back to its original white, allowing the words and letters a dance floor to spin and twirl upon. William retouched the Hadron-Tool to the page, began to imagine again and the colour changing process started to flow again.

As the purple colour spilled across the page, any letter it touched slid back into place and stayed put. Once the whole page was purple and all the words were in orderly lines, he quickly scanned the page looking for anything, but found nothing. As time went on William became quicker and quicker at this process and soon was reading pages at a decent pace, but still trying his best to hide this new skill from his friends.

The group spent many more hours poring through book after book, document after document until it was time to head to Belbury Hall for their evening meal.

The group trudged back to Belbury Hall and ate most of their meal in disappointed silence. Even the arms popping out of the table did not raise much of a smile.

"Hours of looking and nothing, not even a scrap or a point in the right direction," George moaned, wishing he could have those hours of his life back.

"It was our first try, these things can take time," said Isabel calmly, but also secretly feeling a little disappointed.

"Take time! How much time? I guess you have looked for dangerous villains' names before and so this sort of thing is normal for you!" said George, annoyed with Isabel's acceptance of what he perceived as total failure.

"It's strange that there is no trace, not even a tiny clue, in any of the Histories of Thomon Families, birth records, newspapers or even in a book called 'The Greatest of Thomon Criminals', written by a criminal and so you would think he would know. It's like Krevak and that family has been deleted from history," William said in an annoyed voice, but also happy he had been able to read so much for once, but stayed quiet on how. "We will just have to keep looking, I guess, and ask some careful questions. We have to know who Krevak is and what he is trying to steal," William said, trying to force some life and direction back into their goal.

12 Glitter and Boredom

William darted left with the egg tucked under his left arm, his right arm out ready to fend off any tacklers. He was running fast; his reactions were on high alert. William jumped over one boy from the Blanchard team who had just been tackled by one of the Starley attack defence players and had fallen in front of him, his head digging a trench in the mud. He had a brief moment of space and willed his legs to move faster, all fear removed from his mind as it was totally focused on getting to the goal.

From the corner of Williams' left eye he spotted a charging bull of a boy. William started to take evasive action trying to veer away but it was too late, as the bull-like boy charged William down. But at the last minute the bullish boy slipped, smacking William on his hip with his forearm and sending him spinning off course but still on his feet. A few moments of panic crossed William's mind as he spun off course, fearing he was about to fall and lose the ball. He fought hard to get his eyes focused again on the Rutherford goal and his body obeyed and sorted itself out. His feet scrabbling for grip in the soft mud, he set off at pace once more for the goal.

The sideways ice-cold rain and thick mud on the floor, gave little traction for his feet or grip on the ball which was struggling to get out of his grip. Poor visibility also made everything a little bit of a surprise with beasts and monsters launching themselves at him from the mists of blurred vision. The goal was now becoming clear and William was not alone, two of his attack defence team mates had managed to break through and they headed straight for the Rutherford goal, where the two Goal Defence players were now in a problematic three on two situation.

"We're with you Will!" shouted one of the Starley Attack Defenders.

"Leave them to us!" called the other Starley Attacker Defenders.

At the last minute the two Starley players darted in front of William intercepting the Rutherford Goal Defence tackles. William had just enough time and space to change course to avoid the bodies, dive and throw the egg into the goal. The match ended with a loud blast on the referee's Hadron-Tool after more play had been completed and goals scored, leaving Starley still in overall second place.

The cold sideways rain during the match was now chasing the spectators from the stands, back to their warm and dry houses at a rapid pace, as the warmth from the excitement of the match faded away from their bodies.

It had grown so cold lately that the Red Lake had frozen over thick and white. Allowing the students to skate on it during their free time, using stretched and hardened icicles, snapped from the branches of trees and beams of the boat houses around the lake. Lessons at the

Weavers Mill became increasingly popular, with students turning up early for class and staying late to make last minute presents of scarfs, hats, gloves and jumpers to take home.

The cold also meant it was very nearly Christmas and time to go home for the mid-year break, which for William would last for a few weeks. The Starley common room had really become home for him and his friends, but especially William who was an Igmon, and who only a few months ago did not know the Thomon world existed. Soon he would be going home to a place where impossible things were still impossible and his Hadron-Tool would need to stay packed away.

The common room had been decorated ready for an early Christmas celebration that would happen before the break. The seniors of the house headed out into the Great Forest to find a suitable tree. The main criteria for the tree being it must be better than the trees the others houses get.

And as normal they had totally forgotten how tall the common room ceiling was and brought back a tree that was far too tall, and they had no intention of shrinking it to fit.

"The needles on a Christmas tree do not scale down well at all!" a senior student said. "Shrinking a tree that has needles makes it look all fluffy instead of spiky, like a Christmas tree should be, and all your decorations have to be smaller too."

So, the tree would instead be installed at a slight angle, with the top bending along the ceiling above. Everyone in the house had been busy making decorations out of everything and anything, using their Hadron-Tools to reshape the object into something Christmassy. William was sure one of the decorations on the tree was someone's manipulated reading glasses that now looked like a small pair of wings.

On one of the final mornings a stack of official academy letters had appeared on William's bed, with large writing on their fronts stating that these must be taken home and signed.

One letter explained about academy trips in the next half of the year, one of which would be to the Igmon world. Another was a hazard acceptance form that required the parent's signature to allow the children to take part in many dangerous but exciting activities. In the letter the parents were told that the medical centre could repair most forms of limb loss and marginal death, and so therefore any other lessor injury would be of no issue meaning they should not be worried about the exact nature of the activities.

Another was from Gold Stones bank, containing a form that William's parents again needed to sign to allow him to open an account with them. The letter stated that this would be very important, as after Christmas the First Year students would be required to start buying their own equipment for academy lessons. The reasoning for this was that the academy saw the first half of the year for First Years as an adjustment period and so were happy to provide equipment. But for the second half of the year the students would need to show and develop increased self-reliance and preparedness, which would need to increase as they grew through the academy.

The academy term ended this coming Friday with the Christmas Fair. Looking out of one of his house common room windows William could see the fair ground under construction, spread like Lego bricks tipped out of a box over the meadow in the south east and spilling onto the frozen lake. With large tents, stalls, bright flags and many strange and wonderful things being moved into place.

However, before the excitement could be enjoyed the last few lessons had to be finished and William and George were running late for one of the last ones and one of the worst possible lessons to be late for. "Looking After Yourself", with Mrs Endorfa Vigor took place in a restaurant called Delights, a small little place with room to seat twenty customers at a time. The slightly interesting meals that were served ranged from a creamy Grantonk Ankle soup, a type of top feeding slug with bay leaves, and the very popular Decaoctanon roast, which is a creature with ten legs, nine eyes and eight ears. Although very tasty the Decaoctanon could never with any confidence be fully killed, as its brain was scattered all over its body. So even once it was cooked and on the plate about to be eaten it could very well come back to life and eat the customer instead. The honey roasted vegetables it came with were very tasty though and well worth the risk.

Mrs Endorfa Vigor, a stern-faced woman, was the owner and head chef of Delights restaurant, and was the one teacher that William could not stand. She was a large round woman, who looked like she had eaten far too much of her own food. She wore a waisted jacket, whose every thread was hanging on for dear life. Tight blue and white chequered britches covered her rolling legs like snow covered hills. All of this mass was covered with a large white apron whose waist tie acted like a ratchet strap to contain the bursting person inside. Her hair was twisted into a cake-like pile on her head and held in place with a fork, and a golden tube around her head called an HHCR device or Head Hair Control Ring, created a dome of air over the hair stack to stop any loose bits from falling into her cooking. The students also wore HHCR devices during their lessons for the same reason. But most of the children thought that a little hair might make their cooking taste a bit better though.

Whenever there was a chance she would stop and stretch her vast bulk, but her rolling fingers of pink fat never did touch her toes, and the students could almost hear her britches start to scream in panic every time the pointless event was about to happen. Most of the time she also carried some nasty green drink concoction that apparently was good for you, probably because it put you right off eating anything else at all.

"Come on George we are really late, she already doesn't like us," said William, stepping in through the door.

"She doesn't like anyone! I reckon she eats anyone she really doesn't like. I have not seen Craig Mucklunkin since he had detention with her two weeks ago," George said with worry. "Maybe he's in what's being eaten now!"

"The rubbish that comes out of your mouth!" William said, partly laughing in amazement at George's thoughts.

"We can sneak in when she is not looking, she won't notice," William said hopefully.

William and George quickly scooted past the restaurant customers who were eating a selection of lunches, some of which looked like they could walk off the plate at any moment.

The customers were seated on simple red wooden chairs, at small round tables covered in white table cloths. The boy's plan was quickly tested as they slowly and quietly opened the door to the restaurant's kitchen.

Mrs Endorfa was currently heating a large pot with her Handron-Tool and instructing the class how to make what she thought was a, "good and healthy meal." This meant boring and tasteless food to William. What she was cooking right now looked like it would have been happily at home in a witch's cauldron.

"Late again!" announced Mrs Endorfa Vigor, catching the two boys sliding through the narrowly opened door and making the class turn around from their tables. The class were all currently using their Hadron-Tools to chop and stir the contents of large pots that were being heated by another Hadron-Tool that was being held against the side of the pot.

"Well... we..." William started but was cut off.

"Is looking after your body not important to you?"

"Ye..." William started but was cut off again.

"Think you know everything do you?"

"Well, no but..." William tried again but was cut off, with Mrs Endorfa now making him feel like a problem to her, which in a way William and George currently were.

"Well class, since William and George are late, they clearly know more than I do and so will be teaching you for the rest of the lesson," she said while showing the boys to the front of the class with her outstretched arm. The boys hesitated, looking at each other and not sure what to do.

"Well boys?" she said with sudden scary calmness. "Can you teach this lesson and teach the class how to make this delicious broth of Hobosh tendrils and Rock leaves? And make it so correctly that it can also cure someone from bowl sneezing?" She paused for a minute to drive home the telling off and prolong the awkward quiet. "No? Well SIT DOWN and DON'T BE LATE AGAIN! I will be meeting with your House Captains and removing house points, now sit. You're lucky they have banned the use of thumbscrews. Those were the days of real discipline," she muttered to herself.

William and George rushed to the only empty desk and then sat still as statues, only daring to move their eyes, not wanting to do anything at all wrong, even in the slightest that could get them into more trouble.

As the lesson went on the smell in the cramped restaurant kitchen grew more and more pungent with more and more students making something that was not quite unlike what Mrs Endorfa had asked them to make.

"I hope I don't have to eat this," said George. "She always makes us try what we have made at the end," he said, peering over the edge of his pot and seeing lumpy, heavy bubbles inside.

"It can't be as bad as what we made last week, that was some sort of curry I think. It made my finger shrink,

I had to go to medical to get them re-lengthened!" William replied.

After a few more minutes of stirring, heating and more stirring Mrs Endorfa banged a wooden spoon on the table at the front.

"Right class this lesson is nearly over, time for the ultimate test, try what you have made. It should taste light, with a hint of rosemary and have a little delayed bite to it." Mrs Endorfa instructed the class.

William and George looked at each other with unwillingness on their faces, each wanting the other to go first. Pleasant noises started to be heard from around the class as students were impressed with what they had made.

"See you are all starting to get better, well done all of you," Mrs Endorfa praised. "And how did the late comers do? Come on hurry up."

George dipped his spoon into the pot expecting the end to be melted off by whatever they had made. He then very slowly put the spoon into his mouth, his eyes were closed tight while he thought about the taste in his mouth. Then like a delayed explosion they were wide open, steam was pouring from his ears and nose. His pale skin slowly turned from white, to blue then to green.

"Quick, outside boy. Don't be sick in my kitchen," Mrs Endofa shouted pointing at the door.

George desperately ran for it, his trousers leaving a trail of green smoke behind him all the way.

"Errrrrr," laughed the class all together, as they heard the faint sounds of George being sick in the road.

"All right, all right, calm down he will be fine," Mrs Endorfa reassured the class.

And with that the classroom emptied, everyone eager to get to the Christmas Fair, which had already been in full swing since lunch time, with an impressively colourful hydroworks display in the air above the fair signalling the opening. But it really came to life when the moon took the place of the sun and the lights of the fair came to life in the darkness.

Since lunchtime, William had been hearing and seeing students in and around town walking back from the fair with toys, sweets and smiling faces, all full of excitement. Now, finally he was also free and keen to explore the Christmas Fair before the night was over. William and his friends ran, slipping and sliding on the icy cobbles and pavements, taking three blinkingly long grooves back to their house to get changed into warm weather clothing. They agreed to meet in the common room at five pm.

"Where on earth are William and George? They always say we are so slow to get ready," Isabel said to Jasmin, who was already starting to become red in the face while standing in a slightly warm common room in a thick jacket, scarf and woolly hat.

"Ha, they're probably doing their makeup," Jasmin joked, just before the two boys appeared running out of the boy's corridor.

"See, I told you we said five!" William said to George who was running behind him.

"Sorry you two, I thought we said a different time, I thought I had time for a quick shower!" George said as he came to a halt in front of Jasmin and Isabel.

"All good! Let's hurry and get going, don't want to miss it," Jasmin said while turning to leave.

They quickly set off down the groove to enjoy the last event of term. Filled with excitement they bounced and skipped through the narrow and winding jitties, allies and roads that had been cleared of ice and snow.

As they got closer to the main entrance of the fair, they joined more and more students all excited for the fun of the event.

The fair's entrance glowed into view, with a towering arch of fire that blasted every person with heat as they entered under it. Once through this dramatic and hot entrance they were enveloped with bright lights, exciting sounds and pungent smells that repelled the darkness and cold of the outside world.

Everywhere were decorative lights, created by fire spheres of all different sizes and containing different shapes and patterns of fire within. There was music from bands, and music machines on all sides, hundreds of small stalls, tents and rides spread out on the lake's thick ice. All of the routes through the maze-like fair eventually led to a large main tent located at the fair's heart. The tent roof was striped with the academy house colours, like much of the rest of the fair.

There were Jugglers, Fire Burpers and Zaramin Tamers paraded around with their beautiful gymnastic animals, and Libras were ridden in jousting matches.

All the games around the fair involved using your Hadron-Tools to shoot and or move objects to knock over or capture other objects.

A great Ferris wheel was turned by a Dragoon, a horse-like creature a little larger than a shire horse. Instead of a long hairy mane it had Hawthorn-like branches that sprouted from the back of its long thick neck. These branches would grow leaves and small white flowers with red berries when it was ready to find a mate. Helpfully the Dragoon did not breathe fire like the dragons of Igmon myths.

William had learnt about these unusual creatures during his "Things We Live With" classes at the local vets. Animals like the Dragoon had been created many hundreds of years ago by Thomon bio-engineers. The engineers had been combining animals with plants, but like with all experiments that sound too interesting and so should not have been carried out, the hybrid Plamal creatures, as they were collectively known, had escaped. They had since bred and adapted even more, becoming widespread and highly prized.

As they carried on walking around the fair, William brought a candy floss hat for himself and his friends along with playing one or two games with great excitement but little success.

Isabel had her fortune read by a Mork, another Plamal creature. The Mork looked like a very fat and well-fed barn owl, and had long, dangling but soft spines, like those on a Lion's Mane Mushroom covering its body instead of feathers. After paying the Mork's owner, she was then instructed to place her head against its soft, white forehead and look into its large round eyes. Isabel started to feel very nervous as the Mork silently brought its sizeable white wings around from its sides and covered her head, putting them into darkness where the Mork's eyes began to glow and stared unblinkingly into Isabelle's.

A few moments later the Mork opened its wings and Isabel emerged confused.

"Well, that was a waste of money! It showed three different futures. The Mork must be broken," she said.

"Broken... no not broken my dear," said the lady who ran the Mork. "The Mork will show you three different versions of the future, none of which on their own are true. It is up to you young lady, to combine the visions together to create the real true vision of your future!"

"Well, that makes it more like guess work, there must be a thousand different ways you can combine three visions," Isabel said as she walked away annoyed with the waste of money.

Jasmin tried a shooting game, where tiny flicks would run around with targets on their backs and people would use their Hadron-Tools to shoot air bubbles at them to try and knock them over.

William was most impressed with the skywalkers, who would run in free air, high above everyone's heads by standing on blocks of ice they formed with the Hadron-Tools. These blocks would briefly take the skywalker's weight before they fell to the floor and smashed.

Eventually they made their way into the big top with all the others to see and hear the end-of-term speech from the Headmaster, Sir Coalbrook. The big top was indeed big. From the outside it looked large but once inside all sense of size was gone. It was a vast theatre, considerably bigger than the outside of the tent would allow for. Rows upon rows of tiered seating filled most of the space, with balconies and comfortably appointed boxes floating around the edges.

"Good evening students," came the Headmaster's voice from the stage located in the centre of the tent. "Welcome to our annual end-of-half-year Christmas Fair, I trust everyone has been enjoying the event so far and so I won't keep you from your fun. Thank you for a great first half of the year, you are all showing fantastic academy and house spirit and long may that continue. You are now to go home to see your families and friends, relax and recharge, but I must remind you that if you are going back to an Igmon home, use of your Hadron-Tools is not allowed. We don't want to start seeing people dropped into lakes on ducking stools or burnt at the stake again just for being highly skilled and caught showing off.

For those who are staying in the Thomon world you are limited to the skills you have learned so far only, and no further progress is permitted to be made away from here. These are limitations put in place by the Thomon Protection and Security Council and so it is with them that you will be in trouble not me. So now with that said, go and enjoy to your heart's content, as tomorrow you leave to go back to the many different and fantastic lives you all come from." With that Sir Coalbrook walked quickly down into the floor and the noise in the tent rose once again.

The students were once again up and moving around after the short speech, some would stay to see the circus and trickster shows that would take place. Others made their way back out into the warm flickering light outside to continue playing games and eating sweets until they dropped with tiredness.

As the Christmas Fair drew to an end, the tired friends were slowly making their way to the exit which was just as tall and hot as at the start, when William saw in the shadows behind one of the game tents, a dark profile wearing a long jacket and a head of unkept hair. From the shadowed profile's movements William could tell he was talking very aggressively to another person also in shadow, but whose body position was clearly of someone not enjoying the interaction.

Out of curiosity to what was happening William made his way closer, slipping through small gaps between the stands, while trying to stay out of sight. He saw the man with the wild hair take what must have been his Hadron-Tool out of his pocket, put it under the other person's chin, lifting him clear off the ground. The person was now dangling in the air, scrabbling around with his hands trying to breathe, his feet flailed around hopelessly in free air. William suddenly felt a shiver of fear ripple over his body, causing him to pause and listen, hoping he had not been seen yet.

"You will do it or you will not live much longer. We are coming for it whether you like it or not and you can either survive or die when that happens!" The dominating figure snarled at his victim.

"Iii... ccaannnttt," came a choking answer from the struggling man.

"Then you are of no use to me," the dominating man said dismissively, before up-ending the man and slamming him into the ground with brutal force, the victim's body making a sickening crack as it hit. The man now lay contorted and unmoving.

William, without thought for what might happen, ran forward shouting, "Hey, hey you, *STOP*! George, Isabel, Jasmin come quick help!" He ran straight at the wild haired man without fear, pulling his Hadron-Tool out of his pocket as he went, but unsure what he would do with it. The man turned to face him, stepping out of the shadows into the glowing light of the Christmas Fair.

William saw it was the same man with red hair he had seen on level five, it was Krevak Ragwort. Using his Hadron-Tool Krevak hurled a stout wood barrel that was standing on the floor next to one of the fairground tents towards William with great speed and force. He then turned and ran, his long jacket spinning out like a sail.

William gave chase. As he ran, he bent over to touch the floor with his Hadron-Tool, dragging it up into a barrier to shield himself. William was not thinking, just acting, imagining a shield to protect himself from the wooden barrel that was hurtling towards him at alarming speed. The barrel hit William's floor-coloured barrier with a deafening crash and split into splinters, throwing the rainbow-coloured liquid everywhere. William carried on, working on instinct, dropping his arm and allowing the barrier to slither back into the ground. He raced around the corner of the next tent only to see Krevak flying up into the sky with a great leap and was out of reach, leaving only a cloud of dust behind him.

William looked around and saw his friends running up behind him with their Hadron-Tools also drawn. Instantly he gave instructions, "George, go get the Headmaster, and hurry. Isabel, can you help that person on the floor? Jasmin, tell any teacher you find to come here now! Krevak was here!"

Off they flew to their tasks without hesitation, understanding the urgency.

Sir Rudyard must have been walking very close by because before William had time to get his breath back and think about what was next, he came running around the corner with Jasmin in tow.

"Everyone ok? Any of you hurt?" he said looking around in panic at the remaining children. "No! good… You have done really well here but it is now time to return to your houses, I will take it from here."

"But Sir I saw…" William complained before he was cut off.

"William please," Sir Rudyard snapped with the rush of adrenalin. "What you have done here is good but please go back to your house and you will be questioned later. *Now go!*" Sir Rudyard said with force and control.

Isabel and Jasmin followed the instruction with relief, but had to drag William away who wanted to keep helping.

They had to push their way through students continuing to have fun at the fair and who were totally oblivious to the man lying dead on the floor behind one of the tents, and how close they had been to such a dangerous man.

Once in the quiet safety of their common room the three sat in front of the bobbing fire, talking frantically and trying to make sense of the event that had just taken place. George appeared a few minutes later and instantly joined in the panicked conversation, telling his story of trying to find the Headmaster.

"Will, how did you pull that ground up like that, we have not learnt how to do that yet?" Isabel said, amazed by what William had created and how strong it was. "Did you see that barrel just smash against it, just amazing," she carried on talking quickly.

"Yeah, that was awesome Will, but you said you heard Krevak say something before he killed that man, what did he say?" George asked William, trying to catch up with the conversation.

"You will do it or you will not live much longer. We are coming for it whether you like it or not and you can either survive or die when that happens," William said, repeating the words that were now permanently in his memory.

"But what are they coming for? What is behind that wall at the end of the Dead End corridor?" Isabel said in a flustered tone.

"Any idea who the man was on the floor?" George asked. But before an uninformed answer could be given, Sir Coalbrook and Arthur Rebibox interrupted their conversation.

"Well now, I can tell that one or all of you are always going to be in the right place at the wrong time," came the Headmasters low and controlled voice. The tone helping to calm the already on edge group from the surprise visit and letting them know they were not in trouble.

"Who's the man going to a funeral?" Isabel whispered to William.

"That's Arthur Rebibox from the PSC," William whispered back. Isabel nodded in understanding, while Sir Coalbrook and Arthur walked across the room.

"Thank you George for finding me so quickly, as I believe you all have a story to tell me," the Headmaster said while lowering himself into a chair and offering another to Arthur.

So, the group led by William began to tell the story of what had happened, who they had seen and what they had heard. The Headmaster and Arthur listened quietly, only interrupting to ask small questions to gain more detail where required.

"Any more questions Arthur?" Sir Coalbrook asked.

Arthur shook his head without saying a word.

"Good, please get back to the PSC as quickly as possible and alert the Tutelaries, they will want to be briefed."

Arthur turned to leave, but did not get far before Sir Coalbrook gripped Arthur's upper arm and turned fully towards him saying, "I think we may need the Sentinels here sooner than I thought."

Arthur nodded in agreement and once again started to leave the room. But before he had a chance to, William stepped forward saying, "Wait! Who is Krevak? And who are the Hemlocks? We have been looking and looking in the library and found nothing!"

The Headmaster and Arthur looked at each other before Arthur gave Sir Coalbrook a nod, allowing him to enlighten the four students.

"The great war was started by a family called the Hemlocks. They started it as they wanted to control the whole word and have everyone do their bidding. When they finally lost, all evidence of them was destroyed, as no one wanted that level of destruction and death to ever happen again. The man you met tonight is a distant descendant of the Hemlocks of an obscure family line that was never fully destroyed. Over the last few years, he has been trying without success to rebuild his family's power and name." He finished and looked around the group who were standing wide-eyed and amazed with this new information.

Changing his tone to be much lower and firmer, Sir Coalbrook started to talk once again. "Arthur here will take care of the matter so there is no need for you to worry or do anything else. You were very brave and lucky doing what you did this evening William, but he could have easily killed you, Kevak is immensely powerful. You must stay out of these matters in the future and leave it to the teachers and Arthur here." Seeing that the group understood, he relaxed his tone again, "Please enjoy the rest of your evening and have a great Christmas holiday." Sir Coalbrook smiled widely to help lighten the mood in the room, then turned and left down the groove with Arthur following, leaving the four standing in quiet silence.

William, undeterred by the warning, turned to his friends with determination in his eyes and voice saying, "We may be going on holiday, but we must keep looking and finding out more about what is behind that Dead End, and why Krevak wants it so badly that he is willing to kill to get it. If he wants to build his family back up then we must know what he is trying to get his hands on."

The group agreed to keep thinking and looking over the holidays and share what they had learned when they returned.

👁👁 Everything is impossible

The infinitely long minibus snaked round the final bend onto Downhole Road, where William could see his parents waiting by the post box, as if they had never moved after dropping him off all those months ago.

The minibus drew to a halt with a squeal of worn brakes and the side door slid backward, giving William the first proper look at his parents in half a year. Before he removed his bags from the warmth of the minibus to the cold hard tarmac of the pavement he and George shook hands, promising to stay in touch over the holiday. William then dived out of the open minibus door, wrapping his arms around his mum and dad who responded in kind.

"It's so good to see you," said William, beaming up into his parents' faces.

"You too boy. What have they been feeding you? You must have grown about a foot," Mr Taylor said, smiling along with his wife.

"You may have grown but you're still my boy and it is good to have you back. But have you brought your bags back with you as you look a little light," his mum said, looking forward to having her boy back in the house.

William quickly jumped back into the bus, grabbed his bags before the minibus left and dropped them on the cold pavement.

William waved and said a general goodbye to the others on the minibus before the door slid back in place with a hollow bang, allowing the rest of the passengers to be delivered back to their waiting families.

As William walked home between his mum and dad he looked back once more to see the back of the very standard sized white minibus driving off, remembering the infinitely large secret hidden inside.

The walk back to his house was a time of sadness, but also happiness for William. He was finally back with his mum and dad and loved that as he had missed them. But at the same time, he missed being in the amazing Thomon world where impossible things were made possible every day.

Sitting on his bed in his room, it was just as he remembered it. He bounced gently while taking it all back in, as if he was remembering an old friend. He turned his Hadron-Tool around in his pocket and his body ached, knowing he was not allowed to use it.

His mum was already washing all his clothes and was very impressed with how neatly everything was packed.

"Would you look at this? It's all so neat and even clean! I'm not really sure I need to wash any of it!" Mrs Taylor said in amazement to Mr Taylor who then peered into the bag.

"That is impressive, he can't have packed that! Surely not," Mr Taylor said in equal amazement.

William had the 'anything hole' to thank for that, as his bag had been the picture of messy, with dirty clothes in no order at all before he tossed it in there.

The holiday passed with the traditional events of the Igmon Christmas. A lot of exhausting time was spent with his immediate family attending carol services and Christmas markets. However, since being in the Thomon world all the magic of an Igmon Christmas did not excite him as much as it did before. When meeting William's wider family they all remarked how confident William was now and how much he had developed over the six months.

This made William feel very proud that so many people who normally pitied him, saw a positive change in him for once. But he had to work hard not to tell the full truth about Belbury Academy. William had to use his imagination to lie as the Thomon Protection and Security Council monitored all the Igmon children when they left the Thomon world, to ensure they didn't reveal the Thomon world to Igmon families. If they did, they would be expelled for putting the Thomon world at risk. So, William created a new imaginary school called Landsbourgh, as being the real reason for his recent change. As the Christmas holiday went on the imaginary school became more and more detailed with imaginary lessons, imaginary friends, teachers and sports, but it was still not as good as the real thing.

After hearing William's detailed and interesting descriptions of Landsbourgh school, many of the parents tried to find out where this school was, to send their own children there, but with little success.

Throughout the holiday he had received circular letters from Isabel, George and Jasmin telling him about what they were doing, and how he should have stayed with them instead of going home. William so wanted to go visit one of their houses and see what a normal Thomon family life was like.

This again made him feel sad that his parents would never be able to join him in the hidden world, and see the things that he had seen. He made a mental note to ask the Headmaster if there was any way to let his mum and dad into the Thomon world.

William and his dad had gone to the Royal Arms pub to watch the boxing day football between Aston Villa and Millwall, which always proved to be an interesting match. It was almost as entertaining, William thought, to watch the spectators in the stands as the players on the pitch. However, after playing 4's he just saw a load of adults, sort of running around and falling over, clutching their ankles whenever another player came within shouting distance of them.

At half time Mr Taylor went to the bar to buy two more drinks. When, from over William's shoulder, two coasters appeared held by the long arms of Mr Stephenson.

"Happy Christmas William, how are you?"

William turned in his seat and beamed at his old favourite teacher, feeling that finally there was someone who knew his secret.

"Hello Sir, I am really good, how are you?"

"I am well, thank you for asking. How about you swap your dad's coaster for one of these, so he does not need to buy another drink."

The two were clearly happy to see each other. Mr Stephenson because he had sent William to the Thomon academy and had heard a lot about how he was developing and what he was achieving, and William because this was still his favourite teacher, who had started him on this new journey in an amazing world.

"Is there any news of the PSC catching Krevak yet?" William asked quietly.

"Ah yes, I hear you got to meet that dangerous man, well done for surviving," he said with quiet excitement.

"I think it was more luck than skill Sir," William replied.

"Yes I would agree with that, and no they have not caught him yet, despite having so many Sentinels out looking for him! Hundreds I last heard."

"Sentinels, what are..." William was cut short by his dad coming back from the bar with a drink in each hand.

"Ah, Mr Stephenson isn't it?" Mr Taylor asked, wiping his damp hand on his shirt before holding it out to shake Mr Stephenson's, happy to see the man who had done so much for his son.

"Yes it is," came the reply. "I am really glad that your son is fitting in so well and by all accounts doing really well also."

"Yes, he is, Belbury Apprenticeship Academy seems to have waved a magic wand over William. He has changed so much and it makes me very proud and very happy."

"That is great to hear. Well, I can't stay I am afraid, I have family to see but good to see you both and continue the great work William when you go back."

Both the Taylors stood and said goodbye, and sat back down just before the match started its second half of people falling over. In the brief pause before the football started again, Mr Taylor ruffled William's hair with his hand, looked his son straight in the face, with eyes that William had not seen before.

"We are truly proud of you boy, well done." With that brief moment of softness done, he turned back to the match.

William felt amazing joy in his chest and a lump in his throat. Finally, after causing his parents so much difficulty, disappointment and stress over the years he had changed all that, and it was the greatest Christmas present William felt he had ever been given and been able to give to his parents.

🏛🏛 Bunches Market

The new half year term was about to start and William was now required to buy his own equipment for his lessons. The academy had helpfully given all the First Years a long list of equipment to acquire before lessons started the following day. This meant William had to go to the Gold Stones bank to set up his account, using the form his parents had signed, and convert the money he had been given by his parents for Christmas into Thomon money.

The bank felt far colder, more powerful and overbearing now that William was on his own. He approached the main, high and angular counter and slid the signed form across its white marble table top to a young-looking dwarf, who was dressed in a far plainer manner than the head of the bank, Turpit Cointis. This identified the young dwarf as a lower rank, probably a newly appointed clerk William thought.

The clerk slowly slid the paper off the table towards himself with a short solid finger, while never taking his keen eyes away from William. Giving William the feeling of being distrusted until he had proved himself a customer.

After the clerk had flipped the paper over several times, folded the paper somewhat randomly a few times to read all the information and check for the right signatures he spoke. This startled William, as he had started to daydream in his head while waiting.

"Well, I see everything is in order William Taylor," said the clerk, changing his tone as William had now moved from being a passer-by to a valued customer. "How much do you wish to deposit?"

William reached into his bag and produced two hundred pounds of Igmon money in twenty ten-pound notes. His parents had reassured William that they could afford such an amount, even so he felt they had over-stretched a little. The clerk's eyes glinted with happiness, while his mouth restrained a large smile from breaking out across his face.

"Well Sir, that is a very sizeable first deposit, thank you. Will you also be wanting to make a withdrawal at this time?"

William, not knowing how much everything on the list would cost and not being able to remember how much Igmon money was in Thomon money, said, "Everything?" In a questioning tone, unsure about how much this would be.

William knew he should have been able to work it out, as he had been taught this in his lessons at the bank. He did know that Igmon money was very rare in the Thomon world and so was very valuable, but could not remember how valuable it was. His teacher Turpit Cointis was sitting nearby slowly flipping through a stack of papers, so William was trying to be as discreet as possible.

"Are you sure Sir?" the clerk said with wide eyes of surprise.

William thought for a minute, "Well... how much is two hundred pounds?"

"Sir you will not need to worry about money for this term or the next one, Sir has plenty of funds."

William had never been in this position before. But this still left him in a difficult position. How much Thomon money did he need for all the academy equipment on the list?

"How much is one transom in Igmon money?" William asked hoping his teacher would not overhear and so focus on him with questions in the next lesson in the bank.

The clerk looked up at the moving marble ceiling, "At this moment Sir, about fifty pence."

"Do you have any idea how much I will need to buy all my equipment for my lessons?" William asked, hoping the clerk might have an idea, surely other First Years had come to get money out for the same purpose.

"For Sir's information, other students around your age have made withdrawals of thirty transoms, but I do not know for what purposes the withdrawals were made," said the Dwarf with professional courtesy.

"Well, that will have to do then, I will have that please!" William said happily.

"Yes Sir. I will also need your Hadron-Tool to link to your account," said the clerk, holding out his small hand, covered in body armour thick leather skin.

William took it out his pocket and placed it into the solid looking hand.

With that the clerk strode off out of sight, leaving William to watch the ceiling ripple and slosh around.

A few minutes later the clerk strode back with William's Hadron-Tool and a bag about the size of a one-kilogram bag of flour, full of bright and shiny coins that were round and square at the same time.

"To access your account in the future, all you will need to do is show us your Hadron-Tool. Is there anything else I can do for you today Sir?" the clerk asked while gently pressing his hands together, linking his fingers.

"No, thank you," William replied, while he hefted the bag of coins, which the dwarf had carried so easily, into his rucksack, commending himself for remembering to bring the bag just in case.

William left the bank and met up with Isabel, George and Jasmin by one of the narrow jitties that entered Bunches Market. A place where everything they required could be bought, along with lots of items that every student wanted but did not need and probably should not buy.

The market was a hive of activity and was spread over five levels. William and his friends walked through the many stalls on the torus-shaped level zero, to the balcony in the centre of the market to have a look into its depths and up at its heights.

Around each of the level's perimeters were many shops, each with a glass bay window showing the best of what they were selling. The windows were made of small square panes of thick glass with a swirl in the centre and were held in place with painted wooden frames. Each window bay bulged out at its centre allowing the warm light from the inside to spill out onto the thick wooden boards that made up the floor in front of them.

Looking up and down from the balcony William could see parts of each new level, he counted four in total, two above called one and two and two below called minus one and minus two, each with its own style and flavour. As the floors went down they grew darker and more cluttered and each floor above became lighter and airier, with the most expensive and exclusive shops found on the very top floor, that was open to the sky.

People moved between the five levels on two counter-spiralling staircases that could either be walked on or by placing a Hadron-Tool into the banister, the user would be slowly pulled up or down the spiralling staircase.

This gave the feeling that instead of using one's Hadron-Tool in a groove to get somewhere quickly the aim here was to go slow and be seen. A user of the spiral stair could glide up a floor and then without stopping or stepping off glide straight back down again. Smooth and elegant, William thought before turning back to his friends to consult the list.

"I will be meeting my mum and dad for lunch at twelve thirty-seven, you are welcome to join?" Isabel said.

"Great, a free lunch!" George said cheerfully.

"I did not say it would be free!" Isabel said, trying to put George in his place.

"We have more things to think about than lunch right now, let's look at that list," William said, trying to focus on the group.

George pulled a single A5 piece of paper from his pocket and showed it to the group, turning it over a few times to show the full list.

First Years 2nd Term Equipment List:

Books

- *1 x Eight Uses for Octopus Legs, by Genindale Octave*
- *1 x History of the Hadron-Tool, by Clarence Contrivance*
- *1 x A Study Into Igmon Traditions, by Layland Lore*
- *1 x Flick Culture and How to Communicate, by Elizabeth Tell*
- *1 x Animals, Beasts and Creatures, by Tobias Brute*

And so the list of books went on...

Hardware

- *1 x Hadron-Tool ghost stand*
- *3 x Half litre tubes of dark matter*
- *1 x Lavarathon flame proof glove set*
- *1 x Medical kit – large*

The list went on and on, page flip after page flip, listing new categories and equipment that they needed. Most of the items were unknown to the group and so they had no clue about where they needed to go to get it, making it very hard to understand where to start.

"Well, that is a lot of stuff we need to get, good thing they taught us how to shrink stuff!" George laughed.

The group, not knowing much about the market, decided to start from the bottom floor and work their way up. This way, Isabel reasoned, they should at least not miss anything. So down the spiral stairs they went, allowing their Hadron-Tools to pull them gently downward, allowing them to relax and look out to see what was on level minus one as they wafted past.

Level minus two, was the darkest of all the floors with very little natural light being able to spill down the shaft that housed the spiral stairs. The level was lit mostly by a mixture of different coloured and shaped lights used by the shops and stalls, giving the feeling that this was the level for shady dealings. Somewhere that underhand dealings could be conducted, and that if you wanted something that was not allowed, you could find it here.

The ceiling of minus two was also quite low, about six feet from the floor, adding to the feeling of darkness and mischief. Anyone tall like the Trolls, Almops, Catoblepas and Druons had to walk bent or even crawl around.

Jasmin did not feel comfortable down on level minus two at all. Normally for Jasmin most people showed no haze of colour at all and Jasmin had to focus on them for her gifting to work, but down on level minus two her gift was on high alert. Nowhere had she felt so many red-hazed people and she was not even trying.

"Guys I don't think we should be down here, everyone's colours down here are not good! Guys...? Jasmin said, but was ignored as the other three were so nervous and scared that they did not hear her, or she had said it in a whisper out of fear herself and so they did not hear her.

After a brief walk past shops and stalls selling severed hands and talking stand-alone heads, or shops where green smoke slowly billowed out of the door onto the walkway. The group who out of fear were sticking very close together, finally came to a shop called, Contrivances and Contraptions. The shop owner had made the letter O in each word of the shop's name into rotating gears, giving it a much friendlier feel. This small amount of friendliness made the shop glow like a torch at night in the gloom of villainous distrust that infused the minus two level.

The shop's battered door was pushed open by the nervous hand of George, hitting and ringing a bell mounted on the inside of the doorframe, making him jump.

Inside were rows of heavy sheet steel shelves, all loaded with a huge amount of mechanical objects, turning the shop floor into a series of narrow corridors running front to back.

An old and very lean man with sharp darting eyes contained by thick blue-rimmed round glasses appeared out of one of the many narrow aisles in front of William. He wore a plain black waistcoat that had a single gold chain running from the central button into a pocket and a blue handkerchief poked out of his chest pocket. A collarless white shirt with thin blue stripes was contained underneath. His black trousers hung perfectly over his heavy-duty boots, with a brown belt that held a holster containing his Hadron-Tool to his waist. On his head was a black flat-cap, which he kept playing with, moving it around as if to itch his head.

"And what might you be looking for? Young bucks like you should not be down on level Minus Two! Don't want no thieving in here!" The man said, showing few teeth and looking for some reassurance that the group was not about to try and rob him. "You here to buy kit for academy lessons?" The question was asked in a gentler tone, as he saw the group were a little scared, standing close together in some sort of protective huddle. "You have nothing to fear from me, what do you need?"

The group looked at Jasmin to get her verdict on the old man standing in front of them before answering. They had to realise that coming down to level minus two was probably a mistake, and they were unsure who they could trust. Jasmin shrugged her shoulders, "He is a sort of a greeny-brown colour, good enough, best I have seen down here so far."

The old man looked at the group a little confused by this statement of him being a greeny-brown colour, but quickly looked happy again when William started to talk.

"The academy has given us a list of kit we need, but don't really know what many of the items are. Any chance you can help?" William said with forced bravery to get the ball rolling.

"Will see what I can do, let me see the list then!" said the man, holding out his hand.

George pulled the crumpled-up list out of his pocket and placed it in the bony and tendinous hand, which promptly snapped shut like a trap around the single crinkly page. The man's keen eyes quickly scanned the page with a long slender finger sliding down the list at a rate of knots, flipping the page as soon as it reached the bottom.

"Ah ha, yes, yes, yes, now I do have some of these things!"

"Enough for us all?" William asked.

"Hmm... yes, I would say so..." the man said thoughtfully.

Without divulging any more information, he disappeared off and could be heard walking up and down the long narrow aisle between the shelves, collecting items into his arms. After a noise that could only be him dumping all the items onto a wooden counter, he reappeared in front of the intrigued group.

"Come along now," he said, beckoning with his arm.

The group followed, still staying close together, with Isabel becoming increasingly nervous as she looked back to see the exit door disappear out of sight. They eventually arrived at the back of the store where a long wooden counter was constructed out of heavy timbers and stretched the width of the shop. The left end of the counter lifted up allowing the man to pass through to the other side. Piled in the centre of the counter was a collection of interesting looking things. The group, clueless to what the items were, asked the man to explain each item and where it was on the list.

"Of course!" the man said gladly.

He flipped the page over four times and placed it on the table facing the group so they could read it. Using a wand-like finger, he stabbed at the section they were to look at that contained four items.

"History viewer," he said, picking up a tube-looking object, then, "Time Counter," as another round object was produced from the pile, "Light Relaxer and Void Contain," were subsequently pointed to.

"Well thank you for getting all of that for us. How much do we owe you?" William asked, careful not to show his bag of money before asking.

The man thought briefly while looking over the items on the table in front of him. "Six transoms each, will cover it."

They all dug into their pockets and bags to find the correct square round coins, and checked with each other that they had the correct type and quantity of coins and were not about to over pay. The transoms were passed over and the group set about splitting the items into four piles and shrinking them down to fit in their pockets and bags.

"Thank you for your help!" William said, about to turn around.

"It's what I am here for. Now if I were you, I would go down no further than level minus one in the future," the man said with caution in his voice.

William nodded in understanding before navigating his way along the narrow aisle to walk out the door, allowing it to shut behind him, ringing the bell as it swung shut. The group headed straight for the spiral staircase and up one level as quickly as they could without running.

With each step that they got above level minus two they felt safer, less scared and able to catch their breath and stand up properly.

Jasmin was feeling exhausted after seeing so many red-hazed people and looked forward to not seeing anyone's character colours again.

Minus one felt much cleaner and safer, with ceilings set higher and the people and creatures dressed more elegant and proper. The whole level was cleaner and brighter with brilliantly beautiful squirrel cage lights hanging in long chains along the walkways and over street food stalls that were dotted around. The bulging windows of the built-in shops around the edge contained used toys, clothes and many other objects and products. There were tailors and many other craft-like shops selling all sorts of handmade goods.

The group found a book shop called Perfectly Good Ink, which was full to the rafters with stacks of any and every second-hand book and paper sheet document one could imagine. All the books and papers, like the library, had been shrunk so they would all fit and were in stacks touching the ceiling, some piles spilling over into small heaps on the carpeted walkways.

William pulled gently at one of the tiny books and the whole pile wobbled, causing him to stop and take a few steps back in case it collapsed into a heap.

There were two distinct areas in the shop. One half was filled with shrunken books of all colours and bindings and the other with stacks of shrunken papers new and old, flat and rolled.

"Good afternoon children," came a polite greeting from behind them at the front of the shop.

The group had walked right past a curved pastel-painted desk just inside of the door to the left, where a young female elf sat tall and straight-backed behind it. She wore her shimmering silver hair up in a bun of elaborate twists on the top of her perfectly proportioned head and a billowing light blue shirt with a frilly neckline.

"Please do ask if you need anything," she said gently.

"Thank you and yes your help would be great!" Isabel said, smiling at the young elf and feeling much more confident in this shop compared to the last.

George once again produced the list from his pocket, and a slim, smooth hand floated out to lightly grasp it between two dainty fingers with perfect nails. The elf took a quick look at the front page and smiled politely.

"Yes, we have all of those, please follow me," she said, getting up to show the billowing shirt was tucked into a high waisted skirt that flowed lightly down to her ankles, finishing off in some delicate buckled shoes.

She exuded calm, self-control and togetherness as she glided through the stacks of untidy books and paper. She gently ran a finger along the stacks as if she were reading braille book names on the spines and did not need to enlarge the books to know what they were.

"Ah, here we are, the first book, Flick Culture and How to Communicate. A very interesting book but I think the better and more insightful read is A History of Flick Culture by Tim E Past. Far more in depth and apparently he spent two years living with the flicks in order to write it. Not sure how he did that as flicks are very small and live in very small places," she said, while pausing and sliding a single tiny book out of the stack like some sort of elite Jenga player. When the book was removed the entire stack dropped perfectly down, it did not wobble or fall. She passed the tiny book to Jasmin to hold. The group continued to follow the elf around the bookshop's stacked corridors, as one by one she collected a handful of tiny books.

During this time William had become interested in a wicker basket in a dark corner that said Thomon Families and Their Histories on its front, on a label that was slowly falling off. William found the basket contained hundreds of paper documents, all crammed in, in no perceivable order. After rummaging for a while, he found that the organised mess contained paper documents showing more details and information than he had found in the town's library. William grew increasingly excited as he delved ever deeper into the basket, papers spilling out into the walkway as he dug and quickly glanced at each sheet as it flashed past his face. A few minutes passed when he came across something that looked like a family tree, with lines connecting different family crests, which he assumed showed loyalists and rank. William was intrigued with one particular area of the chart as it looked like a crest and its joining lines had been painted over and removed. This jolted his memory, remembering that the Headmaster had said that the Hemlock family had been erased from all Thomon history.

"And that's all of them I think," the elf said checking the list once more when they arrived back at her desk. The voice startled William from the depths of his thoughts and he quickly ran back over to join the group.

"Do you mind if I enlarge them to check?" Isabel asked politely.

"No not at all, please go ahead."

Isabel sprang to the task, grabbing the books out of Jasmine's hands and enlarging each one and checking the books.

"They are perfect, thank you. How much do we owe you?" Isabel said after a moment with a smile.

"Each book is three transoms," came a quick answer.

"And I would also like this," William said, holding up the tatty piece of paper he had found.

"All paper documents are half a transom," the elf said with the well-practised phrase.

Isabel and Jasmin both looked at William with bemusement, while George obliviously stared out of the window.

"What!" William said, shrugging in response, "I think it looks good."

This left the two girls shaking their heads at each other in bemusement at this seemingly waste of money.

The group once again rummaged around producing the coins and checking with each other that they had the correct amount. They then handed them over while placing the re-shrunk books into their pockets to join the small hard metal objects already there.

Once out of the shop they paused for a minute next to the centre railing, enjoying watching Thomons going about their days and looking over the rest of the list when a shout came from above.

"Isabel, darling, up here," came a high pitched loud voice that cut through the general noise of Bunches Market.

Isabel looked slowly up with embarrassment toward the familiar voice and saw her mum leaning out over the railing on level one and waving frantically to get her attention.

"Lunch time, make your way up!" Isabel's mum shouted, so that everyone in the market could hear.

Isabel was suitably embarrassed, and quietly hoping that there were no other members of her class in the market today to see and hear that. George began to beam with happiness about the potential of a free lunch.

"Is that your mum Isabel? What a lovely lady, quite the voice," George teased Isabel as he waved back.

Jasmin and William were just looking forward to sitting down, and so all worked their way up to level one, their feet glad to finally be given a break.

Mr and Mrs Howl were a couple of middle rank and dressed in a style that showed this, not showy, not scruffy but practical. Mr Howl wore brown mid-shin tall boots with black trousers with narrow white stripes held high at his waist. A casual dark green wax jacket that ended at his knees covered a dark blue jumper with a bowler hat on his head. Mrs Howl wore a long dress of dark blue with white flowers that ran from her feet through a delicate belt around her waist and over her shoulders. A dark green, long-sleeved cardigan covered her shoulders and arms. Her hair was plaited around the back of her head in coils and was decorated with small golden stars and prime shapes.

*

During lunch they had been severely told off for heading to level minus two by Mr and Mrs Howl.

"You should have gone to Trinkets and Instruments on level zero for that equipment. Who knows what could have happened to you on level minus two," Mrs Howl said crossly to Isabel.

"It is not safe down there for children. Even I will hesitate to go down there, and will only if I have no other choice. It is filled with very unpleasant people and things," said Mr Howl equally cross.

"I have never seen so many red people," Jasmin said in amazement.

"See, you should trust her gift Isabel," said Mrs Howl, pointing an arm in Jasmine's direction.

"Ok, ok, I am sorry, I didn't know," Isabel apologised.

"Well, you should have known better, clearly you are not reading enough of the right stuff," said Mr Howl.

William and George both stayed quiet and paid very close attention to their food, trying to pretend they did not exist as they both felt very embarrassed with all the people watching the telling off.

Once lunch finished, George felt very happy it was indeed free, the day carried on with lots of going in and out of shops and pockets becoming ever fuller with the growing quantities of stuff.

"It is great they taught us how to shrink stuff, but it would also be good to learn how to make it lighter. My pockets are going to rip soon," complained George as he tried to support his jacket pockets with his hands.

"Is that even possible, to make something lighter?" asked Jasmin.

"Must be or you couldn't have picked up that shrunken car at the start of the year," George replied.

"Oh yeah," Jasmin realised.

"Can't be too long before they teach us that," said Isabel, also thinking that would be great to know right now as she thought about the integrity of her own pockets. "There must be a reason they have not taught us that yet, and we only have a few more things to get now so our pockets can't get that much heavier, can they!" said Isabel.

"And you, stop smiling," Jasmin said, pointing at William's grinning face. "Just because you thought to bring a rucksack."

"Hey, my bag is just as heavy as your pockets," said William, while trying not to laugh and defending himself from a grinning George who was trying hard to pull the bag off his back.

It was now five thirty-eight, Isabel had said goodbye to her parents who had helped the group find and buy the last items on their lists, and they were now back in Starley common room enlarging all the items they had bought that day. They wanted to check that all the items were indeed correct and if they were missing anything, and since a large amount was second-hand that it was also working.

George spotted the tatty bit of paper William had bought from Perfectly Good Ink and lunged across the table for it. "Well, what is it then? Look, it's been drawn on already!" George said, successfully grabbing the paper and peering at it.

William snatched the paper back and placed it flat on the table for all to see.

"Well, look, the Headmaster said the Hemlock family had been erased from Thomon history right?"

The others nodded in agreement.

"Well, look this is like a family tree but of Thomon family crests, I guess a sort of hierarchy or allegiances.

One crest has been clearly painted out and I thought it might be the Hemlock family!"

"Well, yes that is all very well and good if it wasn't painted out, but it is. It's gone Will, you can't see anything," Isabel said, prodding the painted over section and giving it a scratch with her nail.

"Whatever was there is gone now! You can't get that paint off without damaging the paper," Jasmin said, agreeing with Isabel.

"Yes, you might be right, but…" William said while reaching into his pocket for his Hadron-Tool.

"But what…?" George asked.

"Your Hadron-Tool can't help you here," Jasmin said, seeing what William was thinking about trying.

Just as she said that William touched the paper with his Hadron-Tool and purple ink began to spill out of its end, slowly flooding across the page.

"You've modified your Tool!" Isabel cried incredulously. "You can't do that!"

"Sshhh, keep your voice down, don't let everyone in the house know!" William hissed back. "Look, yes it has been modified, but not by me. Ever wondered how I have been able to read so much and so well recently?" William said again in a firm whisper.

George looked up to the ceiling connecting the dots. William could see him thinking, "Oh yeah," inside his head as the light bulb of realisation turned on.

In silence they all watched the ink flow over more and more of the paper. As it touched the painted area, drawing lines and letters became visible through the paint. There, hidden from sight, now appeared a crest showing three triangles stacked on top of each other, above a long narrow banner that contained the name Hemlock.

Other Starley house members were now coming into the common room in large groups and all talking loudly, but luckily ignoring the four friends. William quickly removed his Hadron-Tool from the paper so as not to be caught, removing the purple ink along with it and once again hiding the amazing hidden image. William rolled up the paper and tucked it away in his jacket, ready to be explored again, once alone.

ⓘⓢ Hiding

The heat that surrounded the class on the metal casting level of Diesel and Sons Engineering was oppressive and stifling. Ensuring that all the class regretted not taking their jumpers off before setting foot into the hot, sulphur and methane-filled space, that burned their noses and made it hard to breathe.

The casting level was located inside a gigantic cavern located deep underground near the earth's core. Up the walls were old and worn wooden staircases, with each wooden step polished to a smooth curve by thousands of pairs of feet, connecting to wooden walkways that ran around the perimeter and crisscrossed the vast void, like brambles growing through a bush. Large moving platforms slid up and down the walls, with some passing through the ceiling in two locations.

To the left of where William had entered the oven, blazing red hot larva oozed like thick congealed syrup, from the ends of large diameter tubes in the cave wall. The oozing flow was controlled by men running their Hadron-Tools around the outer diameter of the protruding tubes like a lever, opening and closing an elaborate valve. As soon as the Hadron-Tool was removed from the pipe the valve snapped shut, sealing itself against the vast heat and pressure behind it.

The larva flowed along rivers that meandered and carved their way across the cavern's hard grey stone floor, which was also unevenly covered in thick reddish pink sand. Stout hump back bridges with green railings were dotted around, allowing access across the red-hot rivers.

Smaller tributaries led to areas where pools like oxbow lakes held the scorching molten syrup ready to be used to heat great bowls of metal ore, before it was poured into moulds. The oozing lava created glass-like bubbles the sizes of footballs half submerged on the surface, that would pop like the sound of a cork being pulled from a bottle.

William watched through the smoky air as two large bipedal creatures stood next to one of these ponds, each with thick skin that looked like crumbling rock. Their long arms reached to both knees, had chests about twice as thick as a man's, but were not as wide or tall as the trolls William had previously seen. They had heads of stone with a single central eye, which sat upon its wide bouldering shoulders. The two creatures were almost camouflaged against the bare rock of the cave walls around them.

They stood either side of the small steaming pond with a great bowl aloft between them. Steadily they lowered it into the bubbling syrup, their long reach helping them not to get burnt. Once the bowl was stable on its own and partly sunken into the ooze, the two creatures then worked together using great ladles to draw up the larva in spirals around the bowl. Like great red snakes, coiling around a clutch of eggs. Only a short time passed before the whole bowl started to glow red hot and the mixture inside melted to liquid.

"What protective suits are those men wearing to work the larva?" William asked Mr Diesel, after watching the activity for a few minutes.

"They are not men, William! They are Cyrolls. They are like trolls in their rough shape and strength, but they are born of the mountains in the north American Rockies. Their skin is made of the actual rock that the mountain they are born from is made of. So, each tribe of Cyrolls has a different look and are useful for different tasks," said Mr Diesel before pausing to find another group of creatures to point to. "The Cyrolls we have here are known for being able to endure incredible heat and having great strength, making them perfect for the task they are currently undertaking. Also, the single eye means they are cheaper on safety goggles than all the two-eyed workers, half as cheap actually," Mr Diesel said, chuckling a little to himself at the health and safety joke.

Over to William's right, two men this time were using their Hadron-Tools to control one of the great bowls that floated a few feet from the floor. Just as Mr Warthard had done with floating the car at the start of the year. The bowl contained glowing red liquid and was poured into a hole located at one end of a large block that lay on the floor. The molten metal slid thickly down into the hole like soft honey. The pouring only stopped when a molten glow raised up and out of more holes at the other end of the block, indicating it was full.

Mr Diesel reminded the class not to touch anything and to stay on the walkways at all times. Then led them over a series of hump back bridges, with the smell increasing and making it even harder to breathe each time they crossed directly over one of the molten rivers.

"Those that work down here are a special breed, be them Human or Cyroll," Mr Diesel said with a laugh, seeing how the children were struggling with the stench in the air.

"No kidding," George murmured to William, as he struggled not to throw up with the intense smell.

"Today the casting gangs are creating a metal called Tantalium, which is immensely strong against impacts, but as flexible as a linen bed sheet," said Mr Diesel, while continuing to walk through the active work space, where many sweaty looking men with eyes covered with dark goggles walked around and worked in their well-oiled work gangs.

"Sir, where does all the smoke and gas in the air go?" William asked after spotting some large circular vents in the ceiling.

"Well, aren't we full of all the questions today William. All of the gases and smoke created by the larva and processes that happen here, are collected by the large vents in the cavern's ceiling. They are separated into their different components and stored for future use, as all of it is useful for something else! For example, unlike the Igmons who ignorantly let all that goodness disappear out of their exhausts and chimneys into the air," he said while pointing to the plumes of smoke in the air, "we collect the fantastic carbon dioxide given off by the larva instead. It is used to feed the great forest and allows the trees to require less water and grow bigger," Mr Diesel said proudly.

The class tour eventually stopped at the entrance to an offshoot cave that was unlit, located directly opposite to where they had entered the casting cavern.

"This is a very important room," Mr Diesel said, pointing into the darkness. "Each mould we make we keep, we must have thousands of them by now in here, which means we can make nearly anything required again and again."

"But Sir I can't really see anything," said Isabel peering into the gloomy dark cave and straining her eyes to see what Sir was on about.

Jasmin was also trying like everyone else, to see anything of interest in the black gloom when she spotted two faint red hazes. She thought this was very strange as she could not see anyone at all, but it was not like her gift could be broken like an electronic sensor.

"I can," she said quietly to William, "I can see two red hazes. There must be two people in there, neither of which I want to meet."

"Really, I doubt it, don't you have to see the person for your gift to work," William replied, "must just be the fumes messing with your head."

"Nope it's not that," Jasmin reassured herself.

"Ah yes, well this storage room only needs light when you are trying to find that mould in a haystack. But I can shed some brief light in there so you can get an idea of the amount we have," Mr Diesel said, while taking his Hadron-Tool out and striking the cave wall like a matchstick. This sent a shooting star shining with light shooting through the air down the length of the long cave. Allowing the class to see rows and rows, stacks on stacks of all shapes and sizes of box laid out down both sides of the corridor-like cave, and went well out of sight.

As soon as the cave was lit Jasmin was proved right as two dirty, burly men were illuminated. They had been huddled together, facing each other, just off to the right about ten metres inside the dark space, and quietly talking. When they realised they were no longer hidden by the darkness of the storage cave, they quickly snapped shut their pocket watches and hurriedly put them away. These had been fully open in their hands and held between them as if showing each other something or connecting to the other man's pocket watch.

"Javid, Thanok what on earth are you doing in here without any light?" said Mr Diesel in a confronting tone.

"Ur... sorry Sir we were umm... just about to sort the lights out but could not find our Hadron-Tools in the dark. Will be going back to our station now Sir," said Thanok somewhat apologetically, as he and the other strongly-set man walked quickly back onto the casting floor, pushing through the group of children who looked a little confused and had to take three or four steps back to get out of the way of the large men.

"Right everyone, who is nice and cold?" Mr Diesel said jokingly after he had paused for a few seconds to watch and check that the two men did indeed walk back to their stations.

No hands went up and he could see they all needed a break from the sweltering heat of the casting cavern.

"Ok, everyone on the platform and let's go get some air before continuing," he said while swinging open the barrier gate to a lifting platform next to the storage cave.

It floated the class up the wall and through the solid-looking ceiling, all controlled by Mr Diesel reeling in a fish action on his Hadron-Tool.

They were given a break in the cold air of a cobbled court yard located just off to the right of the entrance lobby. The class were allowed to have a ten-minute break, and enjoy the relief that the cold January air brought to their bodies. Many of the workers from Diesel and Sons were also in the square quietly having their lunch break, sitting on many of the benches while enjoying the stillness and cool just like the First Years.

"George?" William said to get his attention.

"Yes."

"What did you think about those two men who were standing in the dark? Did you notice what they were doing with their pocket watches?"

"No, was too interested in the shooting star. Why?"

"Just their behaviour seemed very odd. Looked like they were trying to hide something. And Jasmin said she saw them as red hazes even before the light came on!"

"You're probably just seeing things everywhere at the moment because you're thinking about what happened at the Christmas Fair. I am sure it is nothing, and rough workers like that always have bad characters," George said, trying to settle the mind of his friend.

"I'm not so sure," William said, glancing around the square to see if any of the other workers were fiddling with their pocket watches in a similar manner. None were.

"Right First Years, all over here please," came Mr Diesel's voice.

The group huddled together, now being too cold and looking forward to warming up again.

"This is your new teacher who will be showing you how to design and create the casting blocks you saw on your tour before your break. He joined us only last year as Head of Casting, and has proven himself to be well worth his pay, his name is Hulogus Detre."

Standing next to Mr Diesel was a very ordinary-looking man of average height and dressed in a very similar manner to the others in the workshop. With dark trousers, waist coat and a single gold chain from the centre button that led in a curve to the left-hand waistcoat pocket. This covered a white shirt, and all was contained within a blue knee-length jacket with a bowler hat sitting on top of his head.

What set him apart was his darting green eyes. They would lock onto you as if you were prey and unblinkingly stare, and then dart off to do the same to another. He immediately gave William the shivers.

"Thank you for that kind feedback," Hulogus said in a very gruff voice, while giving a nod of appreciation to Mr Diesel.

Turning to the class Hulogus cleared his throat with a small cough. "I will teach you how to make the casting boxes and create items like you have seen already. I will show you how to tame the earth's life blood that flows from its core to make anything you can dream up." He paused to give some drama. "Please do follow me and we shall begin."

Off the group went happy to get out of the cold, but apprehensive about the huge heat they knew was to come.

16 Mountains

William had kept the paper of family crests, shrunken down and hidden in his socks to keep it safe. He would enlarge it only when he was alone or with George to look once again at the hidden crest. The two boys had spent hours flipping, turning and folding the paper to see if it showed anything else, but with no success.

On this particular evening William was sitting at his desk looking at the image trying to understand what it was and what it meant. He knew that family crests always carried deeper meaning than what was shown at first sight, but the meaning of the Hemlock crest escaped him. The crest showed three equilateral triangles stacked one on top of each other. Every time he looked at the crest he sensed that it meant more than the basic shapes grew deeper and stronger.

It was now getting late and he decided to visit his "Your History, Your Culture" teacher Sir Rudyard Welton in the morning to ask some questions about the crest he had found. While lying in the dark in bed William mulled over the risks of asking the questions, but decided the risk was worth it. William thought the worst that could happen was that they took his family crest paper away, surely it would not be worse than that just for asking some questions. Sir Welton was always interested in odd topics and strange questions so this would be no different. Often in class he could be made to go off topic quite easily and end up rambling on about something totally off topic but very interesting. William fell asleep while planning in his head how he would ask the questions, figuring out what he would and wouldn't say. He also tried to come up with pre-planned answers to questions he thought he might be asked, so that he would not be nervous and so make a mistake.

*

William woke bright and early the next morning and could see his favourite weather outside his dorm window, which he took as a good sign for the day. The sky was endlessly light blue and not a cloud ruined the unending, bottomless colour. The winter sun hung low and bright in the sky, its rays looking as warm as summer cutting through the crisp clean air. William loved the temperature contrasts at this time of year and the feeling of freshness, renewal and optimism it gave the world. He felt good about what he was about to do and the weather definitely helped build his confidence.

William left George fast asleep cuddling his pillow to have an early breakfast, which was spent on his own rerunning his plan over in his mind, practising the questions he wanted to ask and rehearsing the answers he thought he might have to give, while his hand fed him toast and tea at a hearty rate.

Leaving through the vast interweaving door, which only partially unwove to let William out, he immediately spotted Mr Diesel who was walking across the large expanse of a somewhat quiet main square. The hustle and bustle of the working week now had relaxed to a gentle feeling of a slow Sunday morning, with a few early risers enjoying coffee and the paper around the trickling central fountain, bathed in the subtly pink light that shone down through the giant glass bowl in the ceiling.

William ran after him shouting, "Mr Diesel... Mr Diesel..." His voice clearly reached him across the hollow open space, because Mr Diesel stopped and turned around just before he stepped onto one of the lifting platforms. Many of the seated paper readers and coffee drinkers looked at William with strong annoyance in their eyes, at the silence they had got up early for being broken.

"Hello William! You're up early this fine morning," he said, genuinely happy to see him.

"Yes, Sir it is my favourite weather, could not miss it," William replied.

"Good man, get out and make the most of it."

"I will Sir. Ur... question, where would I find Sir Welton this morning?" William asked.

"Most students and teachers try to hide from each other over the weekend, especially early Sunday morning. Want on earth do you want to find him for this early on a Sunday morning?" Mr Diesel said, looking at William slightly bemused as to why a student would be actively seeking out a teacher at this time.

"Well, I woke early and had some questions I wanted to ask, Sir Welton always says in his lesson if we ever have a question to come and ask him, so thought why not now."

Mr Diesel looked happy enough with the answer, and had come to trust William through the quality of his work and the capability he had shown in the workshop.

"On Sunday mornings, Sir Welton is normally to be found taking his boat out fishing from the West jetty. If you're quick you might catch him before he casts off."

"Thank you, Sir," William said, spinning around and running off back across the square. As he ran he pulled his map out, flipping it twice to get to the correct level to find the right groove to take him to the West jetty. If he had to walk it would have taken over an hour.

A few minutes later he appeared at the base of a set of stone steps that led up to a brilliant, bright rectangle of blue sky above. The steps were made of large limestone blocks that allowed green moss and lichen to grow out of the cracks and gaps in and around and between them, showing that the joints needed repointing.

The walls that held back the world behind were also made of large limestone blocks that also needed some attention due to heavy weathering that had broken off sections and turned the large smooth face rough.

William climbed the steps two at a time and came out into the gorgeous early spring weather he had seen through his window. He paused briefly, closed his eyes and tilted his head toward the sun. Allowing its warming rays to soak into his skin and breathed deep and slow the fresh and invigorating air.

Looking to his left he saw an old wooden jetty, built on thick wooden piles driven deep into the lake bed. Small wooden boats painted many different colours and styles were tethered to cast bronze double-ended hooks along the jetty's edge by thick white rope leads, preventing the boats from escaping like dogs tied to a lamp post, waiting for their master to come back.

At the far end of the jetty was Sir Welton loading some boxes into a small dark green wooden boat.

William headed down the uneven wooden jetty, stepping on boards that looked old and dark from many winters eating into their surface and worn into smooth undulations from the many feet that had walked upon them.

As William walked long, he enjoyed hearing the water sploshing against the sides of the boats as they rose and dropped with ripples on the red lakes surface.

On hearing the footsteps coming toward him, Sir Welton turned his head to look back down the dock. Seeing William he stood up and greeted him in the same manner as Mr Diesel.

"Good morning William. You're up early on this beautiful morning, and just in time to give me a hand with these last boxes," he said pointing at two large wooden boxes on the jetty.

"Sure," William said, taking to the task before realising how heavy they were. "What is in these boxes, they're really heavy! Can't you make them smaller and lighter?" he asked while struggling to stay upright from the weight of the box.

"Just because I can, doesn't mean I should! These boxes are full of ice cubes, to keep the fish we're going to catch fresh, and it will melt if I shrink it. I suppose I could make more ice but that will take ages and I don't want to be doing that out on the lake, I want to be fishing. Besides, physical labour is good for the soul and body, you know," he said, smiling at William.

"We! I can't fish."

"Well, there's not a better day to learn, in you hop!"

The next thing William knew, he was sitting on a hard wooden bench in Sir Welton's little wooden fishing boat heading toward the centre of the Red Lake. The boat did not use oars, even though they were in the boat just in case. It was propelled along smoothly, silently and stealthily by Sir Welton's Hadron-Tool, which he lazily dipped into the water next to him.

William started to feel nervous as this was not part of his plan. He was now trapped and could not escape if Sir Welton became angry with him for asking certain questions. But the weather was fine and William thought Sir Welton seemed in a good mood. Plus, learning to fish and making a friend in the process could only be a good thing. William decided to ask the questions on their way back and enjoy this surprise adventure.

The fish Sir Welton was after was a Flimmock. It had a bright red top half and its underside was clear, allowing all of the fish's internals to be seen. Two sharp and pointy dorsal fins were inline along the black ridge on its back, leading to a long tail that was split in two strips, and spun like the tail on a flagellum to move the forearm-lengthened fish along.

The first few locations they tried did not give up their secrets, but after a few more tries they landed their first lively fish.

"Well, it's a little small but I think we will stay here for a bit," Sir Welton said, starting to sound excited.

William even managed to catch one after being given a quick lesson on Sir Welton's spare rod. The two ice boxes slowly filled up until it was lunch time, which meant two things. Firstly, it was time to head back to the jetty and secondly William needed to ask his questions.

"Sir, I was wandering around some of the older passages on the lower levels shown on my map and saw some engravings on the walls and I wanted to know what they were," said William, thinking this might be a suitable story to invent.

"Ah yes, there are many interesting things to see and find around Belbury. I will try my best, what did they look like?" he asked.

"Well, I thought it looked like a family crest, you know a picture above a banner containing some writing," William said, trying to downplay how much he already knew.

"Most Thomon families have some sort of crest, mine is quite good I think. It's a rampaging faun surrounded by stars. What was the one you found like?"

"It was three triangles stacked on top of each other. Kinda strange really as most of the crests I have ever seen normally have animals or shields in them, not basic shapes."

"Yes, that is a strange crest... Can you remember what the name was?" Sir said in a slow thoughtful tone, as he knew what name William was going to say.

William paused before answering, considering Sir Welton's reactions so far, who was still focused on where they were going.

"It was Hemlock Sir," William said nervously, expecting the worst reaction.

"Things like that should not be looked into too deeply. Nothing good can come from it. You must tell the Headmaster where it was so it can be removed," he replied with an uncharacteristic snap.

The two sat in awkward silence for the rest of the trip back to the jetty, with Sir Welton carrying a heavy thinking face the whole way back.

The boat bumped the jetty and William jumped out to grab the rope to tie the boat firmly in place. From the jetty he held his hands out to take the first box, which was full of ice-cold fish, and so much heavier than before, making William nearly topple off the jetty and into the dark cold water.

"What kind of history and culture teacher would I be if I could not answer a question about something as major to our history as that!" Sir Welton said suddenly while continuing to unload. He put the box back down in the boat and looked up at William standing on the jetty. "That name, Hemlock, is the name of the family who started the Great War, this you must really know already." William did not react as he just wanted Sir Welton to tell all he knew. "We are not proud of that part of our history but it is allowed to be talked about, but most just want to forget it ever happened. The Hemlock family were harsh and had a long history of being aggressive, power-grabbing and manipulative, wanting everything for themselves. They always wanted to control everyone and everything, and would fight all those that were above them or in their way. At the Christmas Fair you met a man descended on a very obscure line from the Hemlocks and by now you will know his name. I heard the Headmaster came and spoke with you and your friends after the Christmas Fair event, so that information is probably not new either."

This time William did nod his head, but was starting to think maybe Sir Welton knew no more than he himself had already found out.

"Ok, but what you won't know is that the three triangles represent the three mountains of power. If all are controlled by one person or family, they will have ultimate power and control over the world and its people. The crest showed for all who were willing to see what the Hemlocks were really all about. The Thomon culture along with the PSC has worked hard to remove their legacy from our history, and have successfully cast the three mountains of power into legendary stories. No one with any common sense believes they still exist."

"Does anyone know what the three mountains of power did?" William said, now kneeling on the jetty to be eye to eye with Sir Welton.

"You're a good kid, so keep your nose clean and don't keep digging into the subject too much. I will tell you one last thing and then please leave the subject alone." William nodded again. "I do not know what the three objects or mountains exactly were or what they looked like but there is one strange myth. It is said that after the Hemlocks got their hands on one of the devices or mountains of power, that the weather at key points in battles would change rapidly and suddenly in their favour, almost like it was controlled to fight for them. But these are only stories adapted and changed over time," he said dismissively but clearly interested himself.

"Wow, some sort of weather control device," William remarked.

"Maybe, but remember it is just an old story. Even if something like that did exist, it's gone and should probably stay that way. Look, I can tidy the rest of this up and it's probably time you start heading back," said Sir Welton looking at his pocket watch.

"Thank you, Sir, and thank you for the fishing, it was fun," William said with genuine gratitude.

"No problem, have a good rest of the day and remember don't dig too much into it," Sir replied.

William ran off feeling very happy with himself and relieved he was not in any trouble. He was keen to tell the others what he had learned and guessed he would probably find them in the Belbury hall.

William jogged happily into the hall and immediately found George, Isabel and Jasmin in their normal lunch location. Sitting quickly down inbetween Jasmin and George, forcing them to move apart and interrupting their conversation as he began to tell his story of the events of the morning.

"Oi, I'm sitting here," George protested as he was shoved over.

"And me. What's wrong with that chair," complained Jasmin.

"Come on, budge up. I have some important news," William said, teasing them and wanting to drag out his story.

"This better be worth the rude squishing in. I had just got my chair all warm!" said George.

"Yes, it is. I have found something out about that family crest," William announced as loud as he dared, preferring not to say the Hemlock name in case someone overheard and misunderstood.

"Firstly, where have you been, you were nowhere to be found in the house or anywhere else this morning!" Isabel said firmly.

"We were worried, we thought you might have run away again!" Jasmin said in a more motherly tone than normal.

"No, no need to worry, I have been fishing with Sir Welton on the Red Lake," William said, smiling.

"Fishing!... On the Red Lake!... With Sir Welton!... How on earth did that happen?" said George in genuine fascination.

"It's a long story, but I was up early and thought Sir Welton might be a good person to ask about that family crest that shows through the paint on my bit of paper. It turns out he was and he also taught me how to fish!"

"Well come on then, what have you learnt, other than being able to trick a fish to bite a hook," Isabel said, not really expecting to learn anything of actual value.

"Ha funny," said William sarcastically, "well we already know who the family is that owns that crest right. But what we didn't know is what the picture of the three triangles sitting on top of each meant. Sir said that the three triangles represent three mountains of power!" William said with excited eyes.

"Mountains of power. What, like real mountains?" George asked, confused.

"No, they are not real stone mountains like out there," said William, pointing his arm back out the main hall door. "Sir likened them to objects that gave whoever had all three, total power over everything, you, me, the whole world. It's what the Great War was originally about, that family was trying to get all three!" William said drumming on the table in a dramatic finish and a show of success. "And I bet that it is one of those three objects that Belbury is hiding on level five, and that is why Krevak is after it!" he said, carrying on after a moment's pause and holding a finger up to stop the others from interrupting his moment. "Sir Welton also told me during the Great War, the family did get their hands on one of the mountains, objects of power, and they could control the weather, and get it to fight for them in battles!"

"Crikey, you got all of that while out fishing for a few hours. Sounds better than any amount of time spent in the library," said George while looking at Isabel.

"Well, what do you think we should do, go to the Headmaster?" asked Isabel, unsure about what to do next.

"He probably knows all of this already, right Will?" said Jasmin.

"Probably. But we should try and find out what the three mountains of power actually look like and what they did," William said, realising that this was probably impossible and there was actually very little they could do.

🕯️ Myth Or Fact

"Does everyone have a copy of Looking At The Past To See The Future, By Conrad Sparkle?" Mrs Constanta Lation asked the group of cold students. The First Year's "Future Gazing Lesson" was conducted during the dead of night, when the sky was at its clearest and often to the dislike of the students, also its coldest. Along with the students, adults from the Belbury town and surrounding area who were interested in the stars and planets above their heads, would pay to participate in the lessons. Turning a normal academy lesson into a nice little extra earner for Mrs Lation, who was always at her happiest with a big group to teach.

Mrs Lation was dressed in a long cream-coloured sheepskin coat, done up tight against the cold with large toggles that looked like shooting stars and crescent moons. On her head was a hunter starker hat with the ear flaps tied down, again made of sheepskin.

Mrs Lation taught the students and the non-student customers how to view the great history of the stars and planets that stretched out grandly above them every cloudless dark night. She taught and educated them how to use the stars and planets as a calendar, understanding their intricate precessional movements and what it meant for Thomons now and in the future.

This particular night was the coldest so far and equally dark, allowing the stars and planets a deep, unending black darkness on which to perform and show their sparkle to their best.

William was very thankful that for once he had remembered to wear two pairs of socks, gloves and his hat this time. So, unlike many of the others, he was not dancing on the spot to stay warm, while trying not to get told off for causing a distraction and being unprepared.

All the students produced their books from their pockets and quickly enlarged them to a readable size. Many of the class reluctantly ended up having to share their books with the surrounding paying customers who had not come so well prepared, but Mrs Lation also insisted they did so as she never wanted unhappy paying customers.

"Right, can I please have someone read for me?" asked Mrs Lation.

William kept his hand firmly in his pocket, not wanting to advertise too freely the modification that had been made to his Hadron-Tool. Isabel's hand shot up like a rocket reaching for the stars they were about to study.

"Thank you, Isabel, please read from the start of chapter three," came the instruction.

Isabel quickly found the chapter and began to read, using the light from a red floating ball that had been provided and which only shone downward.

"Our ancient Thomon ancestors created amazing structures, all which have deep meaning. For example, the great pyramid is a vast stone structure which conceals in its physical architecture, amazing insight into the universe. The structure is a perfect scale representation of the north hemisphere of the earth. The ratio used for this to work is one to forty-three thousand two hundred. This is not a random number, those who have read my previous book, Dancing Through Time, will know this is a processional number that relates to the earth's great year."

"Perfect! Stop there Isabel, thank you for the clear reading. I can see many blank faces after that mouthful of information, but don't worry we will work through it slowly, and remember please ask questions at any point if you get confused, this is not an easy subject to get your head around. The lesson tonight is on how, without all the technology we have today, our ancestors were able, all those many thousands of years ago, to measure the earth in such a precise manner," Mrs Lation said with a very gentle voice.

William was fascinated by this subject, he did not understand most of what was read, but was very much looking forward to changing that. In his mind he could see very clearly the world sitting amongst the stars and wanted to know how they all related to each other.

"Could everyone now please take out their history viewers and enlarge them ready to look out into the depths of history. Please don't enlarge them past the recommended max size as the focus will be totally wrong and you won't see anything," Mrs Lation instructed.

"Mrs Lation, nowhere on mine does it say the max size, any ideas?" George asked, while looking at his second-hand and slightly dented history viewer.

"Yes, no problem, the rule of thumb with these pieces of equipment is the front and rear top sights should be separated by the length of a Galumbo's tail. Any other questions? No? Good, on we go then," Mrs Lation said as she turned to look through her own device, which was mounted on a stand behind her.

"What's a Galumbos? And how long's its tail?" George said quietly to William, while looking confused and feeling none the wiser, as the lesson carried on.

"No idea. Look, just match the size of mine, can't be that different," William replied, while trying hard to hear what was being said.

The class had been standing for a few freezing cold, but grippingly interesting hours on Caracol peak, which was located in the mountains many miles to the north east of Belbury Town but was only a single groove ride away, and it was now finally time for bed.

Once the lesson was complete, everyone hurried down to the base of Caracol peak to use the single cast iron pillar. A shivering queue formed as they all waited to use the single groove hole that was available.

"Students, Belbury Academy students! Please wait and let the customers go first," Mrs Lation called, bringing the children to a halt.

"She always lets the money go first, I am just as cold as they are," Isabel complained to Jasmin, who was now jogging on the spot watching the paying customers disappearing down the groove.

Thankfully, after a long wait, William dragged his ice block feet over to the pillar to place his Hadron-Tool that was shivering along with his hand into the single hole and vanished towards his warm bed and soft pillows.

The sun decided to rise far too early the following morning. Thankfully the First Year history viewing lessons only happened on a Friday night when the skies were clear, so most students would be taking full advantage of this and taking Saturday morning to lie in.

William was eventually drawn out of a deep sleep by George punching him hard in the shoulder. He had been trying to wrestle William from the grips of the dream world for a while and got bored of being gentle.

"Wake up Will! Isabel says she has found something. She says it can't wait, the common room's empty, everyone's gone to breakfast. Come on, Jasmin is already with her," George said with increasing force, rocking William at the same time.

"What... no go away," William said, moaning and trying to roll away from the rude awakening.

"Nope, not happening," said George while ripping William's covers off and throwing them on to the floor.

"Ok... Ok I'm up, I'm up, give me a sec. No one deserves to be woken up like that," William yawned.

The two boys wrapped in thick dressing gowns and floating on fluffy slippers made their way to the common room, where Isabel was wide awake and already talking eagerly to Jasmin who looked like she would also rather be back in bed.

Each found a worn chair around the warm floating sphere, which Isabel pushed up, out the way with her Hadron-Tool so they could see each other easily.

"Right, what is so important that it could not wait a few more hours?" William asked, yawning once again.

"Well look, ever since you found out about the three mountains of power and what they would enable someone to do I could not stop thinking about it. So, over the last few weeks I have been reading, looking and digging in the library to try and understand what the three objects could do and what they might look like," Isabel said energetically.

"So you have found something then?" George asked.

"Not really, just a type of confirmation," replied Isabel.

"Confirmation! Is that it! Just more of what we have already found out, I just spent ten minutes trying to wake that one up..." said George pointing at William, "... and you have no new information."

"Look, just listen," she said, frustrated at George's lack of understanding. "I started to think about that myth Will told us about how the three objects together would allow someone to control everything. What things would you need to control to be able to have that level of power over people and the world?" she asked, not expecting an answer. "In a very dusty part of the library I found a stack of papers that detailed the legal rules governing types of technology research and their uses. One of the sections said that all research into the control of weather was to be banned, and all technology linked with this type of control was to be destroyed," Isabel said with excitement.

"So what? That is really old information and sounds more like political people sticking their noses into stuff they don't understand. Like normal!" said George, who was never a fan of being told what to do by people in those types of positions.

"Wait, I think I understand what you are saying. You think that the ability to control the weather was real and it's not just a myth," said William, starting to wake up and understand what Isabel was getting at.

"Yes, that is exactly it. If they had to ban it then it had to be real. To do it so soon after the end of the Great War, when you would have thought something like that would have been quite helpful, makes me think that it was probably something that got used as a weapon during the war instead of for good," Isabel said looking at William, happy that someone was on her wavelength.

"It must be one massive device if it can control the earth's weather. Krevak won't be able to just sneak it out in his pocket, there has to be some limit to shrinking stuff," Jasmin said.

The four were now in deep conversation about how a device like that might have worked and what it might look like, leaning over the low three-legged table that was inbetween them, looking over the notes Isabel had made about the document she had found. The floating sphere of fire gently bobbed up and down above their heads sending warm light flickering down, making their shadows dance.

⚏ Down But Not Out

The final 4's match was now upon all the houses, with the days growing hotter and longer pointing to the end of the year. House points were also growing closer and tighter, with the House Points Clock showing very evenly sized house gears all touching each other. Rutherford though had been holding on to first place on the House Points Clock since Christmas, with Starley hot on their heels, even though they had lost the last few 4's matches.

The morning of the last 4's game had become so hot that the pitch was more like a stone floor than a grass field. The game had been running for thirty-nine minutes, with the teams creating clouds of dust from the concrete hard turf pitch, which swirled around like the players were a herd of buffalo.

The players had shrunk the studs on their boots into small sharp bumps to grip the hard surface. The warming fire spheres that were normally on the sidelines had been switched to small floating balls of rippling water which bent the incoming light away from the ground directly below, leaving a cool patch of shade for the players to sit in.

The game had been going well for Starley who were currently out in front, when William had his first major

4's injury. The injury was so bad that he was unable to walk, he just lay on the ground writhing in agony. He was immediately strapped down onto a stretcher and rushed to the medical centre to be looked at and fixed.

William had been running flat out with the egg tucked under his right arm to prevent it from escaping and protected at the front with his left hand, when his forward motion had been halted abruptly by the immovable object of Dillon Doogle from Fermi House. A very large Celtic boy who was built like a boulder and weighed about the same too.

The first impact had stopped William in his tracks, winding him, causing him to drop the ball. His mind quickly became foggy and the world spun around as he tried pathetically to find where the ball had gone. The second impact that caused the most damage, was when he was driven hard into the solid stone-like pitch surface by Dillon Doogle who then landed on top of him, knocking William out cold with a loud crack being heard by the watching spectators.

Once he reached the medical room, he was laid on a clean and tightly sheeted steel frame bed. The ceiling above him continued to spin rapidly, making him feel even more sick. The pain was everywhere over his body, constantly throbbing and stabbing him without remorse. He moaned in pain, clutching at his body, not sure what to do, what to say or where to clutch.

A nurse dressed in white calmly walked across the room to him, "Who do we have here then?" she said to herself. "Can you hear me, William? Can you tell me where the pain is?" She asked William questions but he could not say anything to her that was understandable or useful as to where the pain was or even what had happened.

This was not a problem for the nurse as she had the gift of mirror touch. This gift allowed the owner to feel the very sensations, pain and feelings that another person they saw or touched was feeling. In fact, most of the medical staff in Belbury Town had some sort of empathetic feeling gift that aided their work of healing those that were unwell.

She investigated gently with her soft hands, looking and feeling for bruising, breaks and blood. Slowly, as her hands moved over William's lower back, she felt a growing pain in her own lower back, as her mind began to create in her the injury that William had. She dropped to her knees with the debilitating pain of the experience, breaking the connection between her hand and William's back. After a few moments she focused hard on the pain she was experiencing to understand it. The pain faded away after a minute or so allowing the nurse to stand freely again having understood what was wrong with William.

"Oh dear my love you are not in a good way," she said, looking concerned at him and gently touching the hair on his head. "But no need to worry we will sort you out," she said with experienced calm as she placed her Hadron-Tool on William's forehead, making him instantly calm and still.

She called over two other nurses similarly dressed who did not have the gift of mirror touch and explained to them what was wrong and what needed to be done. They set to their healing work with well-practised order, using bandages and delicate cutting and stitching movements of their Hadron-Tools. After an hour's work they had William patched up and resting for the night ready to be discharged in the morning.

The bright light of the rising morning was thrust upon William with the opening of curtains that covered a long wall made almost totally of glass. The rays of light hit William's eyelids like an alarm clock and shocked him awake. He awoke exhausted, feeling his sleep had been like a twig in a storm and confused about where he was. The last thing he could remember was running into something very solid indeed. It took a few moments to get his bearings and slowly moved his hand to his lower back, which now gave him no pain, but was still bandaged tight, hiding the skilful work that had been carried out.

In the sterile white and calm room he was lying in one of six beds, three down each windowless side wall. The mainly glass end wall looked out over a cricket pitch perfect green lawn that rolled down to the banks of the misting Red Lake, making it look dangerous and beautiful at the same time.

At the opposite end of the room was a door that cut boldly through an equally long wall of glass windows, allowing the nurses and doctors to observe but not disturb. Below these windows and sitting on a polished clean white speckled floor were cabinets containing many of the tools and concoctions of their trade.

Realising where he now was, he relaxed and settled back to look out the window and wondered if there was anything hiding inside the hovering mist.

The nurse who had felt his pain came gliding over from the other side of the glass observation wall.

"Good morning William, I'm Florence Dix, how do you feel today?" Florence said kindly, while looking through a page of notes next to him.

"I feel fine, no more pain!" William said, happy to be so easily repaired.

"Well, that is good news. It was no easy job putting you back together and it is probably best you don't ask what was done. I also don't pick up any more pain from you," she said while looking him over and passing her hands sensingly over him, "so that is doubly good," she said in a happy, job done well tone.

"Does anyone know I am here?" William asked hopefully.

"Why yes of course! The whole town knows you are here. One of the problems with being written about in the paper again! Your team captain I believe, Marcus Mardic is it? Came over last night to see how you were. He has informed your house of your state, so no need to worry." She finally finished by adjusting William's bed sheets. "You will be discharged later this morning and escorted back to your house by a teacher as is academy policy. I have been informed that Mr Diesel thinks very highly of you, so I have sent him a message to come and collect you. Until then, relax and enjoy the view and breakfast." Florence said while moving a mug of tea and a full Thomon on to the table next to him, then swinging it over his lap, turning and walking away back through the door she had come in through.

Hours went by before Mr Diesel's head appeared floating halfway up the door.

"Nurse says that you're all healed and ready to go back to join the fit and healthy. I will give you a few minutes to get dressed, those backless gowns are never a good look!" he said with a friendly smile, disappearing again to give William some time to get ready.

Happily, William jumped out of bed, got ready and met Mr Diesel who was sitting on a chair in the hallway, that was appointed in much the same way as the room.

"Great, you're all good to go. Got everything?" Mr Diesel asked.

"Yep, this is it," said William, holding his arms out to show that he had nothing at all.

"Good, well let's go."

They walked back to the Starley common room, as it was not recommended to use the grooves for a full day after being discharged. The walk took about thirty minutes along cobbled and yellow gravel paths, through stone arches and over ornate woven bridges.

The two talked casually as they walked, enjoying the conversation and similar interest in manufacturing and engineering.

"Sir, do you think you could design and make a device to control the weather?" William asked absentmindedly as they walked, not really thinking much of the question. It just came out and he instantly regretted asking it.

"That's an interesting idea! My guys can make near enough anything so I don't see why not. You would probably need to include a whole lot of 'Sparky' and

'Binary' help for the electronics and controls in something like that, but yeah sure," he said positively.

"Why aren't there any then, would seem like a good thing to have?" William asked, realising he could probably probe for more information.

"Sadly we're not allowed to create tools that control the weather anymore. That's been banned for ages. Shame really as you are right it would be very useful. You could've got it to rain over the 4's pitch yesterday to make it soft. Which would have stopped you getting injured," he said, talking to William as a friend and not as one of his students.

"Banned! That's a shame, would be a really interesting project," William said, faking surprise. "Isabel was right," he thought to himself.

"Yes, banned after the Great War. Not sure why but the powers that be thought it needed to happen."

"Have you ever seen what they looked like?" William asked.

"Seen them, no, I'm not that old. Not even my father was old enough to have seen one!" Mr Diesel said before pausing for a few moments. "I have not seen the real physical thing, no, they were all destroyed, but..."

"But what?" William said, keen to know more.

"This is not known outside of myself and father, so don't say anything to anyone," Mr Diesel said with slight firmness. "In the company archives, I believe I have seen engineering drawings of them or at least parts of them. When the company was first started I am sure we made parts for them. When they were banned the PSC would have taken everything to do with them from our company

stores and archives to ensure it was destroyed, but I
would not be surprised if they missed the odd drawing.
Finding all that paperwork and all those drawings for an
old project can be very hard, often hard even for a new
project." Mr Diesel said with what William thought was
a smile, hinting that he knew this might well be a fact
and probably not an accident.

The two kept walking along the winding passageways,
at one point passing through a neatly kept garden. A
clean and soft-looking grass lawn was surrounded on all
sides by a wide, yellow gravel path. Outside the path
were deep planting beds full of dark, rich loamy soil,
piled up so it sat a few inches higher than the path. The
beds were full of flowering plants, small in height closest
to the path and slowly getting taller as they got further
back. As William and Mr Diesel walked around,
flesh-eating plants snapped their hairy, flexible jaws
in their direction. The enclosed garden smelt like the
intoxicating fragrance that would often delicately waft
out of the girl's dormitory as they put on perfume ready
for the day.

This was one of the town's common spaces that was
looked after by the local gardening group and who also
ran lessons on how to plant and grow food, plant health
and how to make medicine from plants that are freely
available.

As they walked around two of the sides, gravel
scrunching underfoot, they approached a group of girls
from Fermi house, who were talking loudly, and suddenly
went quiet as William got close. One of the girls stepped
out to block William's path, asking, "Will, how are you?

Quite the fuss was made over you at the game!" she asked.

The girl was Henady Tipleton, who William thought did not even know he existed. He did not know what to say.

"Ur... yeah fine now thanks," William said, feeling his face getting hot, but hoping it did not show.

There was a moment's awkward silence between the two, with Henady waiting for William to ask her a question in return.

"Well... see you in class then," he said, trying to fill the silence with something, instantly feeling pathetic that he could not even ask her a question. He stepped around Henady to catch up with Mr Diesel who had carried on, understanding this was something William did not need a teacher around for.

As William quickly walked away with gravel crunching loud with each foot step, he dared a look back hoping that he had not been as totally pathetic as he felt. Henady was still watching him and gave him a little secret hip height wave, which he gladly returned before she turned back to her friends, who all then exploded in excited noise like a gaggle of hens.

"No need to say anything William, just keep it out of lessons," said Mr Diesel smiling to himself, thinking back to his first crush when he was at Belbury Academy himself and thinking how time flies.

Mr Diesel delivered the healed William back to a hero's welcome from his house, who all wanted to know the story and talk about what they saw. Marcus pushed his way through the crowd and put a heavy hand on William's shoulder and the room went quiet.

"I knew you were a good choice, no regard for your own safety at all. Great to have you back."

With that Marcus whacked William on the back, jerking him forward a little from the weight of the friendly blow and then left him to be swamped in hugs from Isabel and Jasmin.

That evening at dinner all of the Starley tables were loud with excitement. They all looked to the front of the hall to watch the house points clock slowly move. The Rutherford house gear had been the largest and closest to the top for most of the year, but finally it now rolled back with a mechanical metal on metal "clack clack" noise into second place. The Starley gear grew in size and rolled up, passing the Rutherford house gear into first place. When the gears had finished moving the whole Starley house erupted in cheers and celebration. Fermi was last with a gear half the size of Starley and Blanchard were in third. Nothing could stop Starley winning this year's competition.

After all of the excitement had died down, William finally had a chance to sit and think about the day he had just had. As if an explosion had gone off in his head he suddenly blurted out to his friends. "Guys, I learnt something else about the device hidden on level five."

George and Isabel were talking happily with each about their last, "You Are What You Eat" class, when William interrupted them, Jasmin also lifted her face from her sketchbook to listen. Once William knew he had their attention he began.

"On my walk back from the medical centre with Mr Diesel we were generally talking and I asked him, without really thinking, about the weather control device."

"How did he take it?" Jasmin asked.

"Did not really change at all, he was just happily talking," William replied.

"Ok, so what did he say, that you have waited till now to tell us," said George pretending to be annoyed.

"Sorry, just been a busy day. He said that he had never seen a physical weather control device because they were all destroyed after they were banned."

"So I was right," Isabel said, happy with herself.

"Yes, what Mr Diesel said confirmed what you found out; they were banned. Now he has never seen a physical device," William said, repeating the point, "but he hinted he had seen drawings of them or at least parts in his company's archive," said William to interested faces.

"So did he say we could look at them or anything?" Isabel asked.

"No, he didn't, I didn't ask, it sounded like he wanted to keep it a secret. Even so, I think we should try and find those drawings. We need to know what Krevak is looking for, maybe even understand how it works," William said, beginning to ponder how they would be able to get access to Mr Diesel's archive.

They started to create a plan when they were interrupted by a ball being thrown onto the table and knocking over two jugs of red sluck juice, which promptly flowed like a tsunami wave across the table, bringing bowls and cups with it. The ball had been thrown by Goran Henbane who then started to shout at and taunt William.

"Told you we would put you in medical before the year was out," Goran shouted.

William turned to react, but Isabel stopped him.

"It wasn't even a boy from Rutherford House who tackled you, the big lump was from Fermi, let it go and let's leave," Isabel said, stepping over her seat, signalling to the others to do the same. They followed suit and left Goran spouting rubbish about how he had arranged William's injury and trying to bait William to come back.

⚙⚙ Sneaking

Lessons wound down as the last week of the academy year was now upon them. The students would soon all be going home, but there were still lessons to be had in the fabric factories, bakeries, garages, metal ore mines and Gold Stones. Everyone including the teachers were eager for the week to end and the summer holidays to begin.

The First Year students were again in Diesel and Sons Engineering, but for once not in the regular old school workshop. Today they were walking through a very clean and sparse lobby of the spiralling glass tower that was slowly enveloping the old iron and brick-built workshop next door.

The building did not excite William's nose and ears in the same way as the older building did, but his eyes were very much captivated.

From the outside the building reminded William of the Gherkin and The Shard in London somehow mashed together, but there was no comparison he could think of for how the inside looked.

The internal structural frame for the building was white and smooth like bone with branching spars, some as thin as a strand of hair and others oak-trunk-thick, reaching across the space, smoothly joining and blending to where each met another. They made a web of curving squares and triangles above the children standing in the entrance lobby.

William could see that all the floors above were suspended and had to weave around the many arms of the building's organic frame. The whole structure was delicately draped in sheets of glass panes, allowing light to freely flow in and make the white clean structure sparkle like a diamond.

Mr Diesel, with his dirty blue jacket and black hat, looked very out of place in this clean new workshop.

"Welcome all to the morphing shop," he said with great pride. "Here we will begin to learn how to make objects by stretching, compressing or curving materials using your Hadron-Tools. This will start to bring together many of the other lessons you have been having around the town. The same rules from the old workshop apply in this new space, which I am happy to say, you have all been keeping really well, we have not lost any fingers, ears or kneecaps so far, so thank you. Please follow me to the working area." He set off with a spring in his step, clearly very happy to show the students the building. However, William remembered he seemed to be a man who preferred the old ways of doing things.

They rose to the fourth floor of the building using grooves located in a central column that looked like a tree trunk, with the grooves giving the column a bark-like texture. The fourth floor was a spacious work area with rows of small workstations, with employees busily moulding and drawing out metal shapes as if they were working with clay.

"Right, all into the lab, come on, come on, in we go, find a space at a bench, and get your practice cubes and Hadron-Tools out and ready!" he said, shepherding the marvelling and amazed students through the door.

The class all found places behind standing tables in their new lab area and all placed their practice cubes and Hadron-Tools on the surface in front of them, which had become a very practised routine.

"Fantastic, all ready!" Mr Diesel said as he walked to the front of the class. "The first task today is to enlarge the practice cube to roughly the size of your head."

The class started immediately with generally good all-round results, for this now basic task.

"Good, good well done Jasmin, you have come a long way this year, great control, well done," he said as he walked around giving feedback and tips.

"Well done everyone, now we will learn how to pull a point out of the cube. Now we don't want to enlarge the cube any more, we just want to pull out a single point. This is where being able to strongly imagine with great controlled detail and see exactly what you are wanting to happen comes into play. All uncontrolled imagining and wondering of your mind must be controlled to succeed in creating the desired shape. Now watch me first," Mr Diesel said, moving over to his bench at the front of the class.

He produced his own small practice cube and quickly enlarged it to a cube with perfect dimensions. He then placed the very tip of his Hadron-Tool against the top flat face of the cube and paused, so everyone could see. "Remember you must really see it in your mind for it to happen. You must see the details like the size of the base, surface texture and how solid or not you want the spike to be, now watch!"

He pulled directly upwards with his Hadron-Tool and a round spike grew out of the cube's top. The round spike grew taller and taller as it followed Mr Diesel's Hadron-Tool, with its base never changing diameter. He stopped when the spike was at arm's length above his head, and brought his arm back down to his side, leaving the round spike standing tall.

"Now, as I was pulling this long round spike out of my cube," he said, pointing to the smooth tower next to him, "I could have started to change its shape as I went if I wanted to, but that is all in the future for you for now. So over to you, try and pull a round spike like mine out of your cubes."

The class set to work trying to mimic what they had just been shown and the room became a hive of facial stress and quiet activity. Jasmin had looked initially like she had mastered it at the first attempt, but this was quickly undone when her entire cube and round spike suddenly melted like a chocolate on a hot day, spreading out all over the desk and floor. While William, George and Isabel were making some steady progress.

The four began talking quickly and quietly with each other about where to start looking for Mr Diesel's archive room. They all shared the same standing desk in a corner of the classroom to try and prevent others from over-hearing what they were planning to try and do.

"It must be in the basement somewhere, they always are, you know somewhere out the way," William whispered.

"Yes, that is a good thought and I would doubt it would be in this new building, you would have to move the old archive from the old building into the new one, and that just sounds like hard work," Isabel said with Jasmin agreeing.

"You have been unusually quiet George, you must be thinking too hard!" Isabel said, teasing him.

"I am thinking," he said and paused for a moment while the other three looked at each other and started to laugh under their breaths.

"Well look, it seems sensible to me that we should start looking down the corridor that Mr Diesel went down to drop the papers off he had under his arm at the first lesson we had with him. You remember he ran off to the left at the far end of the entrance lobby. He must have put them somewhere, an office maybe? I would have also thought that you would like your drawing archive close to hand," George said, not breaking his Hadron-Tool's contact or his stare from his cube as he attempted again to create a long round spike.

"Gosh you must have been thinking hard," Isabel said.

"Think too much harder and you might explode your cube," William said with a laugh. "It sounds like a good place to start though. Good thinking George."

The group continued to talk and plan while Mr Diesel continued to walk around the class giving tips and advice. When suddenly the whole room erupted into screams and fits of laughter at Goran. He didn't like most other people in his class who were not members of his house and so picked on them constantly. This though was a mutual feeling of dislike as those not in his house disliked him just as much and it pleased them greatly to see the enormous error he had just made.

He had lost control of the spike he was creating and sent it piercing through the ceiling, showering the class with dust and scraps of whiteboard. Above, the sound of someone squealing in pain could be heard, making Mr Diesel rush off to see what had happened. He appeared back in the lab a few minutes later and shrunk Goran's spike back into the cube and then the cube back to pocket size.

"This lesson is now over, thank you for all trying so hard, please follow me out of the building," Mr diesel said, very flustered from what had just happened.

"This is our chance," William said to the other three.

He was right, the whole class was leaving in rushed disarray, with everyone talking loudly about what just happened. Mr Diesel was not really concentrating on the class as much as he would normally, so wouldn't be able to tell if the whole class had left or not, William thought to himself.

The four friends faffed around a little at their tables to make sure they were the slowest to get ready and leave, and took the same grooves back down they had used to come up to the fourth floor. When each one of the four appeared at the bottom of the groove they ran to the rear of the large column to hide from the rest of the group and especially Mr Diesel.

They could hear the voices of their classmates getting quieter and quieter and then gone completely once they left the building. Now all they could hear was Mr Diesel walking quickly back, with short, hard footsteps on the solid white floor. He was muttering to himself, trying to work out a plan to firstly sort out the hole in the ceiling of his new building, and secondly how to fix the person who had been impaled on their chair, as the spike had driven straight through into their bottom.

Mr Diesel walked past the groove in the central column towards where the children were hiding, but stopped short. William could see the tips of his shoes and dared not move a muscle as he thought this might attract attention. The four breathed out in relief when Mr Diesel turned around and took a groove up into the heights of the building. Willian, George, Jasmin and Isabel were now safe to sneak off to try and find the archive, and find out, they hoped, what a weather controlling device looked like.

They headed off towards a set of double doors just to the right of the main entrance doors, as Jasmin, without looking at her map, guessed they led to the old workshop. William thought that this was probably a good guess as they looked like the same type of doors that were in the old building.

The white expanse they had to cross was an empty desert of places to hide, so they moved at a run on the tip of their toes, trying to stop their shoes squeaking on the smooth, clean floor, which sparkled like quartz. They reached the double doors without trouble and huddled close together, trying to be as small as possible. William cautiously peered through the window in the top half of the door, and saw a dramatically different-looking space, which confirmed that this door was the right choice.

"All clear I think, but where next, there are three corridors on the other side?" William said as he turned back to the group.

"My map!" George said, having forgotten all about it in the excitement of sneaking around. "Right, we need to go left, that is the shortest route to the lobby."

"Any more information about where to go after we go left?" Isabel said, concerned about the lack of planning.

"We go left and follow it around, cross a junction and then take a right to end up by the double doors into the changing area," replied George, speaking confidently to reassure himself that he had read the map correctly.

"Come on, we're sitting ducks out here, let's get moving," urged Jasmin, worried they would be spotted as they were in plain sight of anyone who wanted to look in their direction.

They all took a brief look at each other, a quiet check with each other, that they all understood what to do. No more words had to be said, a look was all it took to reassure each other.

William pushed the left door open just enough to stick his head through and confirm the coast was still clear. It was. He then slipped the rest of his body through the narrow gap followed closely by the other three. The three corridors on the other side of the door were all the same natural colour, and had metallic strips running along the bottom edges of the walls to protect them from impact and scuff damage. The left corridor, which they needed to take, curved around to the right making the group stick close together against the right-hand wall, so they would be on the inside of the bend and help keep them hidden.

Up ahead William could see four of Mr Diesel's employees, all in their blue knee length jackets with black bowler hats chatting in the centre of the cross-corridor junction. He held up his hand to signal to the others to stop. Only William could see the workers up ahead, leaving the others to wonder what he had seen as he said nothing and did not look back.

William finally turned to face them after what felt like hours of waiting to keep going, as the four workers had started to walk off. After only a single step forward William stopped again this time in panic. One of the workers had not gone with the others but was walking down towards them.

"Quick! Hide! Hide!... In there!" William said, turning and rushing to a door that they had just passed.

George tried the handle, "It's locked!" he said in panic.

William looked back around the corner at the man who was getting closer and closer by the second, the sound of each footstep becoming louder and louder. Luckily, he was looking through his small black and yellow booklet that most of the workers carried in their chest pocket, and did not look up to see them. William's heart was pounding in his chest.

"What do we do, what do we do?!!!" Isabel and Jasmin hissed in panic at each other.

"Move!" William said in desperation. He barged past George who was still trying the door handle and placed his Hadron-Tool against the lock, and focused.

The clunk of the door's locking mechanism was just audible and the door swung open, with William falling in behind it. "Quick, in!" He said getting up from the floor and holding the door open for the others to squeeze in past him. He slowly closed the door behind them, shutting out the strip of light. William then retouched the lock with his Hadron-Tool and the lock mechanism could be heard moving again.

The four waited in the dark cloak of silence, none daring to breathe, partly out of fear of being heard but also because the smell in the tiny dark room was terrible. It smelt like an old sweety 4's sock that contained sick and rotten eggs. They all believed that their heartbeats could be heard through the door and they were going to be found.

In the stillness they could hear the footsteps become louder and clearer, with the click, click of hard-soled shoes on the hard floored corridor. William closed his eyes and listened intently, hoping for the sound to pass, but it stopped right outside the door. They heard the sound of the door handle being grabbed from the outside and tried. A single try at first and then a succession of rapid up and down movements, concluding in a frustrated rattle of the handle.

"Not another door! How many times do we need to get a locksmith in this old broken building to get all the doors to work, unbelievable!" sounded an annoyed voice outside.

They heard the handle being released and the footsteps carry on down the corridor, this time with the force of an annoyed worker driving his heels into the ground.

The sound soon disappeared and the tense silence in the stinking dark space relaxed.

"I am going to check," William whispered.

"No, not yet!" Isabel whispered back, trying to stop him.

William went anyway, placing his Hadron-Tool back on the lock and hearing the satisfying clunk of the lock opening again. Slowly he pulled the door open and disappeared out of the thin gap of light, leaving the other three hiding in the darkness. He came back a few seconds later to the relief of his friends who were more than glad to get out of the stinky darkness.

"Come on, it's all clear, quick," William encouraged them.

Without protest they hurried, only pausing for a brief look down the crossroad junction to check the coast was clear. They were quickly through the end doors and into the workshop's changing room, feeling a little safer, as this area was not off limits to unattended students.

"How did you unlock the door Will?" asked George in a controlled hushed voice, as they moved slowly and silently like nervous mice.

"I shrunk the lock, easy really, pulled the locking bolt right out. Worked better than I thought," William said pleased with himself.

"How did you stop that man opening it?" George asked again not thinking of the obvious answer.

"Made it bigger of course, to the point it jammed. Worked better than I thought it would," William said repeating the same phrase.

Isabel was the first to reach the door to the old workshop's entrance lobby and looked through the door's dirty window. She could see the secretary sitting at her desk reviewing calendars and sipping a coffee of go juice to keep her focused till the end of the day.

"The secretary is still at her desk. She's a nice lady, I know her. Wait here until I am talking with her before you cross the lobby," Isabel said.

The rest of the group nodded and moved up to the door's window to watch. They saw Isabel walk confidently across the lobby and start a conversation with the blonde-haired lady, making sure she stood towards the main entrance door so as to make the secretary turn towards her and look away from where the others would have to cross.

William, George and Jasmin gave her a few moments to get the lady's full attention and then with as much confidence, grace and light-footedness as they could manage, went for it, making it across the lobby in a few worried steps.

The three sneaking First Years heard Isabel say, "Thank you," and then saw her casually walk around the corner as if nothing had happened.

"Well?" William asked, confused by her lack of secretiveness.

"I said I got caught short and needed the toilet. She let me use the manager's one down here," said Isabel, very happy with herself.

"Fair enough, but you don't really need to go, do you?" George asked.

"No, of course not, and I would not tell you if I did," said Isabel, annoyed at the rather stupid question.

"Where now then?" asked Jasmin, anxious to get moving.

"No idea, just look everywhere for clues," answered William as he turned to look through one of the many windows that lined the corridor. "George, does it show anything on your map?" William asked.

"No, nothing. No real detail in here, no room names or information at all," George replied.

The group slowly but purposefully made their way down the featureless square corridor and peered through windows in the walls and doors. The corridor was long and brightly lit, with doors regularly on both sides, windows were set midway up the wall and evenly-spaced between the doors. There were measuring rooms, material storage rooms, break rooms, offices and energy control rooms, all interesting but none were what they were looking for.

"Here! This one!" George said abruptly and pressed his fingers hard into one of the windows. The window he was pointing through looked into a drafting room, where four large drawing boards stood on stands, each had a horizontal bar across its surface and a wheeled stool sat in front of each one ready for the next user. There was one of these boards per wall, and were used to draw plans and manufacturing drawing, which would be used to make objects and parts in the workshop.

In-between two of these large boards was a second boring looking brown door with a gold panel at the top of the door saying, "Archive".

"Great spot," William said, pushing the surprisingly heavy entrance door open.

"Finally, some good news," said Jasmin, happy to be out of the corridor, hidden out of sight and in a room that did not smell like sick.

George could feel his pride rising, making him stand a little taller and his shoulders sit a little bit further back.

🔲🔲 Needle In A Haystack

They stepped through the door and the feeling and sound under their feet changed to a hollow metallic clank. After a few moments, floating spheres located at head height started to light up in rows, flowing out in a grid illuminating a gigantic storage space, full of tall shelving, supporting stacks of papers, parts and objects that had been made and never used, all gathering dust.

The hair on Isabel's and Jasmin's heads was suddenly blown around by a gust of fast-moving air above, making them look up and duck at the same time. A wheeled cart careered along a track suspended from the ceiling and off around the warehouse. Moments later sparks could be seen from the bottom of its wheels as it screeched to a halt under a large riveted bronze cone, that smoothly flared out just above where the cart had stopped. Papers and objects then clattered into the cart's wooden bucket, before speeding off once again along the roller coaster track to be unloaded and items sorted in other various locations around the room.

The more they looked the more movement they saw, tens of carts whizzed around on tracks, giant chains clanked around large gears while lifting and lowering large skips and heavily-laden platforms. A red evening sunset glow created by a large furnace could be seen in the far left corner, eating up unwanted items that could not be reused.

"Well, this is a problem! Why can't anything ever be easy, where on earth do we start?" William said, not getting an echo.

"I was thinking that as well," George said, staring out into the expanse.

"Well, the drawings must be really old as they should be from before the devices were banned. So, we must be looking for a very dusty item, probably in a long-forgotten corner," Isabel said, also thinking out loud.

"Well then let's just follow the sign for the long-forgotten corner then! Oh wait there aren't any!" George said, seeing this as a ridiculous suggestion.

"You never know, the Dead End corridor was signposted. Mr Diesel sounded like he did not want anyone to find it so that would be a good way to keep something like that hidden," said William taking the first steps down.

They reached the bottom and found the room's character had changed. From up high they could see over everything, the room felt massive and open, but everything was in relation to everything else. Now that they were on the floor surrounded by tall, oppressive stacks of boxes, shelves loaded with papers and objects, the room felt far more confined and threatening, maze-like, allowing no further view than the aisle they were in.

"Well, I guess we spread out and look for a sign that points to old dusty stuff!" George said, teasing Isabel who returned a narrow-eyed look of annoyance.

"Isabel is probably right," Jasmin said, "what we are looking for must be really old and so probably won't be on any of the easy to reach shelves, probably somewhere in the back."

They decided to stay together in case they got lost and set off walking, up and down the long lines of shelving. They sometimes had to duck to miss a low sweeping piece of track that dropped even lower as it flexed under the weight of a cart careering along it. They looked and looked for what seemed hours, finding many interesting drawings and contraptions but none of which had the right description written on their labels.

"Over there it looks a lot darker and dirtier, look!" Jasmin said, pointing to a messy area located back toward the entrance.

"Yeah, that does look less tidy and more forgotten compared to the rest of this place," agreed Isabel.

"Over there," George said pointing. "That's back towards where we came in!"

"So! Often the best place to hide something is where you would least expect it," replied Jasmin as she hurried over.

The old shelves leaned heavily to the right-hand side, looking like they were about to collapse. They precariously supported a small amount of tatty paper and brown boxes, each box supporting the one next to it, stopping it falling apart.

They reached the disordered mess and immediately began opening boxes and sifting through the paper, when they heard feet hit the metal plate that made up the top of the stairs into the archive. The group shot down to the floor behind the stack of boxes they had just been looking through, all wishing they had reacted quicker.

From where they were hiding they were able to just about see through the railing that surrounded the upper platform, and saw two men in rough silhouette against a floating light.

As the two figures began to talk, William thought he had heard the gruff voices before. Then William recognised the hand position between the two men and the devices they were holding. These were the same two men who had been hiding in the mould store. They had been the two men who had been surprised when Mr Diesel had thrown a shooting star in the dark storage cave. The same two men Jasmin had seen through the dark with a red haze.

"Jasmin, what colour do you see?" asked William, wanting a small amount of confirmation of his thoughts.

"Definitely red," she immediately said.

They once again were holding their pocket watches open between each other.

"It's getting closer Javid! What do we do?" one man said.

"Don't worry, we still have plenty of time left to work it out," said the man who was now identified as Javid. "Look Thanok, stop worrying, we can do this. Krevak has given us this job because he knows we can do it. We just need to keep trying the different passageways. We will find the hidden passage that leads to the device Krevak wants soon. So please stop worrying," Javid said, prodding Thanok in the chest with a finger on his free hand.

"But what if we fail… there are not that many tunnels left to try. Remember what happened to Tilburt at the Christmas fair when he failed, he is now rotting away somewhere. I don't…" Thanok stopped talking and turned to stare towards where the children were hiding.

George had knocked a rolled-up piece of paper that was at the bottom of a larger pile, which then promptly collapsed onto the floor with numerous small thuds.

Javid was now staring hard also, trying to see what had made the noise.

"It's only a Duelat," Javid said, pointing at a small rat-like creature, which had clearly been living inside the stack of papers and now scurried away to find a new home.

A Duelat is a strange little rodent that has two tails, one body, four legs and two heads. The right head controls the right tail, and the left head, the left tail. Control of the four legs was taken by whichever head was more determined at that time. They were well known for fighting themselves to partial death in violent bouts of biting leaving one head dead. The surviving head of the Duelat would then drag around the rotting dead head and tail of its other half.

"You are just getting nervous, show some guts would you, it will all be worth it when we are rewarded. Come let's go, we have to find it soon," Javid said, snapping his pocket watch shut with a click and walked back out the door followed by Thanok.

William, George, Jasmin and Isabel relaxed into the floor, leaning their heads against the boxes.

"That was close!" Isabel said, staring out blankly.

"Too close," confirmed Jasmin.

"I think we should get out of here before we have a third close call," Isabel said.

"But we haven't found the drawings yet! All of this sneaking around would be for nothing if we leave now empty-handed," said George.

"No... not for nothing... look," said William, who had crawled around to the front of the boxes to look through the mess of papers on the floor, and came crawling back with some papers.

In his hands were four sheets, each with the title Weather Control Apparatus. William quickly flipped the pages over and over and saw that they contained a variety of drawings of an object in different sections and perspective views.

"Now we can leave," he said triumphantly, stuffing the papers into his jacket. "We can look at them when we are safely out of here."

"I thought I would never thank those ugly Duelats for anything, but they really saved us there," George said, exhausted from all the stress of constantly sneaking around and hiding.

"Well come on then let's get out of here," Isabel said firmly.

The four retraced their steps back up the stairs and along the corridor. Constantly peering around corners and moving quickly, silently. Always looking through the windows along the corridor to check the coast was clear and that they were not going to be taken by surprise.

Looking through the window into the company kitchen, Isabel saw the blonde-haired secretary was away from her desk and placing her cup on the coffee coaster for a refill.

"Hurry," said Isabel, realising that this was their chance to get out.

The group sped up to a speed that was neither a walk or a run. The sort of thing someone does when they are late but don't want to be seen running, a sort of hop and a skip walk.

The transparent exit doors came into view, the taste of freedom exciting their hearts and minds. They burst through the double doors like bubbles following the cork out of a bottle, to run down the wide cobble street and disappear down the normal cast iron manhole cover and to invisible safety.

The common room luckily was quiet and empty when the group came puffing in. Everyone else was out enjoying the warm evening sunshine and were playing in and around the twinkling Red Lake.

Before sitting down George and Isabel ran and checked their dorm areas to confirm everyone was indeed out and they were indeed alone.

They took control of the corner chairs and table under a window, which felt like a safe space to look at stolen drawings.

William pulled the now even more tatty, scrunched up papers from inside his jacket and gave one to each person to look at. Each attempted to flatten their paper before looking greedily at the pictures and descriptions on the pages, flipping them over multiple times at their own pace.

"I think we have got the wrong drawings here," George said, looking confused at his paper.

"Yeah, it doesn't look like any sort of weather control device," Isabel replied, turning her page upside down.

"It's very nice and beautifully drawn, but definitely not something to control the weather with Will," Jasmin added.

"Well, what were you expecting?" asked William.

"No idea really, I never knew these things existed until last term, but I thought it would be bigger, you know, with big levers, pipes and large dials. It's meant to control the world's weather right and that's a big thing to control," George said, looking to Isabel and Jasmin for backup.

"Yes, I don't think this can be right either, like George said, this is far too basic, too small, too simple to be able to do what the title of the page says. Maybe it is a part of the device, but can't be the whole thing!" said Isabel, disappointed.

William was carefully looking through the pages, pausing briefly after each flip and was quietly thinking. Closing his eyes he created the whole object in his mind, where he was able to fly inside it, spin it around, see it from all angles and get the parts that the drawing showed would move to do so and see what would happen. He tried to get a sense of the object and how it worked.

"Will you're doing your head thing again, what are you thinking?" Isabel asked, disturbing the closed eye meditation of William's rolling head.

William paused the 3D model he had made in his head and came back into the real world after hearing his name.

"I get that it is simple-looking and without the complexity that you would expect of something that is meant to control something massive and as complicated as the weather, but I think this is it," he said looking at the others with his mind made up.

"Go on," said George, waiting for some revelation, which always seemed to happen in class after William did his closed eyes, head rolling thing.

"Ok, well there are two things here, I think. Firstly, the size of it means it can be easily hidden and moved around so it is potentially easy to steal, and we know from Sir Rudyard that the Hemlocks somehow changed the weather during battles. So, the device must have been close by, if not on the battlefield. Something massive would be too hard to move around and protect." William paused while George, Jasmin and Isabel thought about this for a moment. Once he had seen their thoughts settle he carried on.

"Also, you don't always need something massive and complex to affect something that is itself massive and complex. What if this contains something that is released to control the weather or pulls something in. That is what something that looks like this does right, contains stuff! This would still be the weather control device, even if it only contains something which does the controlling," William said, more to test his thoughts on his own ears.

George, Isabel and Jasmin first looked at each other seeing a light bulb slowly starting to glow dim in each other's heads. Each then turned to gaze back to their paper and take a fresh look at the drawings with William's ideas in mind.

"I think you could be on to something with that Will because look," George said, rotating his page so the others could see what he had been looking at. "Some of the detail on the outside of it looks like it shows something shooting up and out of it, like rays of light or lightning. Maybe that could be showing what happens when the object is used and not just there for looks," he said pointing to a side view drawing on his paper.

"Or that could be stuff going into it and being captured, as Will said it could work either way," Isabel said.

Unbeknown to the group they were not alone. A raven as black as night was perched on the edge of the narrow wooden ledge, digging its talons into the imperfections in the wooden surface to maintain its secret overwatch position and not to be blown off by the wind.

From where the raven was sitting it looked over the table that the children thought was away from prying eyes. It sat there for three or four minutes before stepping off the edge and falling for a moment before opening its soft glossy wings to glide silently away towards the Great Forest.

Having looked at the drawings for a good amount of time the four decided they would shrink and hide them with the tree of family crests in William's dorm and head out to join the rest of the house in what remained of the long summer's day.

🎩 Times Up

The following morning Isabel and Jasmin walked out of their dorm to the common room to wait for William and George, before heading down for breakfast together as normal. They found that there was no need to wait as they were already there, but not alone! Mrs Volta, the Deputy Head, who was standing over William and George with anger on her face, with Mr Diesel behind her. Both boys were sitting unmoving, heads down, silent in front of her.

"There is space for you two here as well," Mrs Volta commanded, pointing next to the two boys. She said in a tone that made it very clear that they were in trouble, and reminded Isabel of being told off at home, when her parents would use her full name, letting her know she really was in trouble.

"Stealing will not be tolerated in this academy, especially stealing from one of the businesses that teaches you. All four of you should be ashamed of yourselves. This is not what this academy or this house stands for," Mrs Volta said with great anger in her controlled voice.

William, George, Isabel and Jasmin sat feeling the weight of guilt growing on them, the thought of potentially jeopardising the house cup or worse, expulsion was flooding their minds.

"Now who has the drawings?" Mrs Volta said forcefully.

"I have them," William said, realising there was no way out.

"Do you have them on you now?" she said, holding out her left hand, which showed great strength, hidden under the clean soft palm.

"No Mrs Volta."

"Well go get them now!"

William rushed off to his room and grabbed the four papers, ran back and sat down immediately still, placing the small papers into her hand.

"Is this all of them? Just the four sheets?"

"Yes Mrs Volta."

Mrs Volta turned and handed them to Mr Diesel without looking, who enlarged them to check what they were.

"Are they anything specific My Diesel?" Mrs Volta asked without taking her eyes from the four sad looking children sitting in front of her.

"Ur, no they are just some old drawings, nothing special," Mr Diesel said, surprising William, as he had not been honest about what they were.

"Well, this has not been a good way for you four to end your first year at Belbury Academy. You will be happy, no doubt, to know though that you will not be expelled for such an *outrageous* miss-judgement. You will all take detention tonight! Meet Mr Diesel at his company at six thirty this evening! Mr Diesel it is up to you what task you use to punish these four, but they are all yours once they turn up. Just make sure they are physically functioning tomorrow morning," Mrs Volta snapped.

"Yes Mrs Volta. Thank you," Mr Diesel said, nodding his head.

At this response Mrs Volta turned away, the bottom of her jack flaring out like a meringue as she forcefully whipped around and strode off to the down grove and vanished out of sight. Leaving behind her a room full of the dark and heavy emotion in a room that was normally so friendly and happy.

Mr Diesel took two slow steps forward.

"Look at me!... Own the mistake," he said with slight gentleness behind his stern voice.

The four lifted their heads to see a face of calm annoyance.

"Do not be late, six thirty sharp in the lobby." With that he turned and also left.

"But Sir they're trying to steal it," said William, jumping up and calling after him, but was given no reply. He sunk back onto the sofa in dismay.

"What do we do now, they won't listen?" said William.

"There is nothing we can do! The Protection and Security Council will just have to hope their protections are up to the job," said George.

*

Six thirty came around very slowly, with the feeling of panic and worry of the punishment to come, dragging out every minute of the day. William, George, Isabel and

Jasmin all felt exhausted from how fast their minds had been spinning all day, churning over and over what could possibly happen to them once the evening came.

The wandering and imagining was now over, and they were standing in front of the entrance doors for Diesel and Sons Engineering. Mr Diesel was standing, arms crossed on the other side of the glass doors waiting for them.

Isabel went in first, followed by George, William and lastly Jasmin, all bent over with heavy shoulders of worry.

"Before we begin our task for this evening, I want to know why you thought it was a good idea to steal these drawings from me?" he said with a genuine questioning voice.

"It was me Sir," William said, forcing some confidence and accepting the main part of the responsibility. "I asked the others to help me."

"Why?"

"Because we needed to know what a weather controlling device looked like, so we could find it and stop it being stolen by Krevak," William said with great pleading and honesty in his voice.

"Is this," he said holding up the drawings, "what you think is being hidden on level five?"

"Yes Sir, please listen to us, we..." Isabel said, jumping in, but was quickly cut off.

"All of these objects were destroyed when they were banned and these are only partial drawings, one could never make one again from these! You have let your imaginations run away with you!" He paused and slowly looked at the four children standing in front of him, feeling a little sorry for them. "Follow me down to the casting floor, where you will clean out old larva tubes that have been blocked up for two years. We're becoming very busy and we need the extra capacity," Mr Diesel instructed.

The workshop floor was spooky now, empty of workers, and deeply dark with only small lights illuminating the walkways. Small clicks and knocking noises from the equipment around them made all four jump at different times, sending their imaginations racing as to what was lurking in the shadows and making the equipment seem like slumbering monsters.

When they reached the platform to go down to the casting level, they could now see the walls and guard rails all around them were washed with a rippling red light that got more intense as they looked over the edge, into what looked like the entrance into a dragon's lair deep down below.

Mr Diesel had none of these worries and walked with confidence onto the platform, holding the gate open for the four to follow. Once all were safely on, Mr Diesel performed the ever so familiar fishing reel operation on his Hadron-Tool, and down the platform went deeper and deeper into the glowing red heart of the earth.

The four pipes to be cleaned were wide enough for a man to crawl inside and located to the far right-hand side of the room. Either side were many tunnels that ran back into the rock, some allowing for servicing of the pipe lines and others leading to places people had never been.

The larva channels that were meant to be flowing with the boiling, sulphureous syrup were dry and empty. The channels showed nothing but a torturous mess of jagged black rock.

"Here we are!" he said, stopping in front of four large round pipes. "These are the four pipes you will be cleaning out. The valves back down the pipes have been closed so you won't suddenly become engulfed in larva and melt where you stand when you break through. To clean the pipes, use your Hadron-Tools to quickly shrink and expand the rock. This will force it to crack into chunks that can be removed. It is one pipe each and you can leave once your pipe is cleared. Is that all understood?" Mr Diesel instructed firmly.

The four nodded, all thankful that this was not a sewage pipe. At first, they were only able to create small cracks and small chunks, but over the hours they were there, the cracks and chunks they were able to break loose got bigger and more precise.

A few times Mr Diesel had tried to encourage the four children by saying that this is very good practice, and you will be better for it. But at the moment it did not feel like that at all! They were filthy, hot and their bodies were physically and mentally exhausted from all the lifting of rocks and strain of imagining. As far as George could tell he was not getting much closer to breaking through.

The hours ticked on past, with Mr Diesel warming once again to the four children who had always performed well in his class. He signalled to them to have a break, and they sat on the hard stone floor, starting to feel a growing bond with each other, created by the shared experience of hard physical labour.

"Why did you not say what was really on those papers to Mrs Volta?" William asked Mr Diesel.

"Well..." he said, before pausing and looking around the group, deciding how much he should say. "After those devices were banned and destroyed, one of my great, great, great grandads decided to keep some of the drawings of parts we had made for the machine. They have been passed down through the family and hidden ever since. So that maybe one day we can help remake them, and of course beat the competition. If I told Mrs Volta the drawings would probably have been taken away and I would have been investigated by the PSC, who could have closed my business down. Really, we're both in the wrong. You should not have taken something that does not belong to you, and I should not possess something that has been banned! But wanting to know about things in our past is not wrong, even if most people want to forget it ever happened."

The group sat in relaxed exhaustion, readying themselves for another attempt at unblocking the pipes, when out of one of the tunnels to the left of the pipes, voices could be heard.

Mr Diesel was instantly puzzled by the voices and turned his head to look down the tunnel's entrance.

"That's strange! Everyone should have gone home ages ago. I wonder who that could be?" he said, slightly confused, while getting stiffly to his feet to go have a proper look. "Wait here I will be back in a second," he said, walking towards the voices.

William looked at George, Isabel and Jasmin with slight panic in his eyes and on his face. "Remember what those two guys said in the archive, what did they call themselves... Javid and Thanok. They said they were looking for an unknown tunnel that led to where the object was being protected!" William said this in a hurried and worried voice.

"Yes, quick we must warn Sir before he..." Isabel was cut short by a sudden loud commotion in the tunnel, which then with equal speed went silent.

"Sir, you ok?" Isabel cautiously called and received no reply.

"We should go and check on him," William said, looking around his friends' faces, who looked back with matching scared eyes.

"We don't know what or who is in there. We should go back and get a teacher," Isabel argued, trying to not get themselves into trouble again.

"We don't have time; we must go down there now," said William in a determined voice full of growing self-assurance.

But the eyes that met his did not agree.

"Fine, I will go. But one of you run back, take the platform and find any teachers you can, send them down here. And go get Sir Coalbrook, get him to check the object is safe," William said with increased confidence and command.

"Ok that sounds like a good idea, I will go! I know the teachers a lot better than you do. Just don't do anything stupid," Isabel said, trying to match William's confidence. "Jasmin, you go and find Sir Coalbrook, he's normally around the main square at this time."

"Ok! That sounds like a plan," Jasmin said, already starting to get up.

Isabel followed, and they both ran back to the platform and up out of sight, making William and George feel very, very alone.

"Come on, let's go," William said, partly commanding his friend to obey, who he could see was reluctant to investigate. William stood and ran to the edge of the tunnel entrance, glad to hear the feet of his friend behind him.

He closed his eyes and took two deep breaths to compose himself, and then peered around the corner expecting the worst. The tunnel though was clear as far as he could see into the darkness.

It was not a wide tunnel and had a low ceiling, just taller than a man. Its walls were wavy, smooth and clear of jutting out rocks. William could also not see any offshoot crevasse to hide in if they saw anyone else.

"Come on!" William said not looking back, but moving around the corner and expecting George to follow.

The darkness grew around them, embracing them, and for a few moments not allowing them to see anything more. They paused, crouching down, hoping to make themselves small and unseeable, to let their eyes adjust to the darkness. As tense moments passed their vision started to get used to the lack of light, allowing the boys to make out more basic shapes and details.

Out of the depths of the darkness grew a tiny speck of light. The two boys with hearts pounding and adrenaline charging, slowly worked their way towards it. The light

crept slowly brighter and larger, filling more and more of
the tunnel every step towards it.

"Ouch!" William cried, as he tripped over something
unseen in the dark! Hitting the hard unforgiving stone
floor with a thud.

"Will you ok?" Came a quiet call from George who
quickly rushed over to pick up the dull shape of his
friend.

"Yeah, fine. But I think whoever's down here knows
we are here though," William said looking down the
tunnel, which was now getting ever lighter as the
dull glow came towards them at a suddenly increased
pace.

"What was it?" William asked, feeling back with his
hands. A moment of realisation struck him dumb when
he felt a workman's boot connected to a leg. "It's
Mr Diesel!" William said with concerned panic.

Both boys turned their attention to the faint lump
shape on the floor, their eyes straining to adjust, as their
owners forced more effort from them.

"Mr Diesel! Mr Diesel!" William called, hurriedly
shaking the body's shoulders and getting not much
more than a murmur. "Mr Diesel!" he tried again, louder
this time, bringing Mr Diesel back to the land of the
conscious.

The light was now almost upon them and had grown
bright at its furthest point.

"William! What are you doing here," Mr Diesel said,
coming back around and remembering where he was.
"You must get out of here, they're coming back!" he
worriedly said, looking towards the light.

"We know, but who was it?" William asked in desperation, trying to understand who might be about to come around the corner to do the same to them.

"Who... who...!" Mr Diesel said still not quite with it.

"Yes, who did this to you?"

"Oh, Thanok and Javid," he said slowly getting to his unsteady feet and staying upright with the help of both William and George, who found Mr Diesel to weigh far more than he looked like he should. "There was a third person, but I have no idea who that was," Mr Diesel added.

"I think we might have a good idea who that is," William said looking at a dark patch that was George's face, with neither boy being able to see much of the other's scared expressions at this realisation.

"Come on, let's go!" George said pleadingly.

"It's too late! Get behind me," ordered William, as he drew up the cave floor to protect and hide them.

"Ouch!" Mr Diesel cried as George, who could not support him on his own, dropped him back to the hard floor.

The light that had been prowling its way toward them finally caught them, illuminating parts of them to the two figures, who could only be Thanok and Javid. William could see that they were both holding their Hadron-Tools in their hands at hip level ready to use.

Without a warning Thanok and Javid picked stones from the floor and started to launch them, along with larger boulders down the tunnel towards them, using their Hadron-Tools to accelerate the makeshift bullets to incredible speed. As they shot past William's head they sounded like buzzing bees, and William knew they were close to hitting him as he peered around the drawn-up floor.

William's shield took the impact of many of the rocks, which came thick and fast as Thanok and Javid marched ever closer.

"We must get out of here!" Mr Diesel shouted over the noise.

"No, we can't, it's too late!" William answered, swapping teacher and student roles briefly with Mr Diesel. "Isabel and Jasmin have gone for help, we can't let Thanok and Javid get to the object. We must hold them off!" William said with increased conviction. "George, start shooting some stuff back."

"I can't, I'm rubbish at that, it always goes wrong," said George, feeling useless to help.

"Come on! You just need to imagine it. I have seen you do it before and if you don't, we are all dead anyway."

George nodded his head acknowledging he understood the importance. He started to mutter to himself saying, "I can do it, you can do it." He felt around on the ground and found one of the rocks that had just been shot at them.

Holding it in his hand he placed his Hadron-Tool against it, pointing up the tunnel towards the oncoming barrage of rocks and boulders. Suddenly the rock sped off up the tunnel hitting the wall. George jumped with the surprise of the rock launching off. But now with a little more confidence and steely determination he found another rock and then another and then another.

From the safety of William's stone shield, George was now unleashing his own hail storm of rocks at the attackers, who were still making their way closer and closer, but at a much slower and cautious pace now.

"Sir can you do anything better than shoot rocks," George shouted, hoping for a yes.

"William, can you make your shield any bigger?" Mr Diesel called, starting to feel balanced enough to try and stand.

"I can try Sir," William said, putting even more effort in, forcing beads of sweat to start pouring down his face with the mental effort.

"Great. Can you two just give me a minute?"

"YES!" They both shouted, as they really had no other choice.

William continued to take the impact of rocks on his stone shield, which was slowly growing weaker and starting to crack as his mind became exhausted from the effort of trying to keep it intact. George was still shooting away with ever greater accuracy as the targets came closer and bigger.

"Any time now Sir would be great!" cried William, realising he could not hold the stone shield much longer. With that the shield he had been holding up cracked into pieces and flowed back into the floor.

As soon as the stone shield was gone, Thanok took aim and smacked William square in the chest with a fist size rock, sending him crumpling to the floor in agony and winded.

Mr Diesel, realising his time had to be now, forced his protesting body to stand up fully and brought the ground up with him just like William's barrier but much, much larger. He pulled the ground up above his head until it almost touched the ceiling and then rapidly dropped his arm, like he was cracking a whip. Up and down his arm went, again and again and again, sending the floor of the tunnel into huge waves that raced down its length with an appalling avalanche-like noise, scraping and crunching its way down, tearing stones out of the walls and ceiling as it went.

Thanok and Javid heard the stone tidal wave coming towards them and turned to run, but it was too late. The waves of rock quickly caught them, sending them first crashing into the ceiling and then smashing into the ground, again and again as each solid wave rolled on.

Mr Diesel then collapsed once again. All his remaining energy drained, and this time out cold, leaving William and George unable to bring him back around again.

As if in sympathy to their master's plight the waves of rock settled back into the calm stone floor and the tunnel became deathly quiet again. The light that Javid had been holding lay on its side in one piece on the floor, lighting up the area where William and George now sat next to Mr Diesel looking at each other in amazement that they had somehow survived.

"We need to keep going George, Sir said there was another person in the tunnel, we need to find them," William said in between deep painful breaths.

"Are you mad! Look at what has happened to Sir and you only just escaped with a bruised chest!" George said more than happy to stop and wait for Isabel and Jasmin to return with help.

"Look there is no time to waste, we must go on," William said, painfully getting to his feet with one hand on his chest and struggling to breathe. He could feel a bruise growing under his hand and it felt like his shirt was getting wet with something that was not sweat.

"Someone needs to stay with Sir, we can't just leave him," George said, protesting while also getting to his feet.

"Isabel and Jasmin will be back with help soon. Mr Diesel isn't going anywhere, come on!" William said with increasing desperation, but also understanding what George had said.

"Fine! Once again off we go into the dark unknown," George replied, finally giving in once more to the instructions of his friend and stepping over Mr Diesel, who had not moved since he collapsed but was faintly breathing.

"We will be back in a bit Sir, don't go anywhere," he said to the non-replying Mr Diesel.

The two young boys were a little bit less nervous now, and a little more confident in their basic Hadron-Tool abilities as they set off towards the two ugly and distorted, unmoving heaps on the floor that used to be Thanok and Javid. The two bodies lay just in front of a T junction in the tunnel with a passage heading to the east and west.

The two boys stopped a good few metres away from the limp, squashed and pummelled bodies on the floor, pausing to try and see for sure that Thanok and Javid were not about to somehow wake up.

As they were looking for signs of life and saw none, both boys continued to edge forward, when more footsteps were heard running down the east tunnel and stopping just on the other side of the two unmoving bodies.

"You!" The person said with aggressive anger towards William.

William looked up, hoping not to see who he thought was standing in front of him. There in all his red-haired menace was Krevak, Hadron-Tool in one hand and an object in the other. He cast a monstrous shadow over the boys, making them feel very small, powerless and insignificant.

"Look at what you have done!" he said, snapping and spitting at William and George. Then instantly changed into a soft, loving tone, kneeling down and placing the object on the floor before stroking what was left of Thanok's brown hair. "Shame, but they had done their duty, and found me a tunnel past the protections those stupid people at the Protection and Security Council set up, how pathetic they are. Soon this won't be the only mountain of power I have," he said while patting the wooden box, "and you two little annoyances will be nothing more than slaves cleaning the soles of my boots or better still dead," Krevak said with a horrid snake-like menace.

"You can't!" shouted William out of fear.

"So you're the brave one then, well you will die first," Krevak said calmly, pointing his Hadron-Tool at William.

Its tip started to fizz and spark and grew in brightness until a lightning bolt shot out of the end, crackling and sparking its way to William's body. At the last moment the lightning bolt suddenly darted off course, and instead of hitting William in the chest, it burnt its way through William's right shoulder and created an explosion of rock as it hit the tunnel's wall behind him.

Krevak had been distracted just at the final moment by bullets of rocks and stone that started to pour down from the east tunnel, causing him to change his focus and draw up the floor to protect himself from the threat.

A lightning bolt then shot out of the blackness of the same tunnel, exploding on the ceiling near Krevak's head and bringing rocks showering down, causing William and George to dive for cover. Krevak now stood with his Hadron-Tool pointing up, repelling away the rocks that rained down on him from above, like he had some invisible force field umbrella above his head.

Shouts and the sound of pounding feet could be heard getting louder and louder as more lightning bolts crackled and rocks buzzed, leaving the air thick with dust and loud with crashes, bangs and explosions.

In the mayhem William believed he saw a hurricane whirl past and daggers of ice fly down the tunnel, narrowly missing himself and George.

"NO!... YOU WON'T TAKE ME!" Krevak bellowed back with defiance down the tunnel, before turning to run down the west tunnel, but quickly stopped, turned back and tried to reach for the object that he had forgotten on the floor during the attack.

Seeing Krevak move to grab the object he had left behind in his hurry, William, in desperation, clawed the ground and dived over it, under a shower of falling rock, covering it with his body. He cried with pain as his bruised and bleeding chest crashed down on the hard, unforgiving object. Krevak hesitated, trying to figure out what was more important, the object or his freedom to try again. He turned and ran from the shouting voices, cursing William as he vanished from sight.

Appearing out of the east tunnel came Arthur Rebibox at full run, with Sentinels from the Protection and Security Council, their knee length jackets flapping behind them and all mostly hatless, chasing on behind. They passed William and George without noticing them, only Arthur paused to pay the boys some brief surprised attention.

"You two boys ok?" he asked breathlessly. "Get back down that tunnel, you will be safe there." Arthur said without waiting for a reply and pointing back down the tunnel the boys had just come up.

"Come on Will!" said George, grabbing William under the arms to help him up.

As William was dragged to his feet, Arthur saw what William now had in his hands, "I will have that," he said, holding out his hand.

William glady handed the object over, with great relief that it was now safe.

The two boys then hobbled back to where Mr Diesel was, who was now no longer alone. In the dim light William could see he was awake and trying to explain what had happened.

Isabel and Jasmin ran over to the two boys, "Gosh Will you're hurt! Help over here!" shouted Jasmin, calling for assistance.

"George, are you ok? Are you hurt?" Isabel asked in panic.

"I am fine, just very…" said George but was stopped mid-sentence by a teary-eyed Isabel giving him a massive hug.

*

The last morning of term was now upon them, and having packed their bags ready to go home, the boys thought that they would visit Mr Diesel who was still in the medical centre, before heading to the main hall for the end of year ceremony.

Entering the medical centre through the front door to visit someone was a novel experience for William as all the previous times he had been the one being visited. They found Mr Diesel sitting in a wheelchair balancing it on the back wheels, trying to keep himself entertained.

"Hello Sir, how are you feeling?" William asked, happy to see his teacher having fun.

"Hello William, hello George, nice to see you," he said, dropping his wheelchair onto all four wheels with a clunk. "I am doing pretty well, I should be allowed out of here within the hour, in time to attend the end of year ceremony. The nurses just want to look at one more thing."

"Great," George said with a smile.

"I did have a visit from Arthur Rebibox yesterday, he said that your actions," he said looking at both boys, "had prevented Krevak from getting away with the object, which I have now found out is called the Aeolus Box. So well done. He also said that without the efforts of Jasmin and Isabel you two would probably now be dead."

"Wow! Arthur told you that?" William said, amazed about the level of information Arther had given.

"Yes, he seemed quite open to answering a few questions. I guess it was kind of a thank you for my small unplanned part in helping to protect the Aeolus Box."

"And what else did he say?" William asked excitedly.

"Well, I asked him how the object worked and was it really as powerful as the myths said it was. He did not answer the questions directly but what he said was very interesting. I would have thought something needed to be really complex to control something as complex as the weather, but that turns out not to be true at all."

William smiled to himself in satisfaction that he had indeed thought correctly about the object, the Aeolus Box, he had seen in the engineering drawings.

"Arthur said that the box contained what he called the four winds; he didn't however say exactly what they were though. He said the four winds could be released and harnessed to create many different types of weather, such as storms, hurricanes and floods. The Aeolus Box that they were hiding and protecting on level five was the last weather control device in the world and would now be destroyed like all the others, as it was clear to the PSC that it could not be guarded safely enough."

"Why did they have it in the first place? They were banned! They were all meant to be destroyed years ago! At least that is what we found out was meant to have happened to all of the weather control devices?" George said dumbfounded.

"Yes, that is true George, he did not say why, but you could see he was a little bit more than uncomfortable that it had been found and so nearly stolen. Arthur also said it was now currently in transit to a new location to be destroyed. So, the PSC are, it would seem, trying to correct their mistake."

"I bet they won't destroy it, it's too useful, if something like that is ever needed again!" George said with his normal distrust of large governing organisations.

"Well, let's hope you are wrong George," Mr Diesel said with an understanding at George's distrust.

"Did the Sentinels capture Krevak?" William asked, hoping for a positive answer.

"No, they did not. Apparently Krevak brought the whole tunnel down behind him as he ran, killing two Sentinels with the falling rock before he escaped. More Sentinels are out in the mountains looking for him now."

"Do you think the PCS will ever catch him?" William asked.

"I have no idea. Before this all happened I thought you and your friends were making it all up, it just all sounded so fanciful. I had believed the narrative I had been told about them all being destroyed all my life." He took a brief pause to reflect. "Clearly I should have looked into it more, rather than just believing what I was told," Mr Diesel said with a sorry look in his eyes. "I am sure though Arthur will want to talk with you two later, you can ask your own questions when that happens if he seems to be in a good mood," Mr Diesel said, before looking at the side of his Hadron-Tool. "Well look, both of you should be getting back to the main hall as the end of year ceremony is going to start soon, I will join you there in a bit, but you can't miss the start, especially since Starley have won the 4's trophy. I also think any problems your detention caused Starley House have now been forgotten, at least I hope so," Mr Diesel said with a friendly smile.

"Yes Sir. Well, it is good to see you're on the mend," William said, turning away to walk out.

"Have a good summer Sir," said George following on and out along the clean and crisp hallway.

"Thank you George, you too," Mr Diesel said, giving the two boys a small wave before getting back to looking out of the room's wide window at the sunny world outside. His chair made a sticky, rubbery squeak as it was put reluctantly back on to its rear wheels to entertain its user.

*

Three loud claps sounded from every surface and object in the hall, indicating that Sir Coalbrook was at the front and wanting quiet.

"Good afternoon to you all on this, our last day together, before the freedom of the summer holiday embraces us all. This year has been truly exceptional, with many of you showing the bravery and courage that would make the founders of your house so proud," Sir Coalbrook said, looking unwaveringly at where William, George, Isabel and Jasmin were sitting.

"Over this year the houses have battled it out on the 4's pitch through every type of weather possible. Games have been hard fought with no player shying away from playing the game to its very fullest, of this you should all be most proud." The whole hall clapped and cheered in agreement. "Great efforts have been made in lessons and in your house to maintain high standards to earn and keep house points throughout the year." The room again filled with clapping and cheers, before he started up again. "One house though..." he said, producing a very small thumb-sized cup from his pocket and placing it on the surface in front of him, "... rose higher and fought harder than any other to make history and to win this, the 4's trophy three times in a row." Cheering started to grow around the Starley tables, all just waiting for the announcement of their house name, like the building of pressure in a volcano.

"And that house is... *Starley*, Marcus Mardic please come to the front." Cheering erupted as the volcano finally exploded, the noise grew louder than when the whole academy had cheered and clapped previously. The other houses booed and heckled Marcus as he made his way to the front, but he was striding confidently and standing up straight with his shoulders back, oozing confidence and pride, to the front of the hall, nothing was going to change that.

Sir Coalbrook shook Marcus's hand firmly with his well-muscled, leathery skinned hand while smiling broadly at him.

William though was partially disappointed, after all the hardship of playing the 4's game and the importance of it to the Thomons, he thought the trophy was pretty pathetic, a little bit small.

"Is that it," William shouted to George, over the noise of his happy house.

"Is that what?" replied George, straining to hear him.

"That trophy is tiny!" William tried again.

"Maybe it is made of something amazing!" came the unconvincing reply.

As George said this Sir Coalbrook touched the pathetically tiny trophy with his Hadron-Tool, it grew and grew to the point where it was no longer small and pathetic at all but amazing.

A great golden bowl that looked like half a 4's ball sat on three eagle-like talons, with details of the feathers and skin folds done in silver and bronze. The talons of the eagle's feet sat gripped and digging into its prey of a coiled snake that looked as if it was writhing in protest.

The top of the bowl resembled a wide-open lion's mouth with its giant sharp dagger-like teeth stabbing toward the centre of the bowl.

The two handles were shaped like rams' horns and were made of black diorite stone that was carved as smooth as silk.

Fire raced and raged around inside the golden bowl, burning the blue of Starley House. Sometimes the fire would burst out of the open lion's mouth in great arcs, before being sucked back down to be once again contained.

The trophy was magnificent, as complex and as dangerous as the game itself, a very fitting trophy William now thought.

After a few more moments of soaking up the cheering, Marcus took the trophy into his arms and walked back to the house tables to place it amongst its retaining owners. With all other houses looking enviously and longingly at the jewel they had strived so hard to gain but had fallen short of.

"Well done, well done," Sir Coalbrook said over the commotion that filled the hall. Three more loud bangs were sent out by the Headmaster to get the attention of the room once again.

"Now... settle down, settle down," Sir Coalbrook said, motioning with his hands. "The last prize to be awarded is for Best House," he said, turning to look at the House Points Clock.

The hall fell silent as they all watched, as the house gears with their metallic clack, clack sound slowly rolled their way to their new and final positions and sizes.

"That house is..." Sir Coalbrook began as the gears slowed down to a stop, "... Starley!" He announced, igniting loud cheers from the Starley tables. He then turned around and wrote the house name on a large white, flat mushroom that grew out of one of the roots on the wall behind him. Glowing spots of blue light then shot off along the white mycelium strings, with the blue glow splitting at each junction it found to carry on its journey. As the blue light shot all over the hall, the root system exploded into full blue bloom behind it. William watched as the living, moving and wriggling roots that wove together to make the doors, walls and ceiling of the hall sprouted blue multi-petalled flowers of all sizes and shapes, and shot blue sparkling pollen over all the students as they opened, that then wafted and danced around in the air. Long blue dangling leaves dropped out of the ceiling like streamers and waved about gently like Willow branches.

"And now for our final meal together," Sir Coalbrook said, tapping the end of his Hadron-Tool on his table twice, allowing the centre of the tables to open and the mechanical arms to spring out and get to work. Great golden hams, roasted carrots, dark gravy and thick fluffy cakes were produced with the mechanical arms moving at impressive speed. No matter how many times William saw this mechanical dance happen, it still totally amazed him.

"Please begin!" announced the Headmaster, and every table began to enjoy the food, cake and drink in front of them.

Sounds of happiness filled the blue hall, with students and teachers alike sharing stories of the year and plans for the summer holidays.

"Will, would your mum and dad let you come over to ours this summer?" George asked with a mouth full of pork.

"I don't see why not," William replied hopefully.

"Great, I will get my mum to contact yours and arrange it."

"But how will I get to your house in the Thomon world without the minibus?" William asked, realising he knew nothing about how to travel between the two worlds. He just got on the minibus and it all happened.

"That will be easy enough, you need to use a megalith. My mum will sort it all out," George said confidently.

William looked content with the reply and carried on eating, moving swiftly on to the fluffy sky cake that sat temptingly in front of him.

After the time of celebration and feasting had come to an end, groups of students started to leave the hall heading for the various methods of transport home.

A call came from the front of the hall, "All students travelling on minibus six B please make their way to the collection point, your bags are already loaded and waiting for you."

It was Mr Stephenson who had made the announcement and who now strode over to William and clapped a hand on his shoulder, almost making him choke on his sky cake.

"Well look who it is!" Mr Stephenson said, looking down at William and then over to George. "But I don't know who you are," he said looking at the girls sitting opposite.

"I am Isabel," Isabel said, shaking the hand that Mr Stephenson held out towards her.

"And I am Jasmin," Jasmin said, also shaking Mr Stephenson's hand.

"Well, I look forward to hearing all about your second term on the way home," he said, looking between William and George. "You need to finish up now though and follow me please, we can't keep everyone waiting for you to finish eating your own weight in cake!"

"Yes Sir," William replied, stuffing a last mouthful of sky cake in his mouth before standing to follow on.

George, realising it really was time to leave, grabbed some pastries and sweets, filling his pockets for the journey, before he ran around the end of the table to join William.

Isabel and Jasmin quickly shot up and ran over to the door to give William and George a very large and affectionate hug before they left.

"Have a great holiday, please do write to us and stay in touch. I got your address from George and will share it with Jasmin," Isabel said, looking at William.

"Ok great, I would like that. Have a great holiday too," William said while waving at the two girls as he walked off.

"You four are either very stupid or very brave," came the voice of Arthur Rebibox who had been standing just outside the hall, making William, George, Isabel and Jasmin freeze in the doorway. "Be that as it may, your actions have helped prevent Krevak Ragwort from getting his hands on the Aeolus Box and for that the PSC are very grateful. I hope you understand that you cannot be rewarded for your efforts as the Aeolus Box should not exist!" he said with uncaring dismissal.

"Why was it not destroyed years ago, when all the other weather controlling devices were banned and destroyed?" William asked with a keen tone of anger in his voice.

"Yes, that is true and I understand your anger. Weather controlling devices were banned after the Great War and all of them were meant to have been destroyed. It was decided by the PSC, that as a matter of Thomon security, a single device should be kept in case of natural disasters, like drought. This view along with the change in circumstances has now changed, and the device will be decommissioned," he said with the calmness of any good politician who had just been caught out. "Please know that the PSC has it all under control and does not require your assistance. So please enjoy your holiday fully and with peace of mind," Arthur said smiling, trying to end the conversation and leave, as he never felt that comfortable talking with children.

"Come on boys, or you'll miss your bus. It won't wait for you just because you are part of the winning house!" said Mr Stephenson, seeing that Arthur was also wanting to leave now.

William and George quickly repeated their goodbyes to Isabel and Jasmin, then reluctantly hurried off to follow Mr Stephenson who had already started walking across the main square, which was once again loud with activity.

Arthur smiled at the two girls, nodded his head in goodbye and walked away. His head now churning through how his plans for the future were now jeopardised and how to save them.

William wished he had more time to ask questions, but that would have to wait. He was now torn out of the academy and the world he had grown to love so much, to go back to his home in the Igmon world, where impossible things were still impossible.